for my beloved
teacher Khyongla
and all the
bodhisattvas at
the Tibet Center —

with all my
Love,

Kriti

NYC
November 88

VELOCITY

Kristin McCloy

VELOCITY

RANDOM HOUSE

NEW YORK

Library of Congress Cataloging-in-Publication Data
McCloy, Kristin.
Velocity.
I. Title.
PS3563.c3417v45   1988   813'.54   88-42658
ISBN 0-394-57022-7

Manufactured in the United States of America
2 4 6 8 9 7 5 3
First Edition

In memory of my father

Then how I'd like to hide from this longing. Oh how I wish,
I wish it were still to come, and I was a boy sitting
Propped up on my future arms . . .

From *Duino Elegies,* "The Sixth Elegy," by Rainer Maria Rilke

VELOCITY

Sometimes in my dreams you rise up as if from a swamp, whole, younger than I remember, dazzling, jagged, and I follow you into smoky rooms, overwhelmed by the sense of being in the presence of an untamed thing, full of light, impossible to control. Sometimes I dream I am standing in your room and peeling my clothes off one by one, eyes closed, undressing as if it were a form of prayer. As if my naked body alone could conjure you up.

Days after I've dreamt of you I walk through the streets and hold the memory of what it was to be with you like a sacred lantern burning high up near my heart. I leapt from my world into yours without questions or conditions, because that was the only way that I would be admitted; you lived in absolutes. We ate, we made love, we slept, and each day the sun rose so that we could do it all over again. You were a foreign land to me and I lived there with you as someone for whom pain doesn't exist.

I tell myself, Once he was mine, and that was enough. But it wasn't. It never was true, and it never was enough. You hunted down your needs—simple and precise—and in those days, it was me.

I F O L L O W my father through the woods and suddenly think what a strange vision we present, he in his only good suit, I in my best dress. It is only June, but the air is stifling. I pick my way through the poison ivy, the roots and rocks and nettles, dipping my hand into the plain wooden urn my father carries and throwing what I take in a wide circle around me. He does the same. My tears are quiet tears; they seem to be a part of the humidity, a natural drizzle. He is dry-eyed.

With every handful of fine ash and chipped bone that I loose upon the rich forest soil the same words rise inside my head: Go. Be free. Soar. Find peace.

Half an hour later it is finished. It doesn't seem right that there should have been so little left. My father and I stand in the middle of the woods, the sweat trickling down our faces, staining our good clothes. I wait for him to speak but he says nothing, just holds the empty vessel in both arms and stares at the trees.

"Well," I say finally, wiping my face with both hands, "should we say something?"

In the stillness that follows, I hear the sound of insects, birds, the rustle of leaves—it seems to me I even hear the heat pouring through the trees.

"I suppose so." He clears his throat and begins the Lord's Prayer. Mom wouldn't like this, I think, but I join in at "on Earth as it is in Heaven."

"Amen."

"Amen."

My father looks at me. "Let's go home."

On the way back I want to hold his hand but neither of them are free. By the time we reach the house it is dusk.

"Daddy, you want a drink?"

He sets the urn down in a corner of the living room, stares at it for a second before standing upright again.

"I think I'll just go change." He goes into his room and shuts the door.

I sit in the darkening living room and stare at all the dying plants. I refuse to water them. They were my mother's; I don't see why they should outlive her.

I don't know how long I've been sitting there when I hear some strange sounds coming from my father's bedroom. Slowly I walk down the hall. I put my hand on the doorknob and listen. Strange, strange sounds—a rasping choke that just repeats itself.

It's the first time I've ever heard my father cry. I stand there with my hand on the knob, unable either to knock or to leave, until the sound stops. Then I go out and climb into the hammock, pull my knees up to my chest and hold them there.

Everything around me seems fragile; when I squint I can focus on the twigs in the oak tree that overhangs the porch, bent with the weight of their leaves. I can't believe I have always taken it for granted, this tree, this life—everything around me seems fraught with danger, full of terrible secrets, the sky itself seems ephemeral and as I stare up at it, eyes held wide, it seems to be falling, rippling softly into a thousand fragments to reveal nothing behind it save space, black and void, never-ending.

When the first star appears overhead, I go back inside and softly open my father's door. He is lying across the bed still wearing his suit, even his shoes and tie. He is clutching a pillow to his chest, asleep. I look at him for long moments, then close the door and go upstairs, to my room. Undressing in the dark, I reach out with one hand and balance myself against the wall. A thin coat of dust comes off on my palm. Getting into bed, I have to bend my head

to keep from bumping it against the wooden beams of the slanting
ceiling, and I reach up again, with the same hand, trace its texture
with my fingertips. Small wooden splinters break off, and I have
to sweep them from my sheets before stretching out, coverless and
naked, on my bed.

Everything crumbles. The walls, the rooftop . . . every structure
will fall. Everything known, all that is so familiar, will vanish.
Including myself.

I turn over on my stomach and, blinking against the pillow, feel
how my eyelashes brush against the cloth, and how the cloth
absorbs my tears.

H E   S T O P S in front of Parker's Restaurant and lets the
squad car idle. "This it?"

I point to the sign up on the door. "See? Help Wanted." I
unbuckle my seat belt. "Wish me luck, Dad."

He grunts. "Luck! You don't need it." He stares through the
windshield while he speaks. "You don't have to stay here this
summer on my account, Ellie."

"I know that. I want to stay." I push the door open, step on
the pavement.

"To be a waitress?" He looks at me. I can see a small nick where
he cut himself shaving. "You're a college graduate, for Chris-
sakes."

"It isn't for the rest of my life."

"Wastin your potential," he mutters, looking ahead again.

"It's just a summer job, Dad," I tell him, leaning in through the window. "I didn't have anything better in New York."

"Okay," he says, but I know he doesn't believe me.

"Anyway I hate the summer in the city."

"You want me to come back and pick you up?"

"No thanks." Stepping away from the car. "I can walk."

In the restaurant I can smell hush puppies frying. At three o'clock hardly anyone's there. In back a woman is pouring the remaining ketchup from several bottles into one. Her hair is bleached blond, she wears bright pink lipstick. When I tell her why I've come she stops what she's doing and puts a fist on her hip.

"You got experience?"

"Sure," I lie. "Should I fill out an application?"

She smiles at me then, her eyes crinkling up at the corners. "Honey," she says, "you'll get the job."

––––––

Dusk falls like a shawl around my shoulders. My arms and legs are bare. I am nearly naked, I think, and for one brief second fantasize that I have someplace else to go besides home, but it is nearly suppertime and I know my father is there by now, alone. I am burdened by his solitude; although I cannot assuage it, I feel compelled to be around it; I feel responsible.

I bang in through the screen door. The house is dark, lifeless.

"Dad?" I look in the kitchen, peek into his room, then finally walk out to the back porch to find him sitting in my mother's rocking chair, drinking Seagram's and staring out into the trees. It seems a radius of silence stretches out for six feet around him.

I go over and give him a kiss, which he receives awkwardly, as he always has any small affection. I sit on the steps.

"Hot today."

"Sure was."

"How was your day?"

"Fine," he says. "How was work?"

"It was easy. The restaurant's only open for breakfast and lunch, so I never have to work at night."

"That's good."

"Yeah, I didn't want to work at night."

"No." We sit in the silence then, the dark thickening around us.

"Want me to fix you some supper?"

"No thanks, honey."

"How about another drink?"

"No thanks, Ellie."

I look at him rocking ever so slightly, still wearing his uniform, even his holster, as if comfort were a thing of the past. His large callused hands wrap around his glass.

"Miss Mom?"

He nods, but he doesn't look at me. "Yup," he says. "I sure do."

"Me too." There doesn't seem to be anything left to say after that, and nothing I can do save sit with him, which I do until he goes inside to watch the news.

———

My mother and I are in her green VW, she's driving, we have the windows down and a cool breeze blows in, I keep looking at her and looking away, then looking back to make sure it's really her, sure she'll disappear in between glances, but every time I see her again, driving like she does with one elbow out the window, wearing a dark blue scarf around her head, small wisps of blond hair sticking out. She's smoking a cigarette, I'm in the car with my mother and we are going somewhere and I think, Everything's fine, but my stomach is queasy, something's bothering me and I don't know what it is. I sit back and realize I'm not wearing my seat belt, and neither is she. Put your seat belt on, I tell her, but she doesn't hear me, she acts like she doesn't hear me, and then I realize how fast we're going, we're hurtling down the road, I tell her, Slow down, I start screaming, Slow down, but her foot keeps pressing on the gas, she isn't wearing her seat belt and she isn't listening to me, I realize she's not in control, she can't hear me, she isn't wearing her seat belt and she shouldn't be driving—

I wake up soaked with sweat. Around me, my room feels as still and hot as a coffin. I get up and dress, tiptoe out to the front porch. A warm breeze is blowing and a full moon illuminates everything. I climb into the hammock and breathe deeply to make myself still, staring up at the sky—but it doesn't work, I am overcome by a terrible sense of urgency, the sense of time running out, it seems to me I can see the moon crossing the sky, and feel us grinding on our axis beneath it.

Abruptly I disentangle myself from the web of cloth and jump down.

———

Used to pass that gleaming Harley on my way home from Parker's and my knees would freeze, my elbows come in tight against my sides and stiff-armed I'd walk by your house, still wearing that stupid uniform with the skirt that was too tight, my sleeves rolled up and my shoes in my hands, eyes staring straight ahead so hard they stung—and still I'd see you, how could I miss you, that crazy height and that straight hair down to your shoulders, even from the shadows of your porch, the way you stared at me would've burned a hole in a blind woman's side, but you never made a sound, not a word, not a whistle or a murmur or a hiss . . . and if I flicked my eyes sideways even for a second you'd catch them, never pretend you weren't looking but nod instead, real grave, as if we were solemn neighbors with a brief history of courtesy between us, so I'd nod back, just the briefest incline of my chin to say I wasn't a snob, I was as Christian as the next, and besides, you didn't scare me . . . but you did, because from the first, I knew you were beautiful.

T A K I N G off my shoes to feel the road beneath bare feet, I walk the edge of blacktop and woods alone, moon so bright my figure casts a shadow, the high whine of crickets rising up like steam and the air still damp with early summer's humidity. The forest on either side is dense, sweet-smelling and secretive. I know where I am going, I have spent the last ten days fantasizing about it, but I walk as if aimless, walk without thinking, I whistle as if to fool myself when in fact my heart is pounding so hard it makes me sweat . . . and then I round the corner and there, like a miracle cure, he is: standing outside that run-down old place like an Indian chieftain, arms folded, surveying the night.

I slow down just before I get there, run my fingers through my hair and let everything go, hips swaying like an African woman's by the river. Beneath my T-shirt, I am free-breasted and brown.

Walking beneath that gaze I come up to meet him like presumption itself. "Hello."

"Evenin."

"Nice night to be out," I say, casually, as if I just happened by. "Not too hot."

"Yeah." He tilts his head so that his hair falls back behind his shoulders again. I can see the silver streak in his hair that runs behind his temples like a vein of ore. "Heat's good too."

"If there's a breeze."

"Good breeze now."

"It's beautiful."

He smiles. His teeth are crooked and brilliantly white. "Beautiful, huh," the word weighted in his mouth. I stand very still, wanting it to be for me, and look away, afraid of betraying myself.

There is a silence. He shifts his weight, dips his hands into his back pockets and settles there, seemingly comfortable in the pause.

"Yeah, I couldn't sleep. I thought maybe I'd come by, see if I could get a ride."

"Where you need to go?"

"I don't care, I just want to go fast."

He nods, accepting this gravely, a piece of information he asked for and received and now is storing somewhere, for secret purposes.

"You work around here?"

I nod. "Just up the road, at Parker's."

He nods too. "I seen you around."

"I've seen you too."

I like his voice; I like the way the whites of his eyes gleam in the dark, and I like the way he holds himself, as if he's drawing power from deep inside some inner well.

"What's your name?"

"Jesse."

"I'm Ellie."

"Ellie. Huh." Again the nod; so serious . . . as if it's business we're transacting. It makes me want to make him want me. "So why can't you sleep?"

I shrug. I don't want to tell him.

"No one to keep you company?"

I shake my head, stare off into space.

"No boyfriend?" he asks. I shake my head again, and when I turn to look at him he unfurls that smile, radiant, like the sun coming out, holding nothing back. In the middle of that moonlit, deserted road, it makes me feel famous. I smile back.

"Hard to believe," he says, and yet I sense a restraint for all the lust in his eyes and it occurs to me, a thousand women, he's had a thousand women, and every one of them has fed him everything she had.

"What about you? How come you're out here all alone tonight?" I hear myself speak and my voice sounds brazen, high-pitched.

"I like it."

I marvel at the simplicity. "You're not bored?"

"Bored?" He frowns. "Nah, I ain't bored. I'm never bored." Looking right at me. "I ain't borin, you know what I mean?"

I have to look away to keep the smile down. "I'll take your word for it."

"Why? You don't even know who I am. Maybe I'm a psycho. One of those guys always tells lies. Maybe I got a knife in my pants."

I look at him. His eyes glitter, all pupil.

"I know who you are," I say slowly.

"Yeah? Who?"

"Jesse. You're Jesse, right?"

"Maybe. Maybe not. Maybe I lied about my name, too."

"No you didn't."

"How do you know?" His look is uncompromisingly direct, like being under white light; suddenly I realize he reminds me of my father.

"I just know."

"You got that—what d'ya call it—feminine intuition, huh?"

"No," I say. I didn't know my mother was going to die. I didn't know it when she was dead. My father had to call me. I didn't know anything. I didn't know anything about anything.

———

I stare at him. A hot breeze is blowing my hair around and a few strands get caught in the corner of my mouth. He reaches out and with two fingers gently sets them free again. We stand there, two feet apart, and all the while I know I am going to sleep with him and yet I cannot think of it, not even for a moment—it's as if the whole time I believed I was going to turn around and walk away, walk home alone and go back to sleep, because if I didn't believe this, I couldn't be here at all, not like this, now, at three-thirty in the morning; it implicated me far too much.

"You know what I do when I can't sleep?" His eyes are a piercingly pure bright green, undiluted by even a fleck of hazel.

"What."

"I drink a little red wine."

"Red wine, huh."

"Yeah. You like red wine? You probably like white wine. Chicks always like white wine."

"No, I like red wine better."

"Yeah, me too."

"Do you have any?"

"Red wine?"

"Uh huh."

"Why, you want some?"

"Yeah. I want some." I did. I wanted it. I wanted him so badly I could taste it . . . so badly I was out there, asking.

He says, "Wait here," and I do, one foot sideways up against my leg, hands holding on to my elbows, maintaining my balance till he returns with an open bottle of Burgundy. "This way." He takes me around the side of the house, hoists me up on a windowsill and tucks the bottle of wine halfway into his jeans. I stand to one side while he climbs up next to me, so close I can feel the heat his skin gives off, and then he's climbing up the wall of the house, stepping on nails hammered so that they stick out all the way up to the top, inviting the spread of your feet. I follow, terrified, with sweaty palms, my body clinging to the wall—but I make it up there all right. The tar feels smooth and cool through my jeans. We sit side by side and look up at the sky. Can barely see the stars for the light of the moon.

Twisting around I can see the curve of the road that leads to my house. "Have you lived here long?"

"Year." From his back pocket he produces a pack of cigarettes, shakes one out. "Smoke?"

"No. Thanks." He lights a match on the roof, I watch him inhale. "You're not from around here, are you?"

"No."

"Where you from?"

"Georgia." He grins at me. "Swampland."

"Why'd you come here?"

Squinting at the moon, he shrugs. "It's where I ended up."

I hold out bare arms, as if to catch the light, and noticing, he grins again. "Witches' moon tonight," he says. I sneak a sidelong glance. "My mother used to say. Good for spellin."

"Your mother was a witch?" I open my throat, feel the wine go down like a ribbon of raw silk, bitter and red.

"Indian lady," he says, terse. I wonder if I've stumbled on some forbidden ground, pick the bottle up.

"You look Indian too. What kind?"

"Cherokee."

"Was your father Indian?"

"Nah. He was just some white dude."

"They weren't married?"

Jesse laughs, short. I wait, but he doesn't say anything, so I take another drink. He watches me swallow, asks, "Sleepy yet?" as if he really meant the wine for medicine. I shake my head and pass the bottle back. I watch his Adam's apple move, the tip of the bottle not touching his mouth.

"Do you ever go back to visit her?"

"No." It seems perfectly clear that this answer is final, the last answer, the only answer, and I feel an affinity toward him, and this finality he seems to have accepted, or decreed.

We sit in silence then, sipping the wine, and I watch how his glance moves, from the road to me, from me to the horizon, up to the moon, then back to me. Although he says nothing, I can feel his attention on me, a constant sense of observation, and something else—not just a wanting but a peculiar alertness, a sense of being absorbed and left alone at the same time, as if I were a wild animal being tamed.

I become quite still beside that presence, have the feeling that everything will be distilled in the silence between us, silence like a living thing into which we pour ourselves, wordless and clean. I don't think my own thoughts and I don't know his. Somewhere I am aware of my grief waiting for me, patient and thick, but right now it is remote, as if it were days away, as if it belonged to somebody else. I've descended into a state of grace, unexpected, and it's purely a physical sensation, as if all my cells are humming. Beneath that white light, my skin takes on a sheen, a silver coating, unnatural and fine. I stretch my legs out in front of me and feel my heart beat.

———

It's dawn when we finish the wine. We are on the roof of the house, watching the sun rise, flat on our backs. He hasn't touched me; this I find more intoxicating than anything else. If I want him I'm going to have to reach for him. I wait for the perfect moment, I have been waiting for minutes and minutes and minutes now, poised to catch it—and then it comes and I freeze: he sits up on one elbow and leans over me to take the empty bottle. I will put my hand on the back of his neck, I think, but I don't. I will pull him down and take his tongue between my teeth—I will grab on to his belt, I will fall through the roof with the weight of him—his presence over me engulfs me, time slows down, my eyes lose focus and suddenly we're kissing and it's me who's on top of him, I can feel the early-morning sun on the back of my calves, I can feel his hands on my waist, thumbs pressing into my stomach, slightly lifting me, and I run my fingers through his hair, I love the length of it, I wind it around one hand while the other slides down smooth skin to his flank, I can feel the hollow squares of his hips just inside the jeans, his thighs as big and hard as young trees.

The whole time he's touching me as if he already possessed me, as if he knew my body would be like this, ripe beneath his hands, my chest arching up to meet his mouth—our jeans come off and then he's up in me hard and I'm on my back, toes gripping the heels of his feet. I open my eyes and he's staring down at me, that gaze is bearing down on me, tense, naked, not just a seeing but a having to see, a having to *know*. He's watching my face as if everything's at stake, and I don't want to meet him, I didn't expect it, this asking, but somewhere I sense that if I shut my eyes I might never see him again, and already I know I want to see him

again, have to see him again, so I force them open wide, and let
him see that I have been abandoned by any self-possession I may
have claimed before; around his neck, my arms twitch. He slows
down, slows until I start moving on him, sliding myself up; his
body absorbs every response, I open my mouth, our hips are glued
together and then we're riding each other as if on the same horse,
it reaches everywhere, this climb, this terrific ascent, it reaches up
to the back of my throat, dry from breathing so hard. My hands
on the back of his neck, I pull him down and hold his mouth on
mine, sucking the sweat off his lower lip, and then we're breathing
together, into each other, carbon dioxide sweet poison makes my
head light—

I come with my head hanging off the roof's edge, my fist in my
mouth to keep from screaming.

W A L K I N G home in daylight, I try to think of how the
time passed, what we talked about for all that time before but I
can't remember anything—all I can think of now is how he moved
me, how he made me move with him, as if this is what he'd been
made for, and me, I was made to do this with him, and it's enough
for me to know this, to do this, I am caught up in time, I am back
in the river, I am in the thick of it, nature itself—

And then there's my father, drinking a cup of coffee at the
kitchen table when I get home. Adrenaline rockets through my
rib cage. I feel like I'm in high school again; I remember his
omniscience then. He looks at me as I walk by, open the fridge

to get some juice. He can smell it on me, I think, if not the sex
then surely the fear. I move as far away from him as I can get and
force a yawn.

"What're you doin up so early?"

"I fell asleep in the hammock and the sun woke me up, so I
went for a walk." I sip some of the juice and pretend to swallow
but I can't; my throat is too constricted.

"Still can't sleep?"

"Not really," I say. "What about you?"

"Maybe you should see a doctor," he says.

"I'm fine," I say. I realize he has no idea that I've lied to him
and I feel relief like a hot flash wash over me. Over the rim of my
glass I look at him. He looks so tired. I remember it's Saturday,
and I'm free.

"Going to work today, Dad?"

He nods. Can't spare the extra words.

"Don't you ever get a day off?"

"Don't want one," he says. This is the closest he comes to a
confession of loneliness and it's close enough to leave me speechless.

"You should rest," I say finally, inanely. He doesn't answer. I
want to tell him with my newfound pulse that he'll get over this,
that this will pass, I want to say life is good and full of strange
surprises, I want to tell him *know* this—but of course I don't. His
wife is dead and that is all he knows. He puts his cup of coffee
down and leaves the room.

At the kitchen table I listen to my father pulling out in his car
and driving away. The house and I sit quiet in the wake of his
leaving. The sun, already heavy, pours in through the windows,
but the light seems part of another world—the one I just left

behind. I get up and yank the curtains, always open, shut. As I pull my hand away, something falls from the sill.

It's my mother's gold lighter. It feels slim and heavy in my hands, a thing of value. I rub the dust from it and click it open. An even, civilized little flame springs up, flickering only slightly. I stare at the flame until I can't see anything else; in the hallway, I can hear the clock ticking off the seconds and the small, thick silences between. I close my eyes, hoping to conjure up my mother's spirit, hoping to feel her presence, to smell her perfume, to hear her footsteps in the hall.

Nothing happens. When I open my eyes, I see the flame has died.

Rising abruptly, I go upstairs to take a shower.

When I come out, naked and clean, I pull the blinds in my room shut and crawl in between clean white sheets. The minute I close my eyes everything comes back to me in a flood, so vividly I catch my breath: the way the muscles of his back moved under my hands, how clean his skin felt, how clean his hair, and how his mouth tasted faintly metallic, as if he had traded parts with his Harley.

Turning over in bed I think again of how gently those callused palms brushed over my ribs, how his stomach slapped hard against mine, and my hands sneak under the covers.

Against the blinds, the sun beats hard.

I WAKE UP at dusk, the hair sticking to the back of my neck. I feel languid, well used, and the feeling is strange; I realize it's the first time I've felt good since my mother died. Guilty, I rise quickly and dress, forcing myself to move briskly. Downstairs I pour myself a tall glass of ice water, crush half a lime into it, then go outside where I sip it slowly, swinging in the hammock.

I wonder what my father does at the station when he's gone so long. I picture him drinking weak instant coffee from a small Styrofoam cup that he gets for fifty cents from the machine, stretching out on the couch in the corridor for a nap, not wanting to come home. Behind me the house looms, offering nothing.

I wonder where Jesse is tonight. The thought sets my heart beating—and then I think, what if Dec were sleeping with somebody else . . . he wouldn't, I think, I'm sure—but I get up and go inside, dial his number for the first time. His machine answers, and I can hear a New York radio station blaring in the background. Dec's voice sounds thin, his message is brief. At the sound of the tone I am dumbstruck; I love you, I think, and it's true, but I don't say it. Replacing the receiver gently, gently, I close my eyes, try to imagine what he's doing, right now . . . sitting on his stoop, maybe, drinking a beer . . . or at some cheap movie theater on the Lower East Side, hunched inside its air-conditioned cool, absorbed by plot.

I think of the city, that impossible verticality; and with my eyes closed it's all right there, rising up against my eyelids, the streets, the staggering array of human traffic, the sirens and the shouts and the horns, and its pulse, how everything seems to rise into one supersonic hum, how it propelled me through every day, made my thoughts race, kept me awake at night . . .

I had gone and stayed for six years, and it never ceased being foreign to me, surrounded as I was by whole populations of people who would never learn to speak English, because they didn't have to. I had loved learning to call it home. My mother never once visited me there. I don't like cities, she said. They sweep me away and drown me.

Back outside, swinging gently inside the unhurried silence of a long North Carolina summer night, I suck on what's left of the lime, concentrate on not making a face.

When the light fades from the sky, I go inside.

———

I'm upstairs in my room when the phone rings. It's Dec, I'm sure. I reach down and pick up, but when I say hello my father says, "Ellie?" He tells me he's going to fill in for someone, that he won't be home till early morning. When I ask him if he's slept, he says he's okay.

It's ten when we hang up. I lie still, thinking I should make myself a sandwich, but I'm not hungry, I'm just wide awake, and restless . . .

I wait till the clock says ten-twenty before I venture out of bed and down the stairs, acting as if I'm just going to the kitchen for another glass of ice water. Pausing at the foot of the stairs, I can feel the house's stillness settling around me, a humid blanket of silence through which only the clock ticks. Dec's name crowds my thoughts, repeats itself like a moth beating at a flame, soft, insistent—

I walk quietly out onto the porch, easing the screen door shut behind me. The moon blazes overhead. A slight breeze dries the hair that sticks to my skin. I sit on the front steps and begin counting, one mississippi, two mississippi, three mississippi . . . I make myself say all the mississippis, pronouncing each syllable, giving every number equal time. When I get to ninety, I start walking.

Rounding the corner I see Jesse's bike, a large shadow looming near the porch, but there's no noise from the house. Slowing down with every step, I approach the porch and stand there, not knowing what to do next. Clearing my throat I decide to say his name but it won't come out. The front door is shut and I don't want to knock. I consider going back home, turn around—and there he is, watching me.

"Jesus!" I take two steps back and smile, desperate to seem cool. "Hi."

" 'Lo," he says, not moving.

"I was just—I was at home—I thought that . . ." I shut my mouth, feeling utterly foolish. Jesse looks at me. Taking a deep breath, I step forward. "I wanted to see you," I admit.

"Come in."

I follow him through the house, past an open door through which I can see a battered old couch, a TV, and into his room, which is shuttered and cool.

"Shut the door," he says. I do, but I keep my hand on the knob. When I turn back around, he's across the room, lighting a cigarette by the window. My mother's lighter lies quietly in my right front pocket, a talisman, a small weight against my thigh.

"You nervous?" He is looking directly at me. Whenever he looks at me I have the feeling he's gauging me exactly, measuring my eyes and my mouth and my soul—it reduces me to a helpless truth-telling.

"Yes."

He is still looking at me that way, as if calculating the risk. "Think I didn't want to see you?"

"Maybe." I let go of the knob.

He takes another drag of his cigarette and then he puts it out with the toe of his boot, sits on the windowsill. "Come over here." My heart quickens; it's uncanny, irritating, irresistible, how he orders me to do what I desire.

Walking over to stand next to him, I avoid his eyes, looking through the narrow space in between the shutters instead. I can see a slice of sky, whitewashed by the moon. He sits so still I can't hear him breathing, but I can feel his eyes on me. I can't look at him, I keep staring through the window, every muscle in my body stiff with tension. We stay like this for second after second, and it feels to me as if the whole world is poised with us, as if the grass outside has stopped growing, and the moon hangs suspended in mid-orbit.

Then, with that same eerie noiselessness, he raises his hand, pushes the hair away from my face with the backs of his fingers before letting them fall to the nape of my neck. When he touches my skin, an electrical current runs from the top of my skull down to my crotch.

"Baby you got the bluest eyes I ever seen—"

"They're gray—"

"Blue."

A shiver runs hard through my body, I twist my head to look at him and he pulls me closer, until I'm wedged between his legs and the tip of my nose brushes against his cheek. The smell of him inundates me, already familiar, and I stay like that, breathing fast and shallow. I can feel my hands shaking at my sides. He reaches up, his mouth reaches up to kiss me, teeth nipping my lower lip and letting go, he plays with me like that, like a cat, he turns his head back and forth so I can feel the texture of his lips, they're cracked. Licking his lips with the tip of my tongue, I feel them coming up in a smile and I'm smiling when he pulls me up against him, still smiling though my mouth is open now, and holding me up from the bend in my waist he stands, starts to move, and I hoist my legs up onto his, thighs clamped around his jeans.

He takes me to bed, starts to unzip my shorts when I grab his wrists. Sitting up I reach for his T-shirt. He has it off in one fluid motion and I'm face to face with his chest, I catch a glimpse of a tattoo, letters, over his heart. I try to back off to see but it's too dark and his hands are on me again, I lose my focus, he wants me and he is so sure of himself, all I have to do is respond, and I can't help but respond, he calls everything I am up beneath his finger-tips, he slides my shorts down, turns me over so my face is buried in the sheet, runs his chin down my spine, slow, nosing down, and then turns me over again, my weight fluid in his hands. Electric pleasure like a river of mercury slices through me, I don't know what he's doing, I want to make him stop, it's too much, but instead, I wrap my thighs around his neck, a human sacrifice, my mind taut, strung blank with pleasure, riding the pleasure with one hand in his hair and the other over my eyes, taken.

All the way in, taken.

M Y EYES open onto pitch dark, and when I hear it again, low in the distance, I realize it was the thunder that woke me. I shift in bed and Jesse sits up. Our bodies are damp where they touch. I roll away from him slightly. The thunder rolls again, closer this time. There's a brief flash of illumination outside.

Someone knocks on the door. "Jesse."

"Yeah." Jesse gets up and I watch him dress, same blue jeans, same T-shirt. He leaves the room without saying anything to me. I lie in bed, listening to the storm approaching, wide awake. After a while, I get up and dress.

I open the door cautiously, walk down the hall to the bathroom, which is stark and harshly lit by a single bulb. A black-and-white poster of Sitting Bull with a quotation printed beneath it, THERE IS NO MORE, faces the door, its corners curling with the moisture. Although there is no towel, no razor—no sign at all, in fact, of personal use, except for one cake of hard white soap—it all seems fairly clean. I wash my face in cold water over a big, rusted sink, and then I run my wet hands along the back of my neck, down the insides of my thighs.

Nobody's in the hall when I come out and Jesse's room is still empty. The door to the TV room is shut, though, and I can hear low voices inside. I stop next to it, hold my breath, trying to decide whether to knock or not. Outside, a motor suddenly roars to life, and I jump. As it leaves, there is a deafening crack of thunder, and then the rain begins to fall.

In seconds it's pouring, and when I reach the porch, I stand against the splintering railing and watch it come down. Jesse's bike and another one are covered by a tarp, standing side by side. The earth gives up a rich, moist smell. I breathe it in so hard my head spins.

I've been out there for ten minutes, maybe more, when Jesse comes out.

"Thought you split."

I turn to look at him, but he is looking at the rain. "You're the one who split," I say lightly.

"Got business," he says shortly.

"What kind of business?"

He ignores the question, and suddenly I am struck by the fact that he is an unknown quantity; that I have already slept with him twice.

"Should I go?"

"You got someone waitin for you?"

"I hope not."

"Thought you didn't have a boyfriend." Grinning, as if he's caught me.

"I live at home," I say. "With my parents."

"Your mother wouldn't like me, huh?" I can tell he's proud of this, that he likes to be considered dangerous. I almost tell him that my mother is dead, but then I don't. I look at him, wondering what my mother *would* think . . . surely she would be struck by those eyes. Any woman would. Even a dead woman.

I look back at the rain. It falls like a sheet of water just inches beyond me. "As long as I'm home before my father gets up."

Behind me, I can hear the flare of a match, and I remember my mother's lighter—I pat my pockets, briefly panicked, but it hasn't fallen out. The door opens again and I turn around just in time to see Jesse going back in. I sit there, wondering if that was a signal, if I should leave now, or if he expects me to wait . . .

Just as I stand, the door opens again and my face prepares itself, but it isn't Jesse. It's a man with long dark hair and a craggy face, half hidden by his beard.

"Evenin."

"Hello."

"You here to see Jesse?" He looks at me appraisingly; I can feel him taking in the tangled hair, the wrinkled shirt, and the fact of me still here.

"Yes." I pull the neck of my T-shirt up, but I know he knows that I was in bed with Jesse. I turn my back on him again, not wanting to see him imagine me naked. Thunder cracks overhead. The rain sounds like stones pelting the roof. I am grateful for the storm; it gives me an excuse to stay.

"You his lady friend?" He has the same manner Jesse used the first time I met him, a distant courtesy, more wariness than anything else. I nod, wonder if that was Jesse's term for me.

He walks over to me and extends his hand. "I'm Eddie." I do a half turn and we shake. His palm is callused, his hand envelops mine. He doesn't smile.

"You waitin on him?"

"No," I lie, quickly, not liking the way his question sounds. "I was just leaving." Taking a deep breath, I prepare to walk into the rain, but a sudden blast of music from inside stops me. Mick Jagger's voice rises in competition with the storm. "Please allow me to introduce myself / I'm a man of wealth and tas-te . . ."

The door opens and Jesse comes out.

"I was just about to go." I hesitate, trailing my hand on the porch railing, waiting to be asked back in.

"Yeah." He looks right and left, as if he's expecting someone. I realize he wants me to leave, and for the first time it occurs to me that maybe he has somebody else; another woman. My throat gets tight.

"Okay," I say after a moment. "I'll see you."

"Yeah," he says. "See you."

I walk into the rain feeling like an idiot, conscious of them behind me, watching me.

"Hey!" He catches me just as I'm about to break into a run. I turn around. My shirt is already soaked, and I cross my arms across my shoulders so Eddie won't see my breasts through it. Rain drips into the corners of my eyes. "You want a ride?"

An unreasonable joy surges up in my chest, but I shake my head. I don't want my father to hear the bike. I whirl around and start running. In a minute I'm around the corner and out of sight, but I keep on running. The motion keeps me warm, and I slide into a steady rhythm, breath in, breath out, in-in-in, out-out-out. The rain is clean and cold, and the road feels hard beneath my feet.

I run all the way home.

————

Inside, everything's the same. Same thick air, same clock ticking in the same silence. I can feel it closing around me as I drip down the hall to the bathroom, I can feel the air like lead slowing my heart down.

I'm wringing my clothes out in the tub when the phone rings. I run to the kitchen to get it, snatch it up, it's so late—I think, I can't help thinking, my father, something's happened, some-one's calling from the station to tell me something I can't bear to hear—

"Ellie. It's me." I stand stock-still, unable for a moment to envision his face.

"Dec . . . it's so late—what time is it?"

"Past three. I've been calling all night. Where've you been?" His voice is quiet, but wide awake.

". . . I was asleep. I fell asleep outside, in the hammock."

"Oh." There's a silence and I hunch down, naked and cold, wrap one arm around myself.

"How are you?"

Automatically I answer, "Fine," then catch myself. "I mean, okay. I'm okay."

"Really?" His tone is so serious. I can imagine Dec in his tiny apartment pacing back and forth with the phone, the extension cord trailing behind him, frowning with concentration as he listens for evidence of my breaking down.

"Yes," I say. "Really." I cover the phone with one hand so he won't hear how fast I'm breathing.

"How's your father?"

"He's okay. Works all the time. He's working a double shift right now."

"So are you going to stay there?" Although he asks as if he's expecting me to say yes, I know he wants me to say no, I know he's hoping.

"I can't just leave, Dec. I can't."

"I know." There's another silence, and then he says, "For how long?"

"At least the summer . . ." I twist the cord around my hand, winding it over and over my wrist as if it were a skein of yarn, and feel the taut elastic digging into my skin.

"I miss you." His voice carries clearly over the wires, almost as if he's calling from the drugstore down the street, but I can't help feeling as if we're trying to communicate across a tremendous distance—as if whole years lie between us.

I can still feel the imprint of Jesse's mouth against my neck; I want to tell Dec I miss him too but shame gags me, and searching for something else, something true, I whisper, "I miss my mother." The finality the words have surprises me, tears spring into my eyes and then I'm pulling the receiver away and swallowing, torn between needing to grieve in private and needing a witness.

"I wish I could be with you," he says softly.

"Me too," I say, and I mean it, but I can't imagine him with his pale face and his cropped brown hair here, in this house, in this town. It seems a physical impossibility.

"Maybe I could visit . . ."

"I don't know, Dec . . . I don't think it's a good idea right now . . ." This time he doesn't say anything, and finally I break the silence. "My dad . . . he's pretty old-fashioned . . ."

"We wouldn't have to sleep together—I mean, in the same room . . ."

"I don't know . . . maybe later." There's another long silence and I hold my breath.

"Okay," he says finally, and I know he didn't want to, know how difficult it was for him to accept this; ordinarily, we would have had an argument, with him growing more and more insistent. I feel cheap, as if I'm using my mother's death to manipulate him.

"I just wanted to call and see how you were doing."

"I'm okay. It's—I can't talk about it."

"I know . . . I can't even imagine . . ."

"Dec, listen. When my dad's home he goes to bed early . . . you shouldn't call after eleven . . ."

"Will you call me? If you need anything?"

"Yes."

"Promise?"

I do. He tells me he loves me. Choked with everything else I didn't tell him, unable to say it back, I say "I know" instead. When we hang up, my skin is clammy with sweat, and I know it's more than the lies: Dec was with me when my father called. That moment seems frozen in time, perfectly preserved; it comes back unexpectedly, with a lethal freshness, as if caught in some eternal present, waiting only for the trigger that springs it free.

"On impact," he had said, his voice far away, brittle. And all night long I kept imagining that impact, I couldn't stop picturing it, the rush and shock and smash of the rest of her life accelerating to meet her head-on through the windshield. I imagined my mother's eyes, wide, her mouth, wide; the soundless "oh," and I wondered if, at that speed, everything slows down. I imagined the terrible creak of steel bending, tires screaming, the trauma of shattering glass—did her soul lift up and out at that sound, did she know it was over, and did she have time to feel anything but surprise?

It was too late when he called to fly out that night, and I couldn't stay at the apartment, inside those four walls, closing the news in around me. I went out onto the streets and walked from block to block, as if by moving I could stay ahead of the ruin, and the vast desolate plain that reached to claim me.

Dec walked with me, kept his arm around me, we must have gone eighty, ninety blocks before he made me stop, said the neighborhood was getting bad, said come on, let's have a drink, and then tried to find words—I remember his face, how distant his every feature seemed; and I remember the dull revelation, revealing itself over and over again through that long, freaked and chilling night, of his powerlessness to console me. He held me and there, with his arms around me and my face sideways against his chest, I was isolated, separated quite neatly from him and the rest of the world.

His love was ineffectual then, and I wanted him to leave me, so I could clutch myself alone and say, "If only Dec were here," and so hold out some final hope, pretend that someone, just one person, if only he were present, could stop the ravage of every passing moment on me. Instead we drank, and later took a taxi home, where Dec fell asleep and I sat up and watched the dawn come in through my bedroom window.

———

I step into the shower and turn it on so hot my skin turns red. I keep hearing my father's voice over the telephone, sounding very far away (Ellie, you have to be very strong). I can remember thinking I *am* strong even as I began to realize, I remember how my back stiffened, What, Dad—and then that long moment before I knew, that long last moment before (Mom) and how I wanted to stop (on impact) snatch it back and hold myself suspended, hang there knowing I was strong and nothing else. (Dead.)

———

In bed, I can hear the branches of the big oak tree scratching against the slanted roof of my room. When I was little it used to scare me, I imagined gnarled old fingers clawing, wanting in, wanting the warmth of my room. Those nights I'd run barefoot downstairs, my mother would be sitting in the living room waiting for my father to come home, music low from the radio, drinking a Scotch and soda and smoking, I could see the lipstick red on the filter. Mama, I'm scared. *They're* upstairs—and I would run over, my nightgown swishing around my calves, and sit in her lap, bury my face in her neck, the perfume of her rising up around me like safety and heaven and everything that would never hurt me. It's just the tree, Ellie, she'd say, putting her cigarette out so as not to blow smoke in my face. Your daddy'll be home soon, don't you worry.

I would pretend to be more scared than I was so she'd let me stay up till he got back, we'd hear the crunch of his tires outside, sometimes he'd flash the blue lights, and then my mother would say, Run and get your daddy a cold beer, and I would hear her kiss him at the door. I'd come back, proud to have opened the bottle all by myself, and hand it up to him. He seemed seven feet tall then, indomitable with his shiny silver belt buckle, the black leather holster, and all that thick brown hair, there was no gray in it at all then . . .

He would take me on his lap while he drank his beer, my whole leg fit inside his hand, and I would lean back against him and grow drowsy, the grown-up music and my parents' voices blurring together, my father's laugh a deep vibration through my back. At some point he would carry me up to bed, tuck me in and then stand up bent, because he was too tall to fit straight, the roof slanted over my bed.

No one's to bother my daughter now, hear? Voice booming in the attic room. Or they'll have to deal with me. It gave me shivers of pleasure to hear him; who would dare disobey such authority.

Right, Ellie?

Right, Daddy.

And then he'd go back downstairs, where my mother was waiting for him.

I think of their room now, empty, her clothes still hanging in the closet, and how he stays away. I reach up under my pillow where I put her lighter, and hold it in my fist, feeling it grow warm.

I lie in bed and listen and listen to the rain, falling down hard over my head.

I T ' S R A I N I N G still when I wake up. Everything gives off
a damp musk; the air is cool, summer's in check. I dress slow; the
day stretches ahead without a glimmer of light. My father, red-
eyed with fatigue, gives me a ride to work. I duck down when we
pass Jesse's, sneaking a look back in the passenger mirror; all I see
is the Harley, covered with a big beige tarp.

It keeps raining all day. Sandra and I stand with one elbow
tucked into a hip and drink coffee, watch it come down.

"I been out last coupla weekends lookin to find someone," she
says in an offhand way.

"Any luck?" I ask. She raises one penciled eyebrow, twists her
lips up sideways.

"Nothin I could keep," she says. "Sometimes you got to have
someone to warm up your bones, though . . . don't hardly matter
who." She looks at me. "Know what I mean?"

"Sure," I say, but she laughs.

"Listen to you, you got that tight skin, them eyelashes . . .
honey, you don't know nothin about bein desperate that wasn't
learned in a book."

"I don't know about desperate," I tell her. "I just feel like I've
been dredged."

My father comes by to pick me up at four when I get off. He
drops me off at home, says he'll be back by dinnertime. When he's
gone I go into his bedroom and push my mother's clothes along
the rack in the closet, stopping to feel the fabrics, stopping to
smell them. I take an oversized camel cardigan of my dad's that
she always used to wear. It's rough against my neck.

When he comes home we eat in the TV room with napkins on our laps, watch the news together.

"Bob Schaeffer's daughter's been askin about you."

"Melanie Schaeffer? Asking about *me*?" I remember her face, pale oval with blond hair, cherry-red lipstick. She was the "it" girl, slim-thighed and narrow-waisted. She wore a thin gold ankle bracelet and showed her midriff the minute the weather turned warm, I remember even now that small span of tan skin, she pushed it out like it was some distant prize and when she walked past them in the hall you could smell the boys lusting after her. I never got too close to her, but everybody followed Melanie.

"She'd like to hear from you." He looks at me briefly.

"I suppose she feels sorry for me."

"I thought you two were friends."

"Not really. She used to say hi to me because she knew her father worked with you, that's all."

"Melanie's a nice girl. Think you oughta call her."

"I don't think we have anything in common anymore, Dad." I don't mention that I never thought we did.

"Ellie, this isn't New York City. You goin to be here all summer, you better make the best of it." I can tell he's thought this out, has decided I need friends, has decided this is what's to be done. I watch the weatherman's stick touching cloud patterns taken from a satellite picture.

"Think it'll flood?"

"No, it'll stop before that happens." I don't question his faith.

"So no one has to evacuate."

"We might evacuate the old people's home, out on Shady Lane. Their roof keeps springin leaks." He puts his bowl aside. "You goin to call?"

I shrug. He presses back into his easy chair, his eyes hooded and dark, fixed on the screen.

"Let me take your boots off, Dad." I stand up, but he says, "No, no, I'm goin to bed soon anyway. Just want to watch the news."

I sit there with him though I dread the parts where they tell about people dying in wrecks, my shoulders tense up and I hold my breath, waiting for I don't know what horror; that my father will break down in front of me, I guess. But he never does. His face hardly changes expression. He waits till the broadcast is finished and then he says, "Got that number right here, in my wallet." He pulls it out of his back pocket, extracts a piece of crumpled paper. "Whyn't you call her now."

"Oh, Dad. I really don't feel like it." I push myself up out of my chair and pick up my dirty dish, but when I go to get his, he puts the piece of paper in my hand instead.

"Go on now Ellie. You don't do it now you never will."

"Dad . . ." I balance his plate on the crook of my elbow like I've learned to do at the restaurant and head for the kitchen, leaving the number crumpled on the table next to him. "I just don't feel like it. What's the big deal?"

"I told Bob you'd be callin over there tonight." His voice reaches down the hall and my fingers tense around the plates; hostility rising like prickly heat, I walk the rest of the way into the kitchen, put the plates in the sink and turn the water on.

"You hear what I said?" He's standing behind me in the doorway.

"You had no business." My back to him, I scrape at the beans still sticking to his plate.

"Schaeffer's the one that found your mother."

For a second I freeze, stare at the water running over my wrists,

and then I start scraping again. Please, I think. I don't want to
know. A silence stretches between us and I tense my back up
against it. Finally, my father sighs.

"You oughta be seein some people your age."

"I don't feel like seeing anybody." The water hits the plates so
hard it splatters back up all over my arms.

"You oughta call her."

"I'll call her! All right?" I let go the plates to turn around and
they fall against each other with a hysterical china clinking. I can
feel my chin trembling; I clamp my jaws together so hard they
hurt. My father rubs his eyes, the other hand on his belt, as if I'm
some runaway teenager defying arrest.

"Here's the number." Carefully, he smooths the piece of paper
out. "Thanks for supper. I'm goin to bed."

He turns around without waiting to see if I'll say good night;
I don't.

If it were the other way around, I think at him, if you had died
instead of her, things would be different. My mother and I, we
would hold each other. We would be close. I could tell her that
I had met someone, that someone was setting my heart on fire.
She wouldn't make me answer questions I didn't want to answer.
She wouldn't make me call Melanie Schaeffer.

I remember the time in New York when I got pregnant. My
freshman year, I slept with someone I never saw again and six weeks
later the test was positive. Shaking, green with nausea, I called my
mother and cried. I expected anger, expected her to tell me how
disappointed she was in me. But all she said was "Oh, honey," and
then she started crying too. She sent me the money for the abortion
from her own bank account, and she never told my father anything.
It'll be our secret, she said. Just between you and me.

Inside my chest, my heart feels like a fist, hard-knuckled and small.

H ARDLY anybody comes into Parker's in the downpour, but Sandra keeps ducking into the ladies' and reapplying her bright pink lipstick.

"You expecting someone?" I ask and from the elaborately casual way she shrugs I know she is. Later on I ask her if she's met Mr. Right.

"Hah," she says. "Maybe if I kept a blindfold on." We both laugh at this and I think maybe she's going to talk to me then, tell me something, but she turns around and goes into the kitchen instead, brews herself a cup of black China tea. Toward the end of our shift she's stopped glancing at the door every time it opens, and her mouth, underneath its girlish color, gets tight. Outside the rain keeps coming down for the third day in a row, and I keep thinking about Jesse, about sleeping with Jesse, sleeping with Jesse and lying to Dec. Maybe he's lying to me too, the thought comes, and for a second I almost feel relieved, but when I try to picture it, suddenly my stomach feels tight, queasy. I can't do it to him. I can't see Jesse anymore.

"They're beginning to talk flood on the radio," I say.

"Yeah, well," she says. "Things are tough all over."

When my tables are empty I go over to the public phone by the door and dial Melanie's number. She answers just after the second ring. When she hears it's me she says she's having a little

party tonight and please won't I come. I look at Sandra, head bent
over an old *McCall's* across the room. From here I can see her
roots, a good half inch of dark before the hair turns blond. Sure,
I tell Melanie. I'd love to.

My father's out of the county so Sandra gives me a ride home
in her old Ford with its rusted hood. I stay sitting upright when
we pass Jesse's, but nobody's there, and his bike is gone.

"You know who lives there?" I ask Sandra, wanting to talk
about him.

"Buncha hoods" is all she answers. We ride the rest of the way
home in silence.

When he gets home, I wait until we're eating before I tell my
father Melanie's invited me over to a little party she's having. He
asks me what time I want to go. Although it's easily two miles
away, I tell him I don't need a ride.

"Don't be stubborn."

"I'm not," I tell him. "I like to walk. In New York I walk
everywhere. I want to walk."

"In the rain?"

"It isn't cold out. Doesn't matter about the rain."

"Suit yourself."

But when I'm dressed and ready to go, he hears me in the hall
and comes out of the TV room. Without a word he opens the
front door for me and we both run out to the car. It's warm inside,
it smells of my father, and I lean my head back to watch the
windshield wipers going back and forth.

"You lookin forward to seein your old buddies?"

I think of my old buddies, my real friends: Kim, George, Ste-
phen, Patrick. I feel a twinge of pride, feel sure we would still be
friends today, but I know that they won't be here, at Melanie's.
Like me, all of them left town years ago and never looked back.

"It's been so long, I've forgotten their names."

"Oh, it all comes back." I look at his profile lit up by the red and green lights on the dash. In the shadows, his eyes look caved in. I am overcome by an urge to hold his hand, an urge so strong it feels like thirst, but he's holding on to the steering wheel with both of them, and after a while, the feeling passes.

He pulls up in front of the Schaeffers' house. We can see the light through the curtains, and shadows moving. Someone pulls the curtains slightly aside, then lets them drop again.

"God." I let my head drop back on the seat and roll my eyes over toward my father.

"Have a good time now," he says.

"Aren't you going to come in and say hi to her parents?"

He shakes his head.

"I'm sure they'd like to see you, Dad." Vaguely now I remember letters my mother wrote to me in college, saying they'd been getting together with the Schaeffers on Friday nights, saying they made a good foursome. I sit up to face him. "They probably meant the invitation for you, too."

He doesn't seem to hear me, checks the lighted windows in the rearview mirror. "Think they're waitin on you, Ellie." When I turn around to see, someone's face is at the window and suddenly I want to ask my father to take me home, but he leans over and unlocks my door.

"I hope we have something to talk about besides the past." I don't move.

"It's good to get out of the house." His voice is firm. What about you, I think, but I don't say it; there's no place else for him to go, besides back to the station. "Call me when you want a ride home."

"That's okay. I can get a ride from one of the kids." I open the door. The sound of the rain rushes in; I can feel the cool wet air in gusts against my skin. I lean over to kiss my father's cheek. "Thanks, Dad."

" 'Night, Ellie." He waits till I've run up to the porch before he shifts to drive.

The door opens before I knock and I know they were watching us out there. Before I can really see her, Melanie grabs me in a hug. Her body is reedlike still, she wears the same perfume she used to wear in high school. The smell overwhelms me more than anything else; I feel as if I'm stepping back into a past life. People come crowding up, and my father's right, names come back when I see their faces, Chuck, Nina, Kathy, Evan . . . all faces I remember from Melanie's crowd. We hug awkwardly.

"Someone get this girl a beer!" Melanie shouts, and immediately a beer appears. It's cold and slippery in my hand but I'm glad for something to hold on to. "Ellie, I am so sorry about your mother," she whispers then, one arm coming around to squeeze my waist.

"Thanks."

"Come on, let's sit down." Melanie leads me to the far end of the room, over to the couch. People leave us alone; she's still the ringleader. She sits facing me, our knees touching.

"Well it's great to see you, Ellie, you look really good."

I am conscious of my tight-fitting sleeveless black turtleneck, my short black denim skirt, my low-heeled black pumps, conscious of having chosen the most flattering clothes I owned, conscious of the makeup on my face, and I feel ashamed of the compliment, as if, since I have so consciously engineered it, it must somehow be false.

"So do you," I tell Melanie, and it's true. She wears a bright blue tank top and fashionably baggy gray shorts. Her skin is still smooth and flawless, her breasts high.

"It's too bad it takes a death to bring us together like this," she adds, and then leans in close, lowers her voice. "Has it been really awful for you at home?"

"Not great." I inch the beer up to my lips and tilt it back, glancing around the room. I seem unable to meet her gaze for longer than two seconds at a time. I feel shifty-eyed, deceitful.

"How's your father?"

"He's okay."

"My dad says he's come into the station practically every day since . . . it happened." Melanie's eyes are fixed on mine. It occurs to me then that she knows all the details of my mother's death (fractured neck, broken ribs, massive internal hemorrhage), and I feel strangely betrayed.

"Work takes his mind off it, I guess."

"He says he practically lives there." She sighs deeply. "God, you poor thing."

"It's not that bad." I can't stand her pity, I shift my legs and Melanie sits back a little. Her eyes widen almost imperceptibly at my words and suddenly I'm overcome with nerves, as if I'm back in ninth grade sitting with the most popular girl in the whole school, helpless to keep from saying the wrong thing. An awkward little silence settles between us and then she clears her throat.

"Will you be movin back here?"

"I'm just staying the summer."

"I'm sure your father appreciates that."

I nod, drink my beer.

"So how do you like New York?" She smiles at me brightly, as if now that we've dealt with morbidity we can get on with our lives, and I remember how many times I said hi to Melanie in the hall, and how few times we ever said more.

"I like it." I know I could never explain my passion for the city to this girl, this prom queen who never left the court; I try to imagine her there amidst the traffic, the winos, the young shirtless Puerto Ricans dancing down Avenue A, and for a second I nearly smile.

"You went there for actin school, right?"

"Directing." I feel as if I've lost my capacity for speech.

"Of course," she says, as if she ever knew, but I smile at her, grateful for the interest. "Are you doin a lot of it?"

"Off and on. It isn't exactly steady work . . . and of course it doesn't pay . . . but I'm learning a lot."

"But what about your bills?"

"Oh . . . I have a day job that pays the rent. Temp work."

"You mean like a secretary?"

"Pretty much." Listening to myself the way I suppose she's hearing me, I feel helpless to make my own case, and suddenly I wonder what I'm doing in New York, what I'm doing here, at this party, what I've got to give anyone in this world at all.

"What about you? How's your life going?"

"Well, I'm gettin ready to be married." She looks down at her hands and for the first time I notice the diamond shining on her slender finger.

"I didn't even see it . . ." I reach over and she puts her hand in mine to show me and suddenly I'm flooded with the warmth of being in her good favor. "It's beautiful."

"Danny gave it to me last Christmas."

"Danny MacIntyre?" I glance around, my hand creeping up to my throat.

"He'll be here later," she says, following my gaze. "Yes, it's goin to be a September wedding. Maybe you'll still be here . . ."

"I'd love to come, but I have to be back in New York in September. I'm directing a play . . . a Sam Shepard play," I say, surprising myself with the lie.

"Sam Shepard? I've seen him in the movies. He's good-lookin." Melanie looks at me, suddenly admiring, and I feel irrevocably compromised, weak-kneed. "Oh, you've finished your beer. Can I get you another?"

"Actually . . . you wouldn't have any vodka in the house, would you?"

I follow her into the kitchen. Chuck and Evan are playing quarters and there are small puddles of flat beer shining up from the table. Melanie makes me a screwdriver, two-thirds vodka, and I lean against the sink, pretend to smile at the game so that Melanie can leave. In the living room somebody turns the music up ("Owner of the lonely heart / you're much better than the rest"), music we overplayed in high school, making up with volume what we lacked in grace, music that staled and still we played it; it reminds me of every high school dance I ever attended, the cafeteria decorated with crepe paper and the boys refusing to dance, sitting outside drinking beers that somebody's older brother had bought while we stood around pretending we didn't care, flesh-colored makeup covering every blemish we could find.

I refuse Evan's offer of joining in the quarters game, finish the drink and make myself another before walking away, skirting the edges of the party, thankful that the lights have been turned off. People whose faces I haven't thought of in years are dancing clumsily between the sofa and the coffee table in the living room, the rug pushed up in wrinkles against the wall. I look at them and

all I can think of is the yearning—standing poised, waiting for
everything to happen to me, in an agony of suspense, the yearning
in the marrow of my bones, a fierce thing, sucking at me . . . in
the mirror nothing was right, hair too short, breasts too small and
nothing around the hips to lure the boys I liked.

Danny MacIntyre. The best-looking boy in the school, I had
a crush on him from junior high to senior year. He was a surfer,
a landlocked surfer with smooth, hairless limbs, a wide chest, curly
hair. Lying in bed on Sunday afternoons I'd spend myself with
fantasies of the curves of his mouth. Empty Sundays dreading
school, planning the outfit for Monday, hoping to sit across from
him on the school bus, glad if I could only drench my eyes with
the sight of his sleep-puffed face. He always wore the same pair
of Levis, till the threads, bared, tore.

And then the summer before college, the last summer I ever
spent in this town until now, Melanie had gone on vacation with
her family, and I had chased after Danny MacIntyre shamelessly.
I remember with a sudden, unwelcome clarity one night our
senior year in a boat, on the lake. A bunch of us had gone out
there, but Danny and I had ended up in one boat, alone. Kim told
me the rumor was he wanted to lose his virginity and Melanie
wouldn't give it to him, but I didn't care what the rumor was, I
was going to go out with him and give him anything he wanted.

Standing there I have the eerie feeling that no time has passed,
that I have no life except the one here, that New York doesn't
exist, that my breasts haven't grown. With every drink I feel less
and less capable of speaking and I keep moving as if possessed with
purpose, flashing busy little smiles at people, until finally somebody catches up to me.

"Good to be back?" Kathy smiles her bland smile from a colorless face, sure of my answer. I remember her being on the debate team, I remember she got the highest scores on the SATs; I cannot fathom why she's still here and I cannot imagine her anyplace else.

"I hate this music," I say suddenly, and realize I'm drunk. Her smile wavers slightly. "It reminds me of high school." She looks at me anxiously, waiting for me to give some indication that I'm kidding. I stand there full of an alcoholic belligerence and say nothing.

"You look good," she tries then and her politeness sets my teeth on edge.

"At least I've managed that," I mutter. "Excuse me."

I make my way back into the kitchen and nearly bump into someone whose face looks vaguely familiar but I can't find his name. He's twisting the cap off a beer; I notice how his wrists jut out and I realize he's young, younger than me. He smiles at me politely, says hi.

"I'm Ellie."

His eyebrows go up in faint surprise. "I know, I remember you. I'm Mike. Melanie's brother."

"Oh." His face looks bloodless to me, clean-shaven and blank. I can see the gel where he spiked up his hair. He picks up a windbreaker thrown across the back of one of the chairs and dips his arm into one of the sleeves. "Why're you leaving the party?"

"I'm goin over to my girlfriend's house." He doesn't look at me and his lack of interest crushes me.

"Well it was nice to see you again."

"You too," he says automatically. "Take care."

As I walk into the bathroom my hip slams into the doorway and when I turn, one of my knees suddenly gives so that I'm left half

standing, supporting myself on the doorknob. Using my weight to
shut the door, I push the lock in with my thumb and slide down
to the cool tile floor. I want to pee but I don't trust the lock, I
can't shake the feeling that someone's going to walk in, discover
me, violate my privacy, break me down. Outside, I can hear music
starting up again. It seems like a cover-up, a false layer over their
voices; I can feel the percussion faintly vibrating through the wall
("Mirrors on the ceiling / Pink champagne on ice / We are all
just prisoners here / Of our own device") . . .

Mouthing the words, I find I know them all. I push myself up
off the floor, go over and sit on the john, put my elbows on my
knees and jam the heels of my hands into my eye sockets. Everything is deeply black, a dense dizziness overtakes me, and I don't
know how long I've been sitting there like that when I hear
someone trying to open the door. Immediately my heart sets up
a wild fluttering.

"I'm in here!" Pulling my skirt up hard, terrorized at the
thought of being caught half-naked.

"Ellie? Is that you?" The voice is familiar and for a brief second
I think it's Dec, but it then comes to me that this is the wrong
context, all wrong . . . it comes to me that everything's wrong or
how else could I be here like this, in the dark, in this house where
no one loves me.

He knocks on the door, three rapid taps. "Melanie wants to
know if you're okay." It's Danny. A rush of adrenaline makes me
break out in a sweat.

"I'm coming out—" Finding a brush in the cabinet I brush my
hair back from my face, check myself in a mirror whose rim is
encrusted with a myriad of tiny varnished seashells. A little pale
but my skin is clear and I can see the bones in my face, the fine
angles they make. I open the door.

"Ellie?" The surprise in his tone gratifies me.

"Hi Danny. It's been a long time."

"Yeah. It sure has." He looks the same, a little older, his hair a little shorter. "How are you?"

Drunk, I think. "Okay. How are you?"

"Fine." He smiles at me then, and it's the same smile that charmed me all through high school, easy and white.

"Did you just get here?" My mouth's gone dry and I look down, lick my lips.

"Yeah, I had some business to take care of."

"Melanie told me the news." I hold my eyes wide and pronounce each word carefully, anxious for him not to know my state. "Congratulations."

"Oh, yeah. Thanks. Guess it's about time we did it."

"You ready for it?" I lean against the wall and cross my legs, run my fingers through my hair. I can feel my skirt riding up my thighs, and Danny looks down, checks me out. When he looks up again I smile at him like I've learned to smile at men in New York, brilliant and careless.

"Ready in what sense?" He smiles back.

"I mean to give up other women." I shift, recross my legs.

"Well," he says slowly. "I'm not married yet."

Our eyes meet and I'm aware of a pact being made. Neither one of us says anything for a minute, and then I look away.

"So how's the party? You been here awhile?"

"Actually, I was getting ready to leave . . ." I don't want Melanie to see me talking to him and I don't want to talk to anyone else. I can see the back door just a few feet down the hall. "Would you mind very much giving me a ride?"

"Uh, no . . . I mean, sure. I'll give you a ride." He lifts his beer, drinks it down. "Didn't bring your car, huh?"

"I don't have one."

"What happened to that VW you used to drive?" I can tell he's proud to have remembered the make.

"It was totaled." I enunciate each word standing up very straight, looking directly at him, and even in the dark I can see the deep flush that rises to his face.

"Oh . . . yeah. Sorry."

"D'you mind if I just meet you out front? I don't really want to face anyone right now."

"No, no, I'll come out the back way too."

The door's unlocked and we slip out and stand on the step for a second, Danny right behind me, just out of the rain which falls like a sheet of water before me. The smell of wet earth clears my head.

"Ready?" He digs into his jeans and pulls out the keys. I nod and step aside, and he runs down the stairs. He still moves like an athlete, and I run after him, both of us staying close to the sides of the house, but by the time we get into the car we're soaked.

"Jesus, it's really comin down." He pushes the hair off his face with one hand and turns the key in the ignition with the other. I slide down in the bucket seat and watch the rabbit's foot dangling from the rearview mirror, the same one I used to watch for whenever I saw a dark blue Mustang drive by. I reach out and hit it.

"You still have it."

"Good luck. Don't leave home without it." We drive away, the headlights shining two beams of wet light.

He asks me directions, and after I tell him neither one of us says anything till we get to my house. Danny pulls up in back of my

father's car and turns the engine off, shifts in his seat and faces
me.

"How long are you in town for?"

"Not very long. Just till summer's over."

I watch his eyes stray to my chest and suddenly I feel sick,
wonder what I ever saw in this small-town boy besides the fine
features of his face.

"You look great, Ellie."

"Misery makes the best diet, I guess."

He reaches over then and pulls me into his arms. "I'm sorry
about your mother," he whispers in my ear and his hands slide
down to my ass. I slam against his shoulder so hard it throws him
off balance, he has to catch himself against the dashboard. My
hair in my eyes I face him. "I don't belong here." The words come
out too fast, knock into each other and I pull myself back as if that
would straighten them out. "I never belonged here."

"You're so full of shit—" He twists the key in the ignition hard
but it doesn't start. "You were always full of shit. You haven't
changed." He twists it again and this time the engine catches.

"Thanks for the ride." I slam the door behind me.

He doesn't wait for me to get to the door before he drives away.

———

Inside I can sense my father sleeping. I take off wet shoes and
leave them by the door, go to the bathroom and start the hot
water in the tub. There's no bubble bath, so I get the dishwashing
detergent from the kitchen and squirt it under the tap so that big
bubbles froth up. His words still burn ("You haven't changed"),
my worst fears realized.

I turn the light off and strip, sink in up to my chin. How many
times has hot water been the only comfort. I hold the sides and

let my body float up, but Danny's face emerges on closed lids, the feel of his hands on me, the hands of the man who stole my sex.

I remember how the boat had rocked from side to side, remember white wine sick and his hands, insistent—it won't hurt (his voice, low, insistent)—

But it *had* hurt. It had made me sober then like it was making me sober now, stone-hard cold sober, but I had kept my mouth shut about it, gripping his wrists harder and harder until I was sure the pressure would cut his circulation off. He hadn't stopped. And he hadn't ever asked me out again.

I remember coming home that night, nausea in my heart; I had filled the tub and flushed my underwear down the toilet. When I was draining the water to run more hot in for the third time, my mother had knocked on the door. Are you okay?

Yes, Mother. Was that the first time I called her Mother? It seems now that it was—

Unlock. Voice low, she learned the command from my father, he's got it down; I was halfway out of the tub before I realized I didn't want her to see me now. Standing calf deep in water filmy with used-up bubbles, I waited. After a moment I heard her leave, and I sat back down but I couldn't relax so I pulled the plug and got out to brush my teeth. She knocked again as I was spitting. Mouth still full of toothpaste, I let her in. She was wearing her old flannel robe, she had that robe my whole life, and holding a cup of tea.

Chamomile and honey, she said. Her face looked soft and worn with sleep, one cheek creased from the sheets, but her eyes were wide awake and trained on me.

Thanks, Mom. I took the cup from her, glad she wasn't going to give me shit for coming home so late; I guessed she'd fallen asleep this time. Her claim was she couldn't ever sleep till I was home. What are you going to do when I go to college? I'd asked her once, lose your eyelids and turn into a snake? She hadn't wanted to laugh at that, but she had.

Rough night? She sat on the toilet lid, put her hands in her lap as if to hold them there to keep from touching me. I wondered if it showed, how she knew. It embarrassed me. I nodded, rubbing my face dry with a towel.

It gets better, she said, and when I looked at her she grinned at me; it caught me completely unprepared. I stared at her. Your tea's getting cold, she told me.

Grateful to have something to do, I picked up the mug and held it with both hands, holding my towel up with my elbows. I'm going up, I said.

It's about time, she answered, following me out the door, but before I'd reached the landing she made me stop and hugged me, holding me to her till I was embarrassed again. I love you, honey.

I know, I mumbled, but I kissed her good night.

———

The bathwater's gone tepid and I get out, wrap a towel around myself and head up the stairs. I don't want to think about the party and I don't want to think about the past. I reach for a book but when I try to read it, my eyes hurt. Me too I'm getting older. Everything leaves you eventually. Everything goes.

There must be some comfort in that, I think, but I lie there, eyes closed, and cannot sleep. I know I'll go back to Jesse when the rain has stopped. The knowledge sits inside me, a fatal rose waiting to bloom.

I W A K E up the next morning with a head aching to the rhythm of my heartbeat. When I move it pounds a high tide of pain throughout my skull.

The bathroom door is open, but my father is in there, shaving. For the millionth time, I wish we had more than one bathroom in the house. I knock lightly and he nods for me to come in. His reflection swings away from him when I open the cabinet and I catch a glimpse of my eyes, smeared with black makeup, as I reach for the Excedrin.

"Good time?"

I swallow three of them, keeping one hidden so he won't see. "Sure." As I walk down the hall it seems to me that something's changed but it isn't till I'm dressing that I realize it's the rain; it's stopped.

At work I run around the restaurant during the lunch rush with plates balanced in the crooks of my elbows, sweat trickling down my spine to catch in the waistband of my skirt. In an hour I'll feel the dampness there, cold against the small of my back, but now I'm too busy—busy serving cheeseburgers and fries to truckers off the highway, one-time-only customers. They eat and pay and tip fast in stoic silence, their eyes still blank from the miles of road that stretch behind them. I serve Jell-O-and-cottage-cheese diet plates to large men with heart disease, house salads with thick orange dressing and stiff little brownie squares to the young women who work for the telephone company down the road, women with fake nails and frosted hair, voices raised high and sweet, always asking will I write out separate checks.

I serve Cokes and Diet Cokes, tall glasses of milk and small glasses of juice, endlessly refill coffee cups, bring the old couple another basket of individually wrapped crackers, bring the woman with the baby ketchup for her grilled cheese sandwich.

Sandra and I pass each other at the window where the food is waiting, gauging our distance expertly, turning sideways so our skirts swish against each other. We never spill a thing.

Later when only two or three tables are left, time starts to slow. Sandra and I lean against the wall and drink iced tea, watch our customers as if they were fitful babies, and gossip about the regulars, people whose names we'll never know.

"Restaurant talk's like junk food," Sandra says. "You do it to pass the time." She smokes a cigarette and looks out the window.

On the horizon I can still see heavy black clouds. "Looks like it's going to rain again."

"It's over."

"How do you know?"

"I grew up on a farm. I could always tell when it was goin to rain and when it wouldn't. My daddy used to say, 'That girl's got a gift in her bones.' "

"Where's your father now?"

"In a home." She blows three smoke rings with great concentration and I know she doesn't want to talk about it. I watch the clouds moving across the sky, weighted and slow.

Before I leave work I change into jeans and a tight red tank top. I put red lipstick on, the kind my mother used to wear. As I trace the outline of my mouth with it I catch my expression in the mirror and suddenly it's as if I'm seeing her, the way she pursed her lips, that vague frown. Tentatively, I repeat the gesture and the echo holds. I rehearse it again, my lips thick with color now, and still, it's her—not so much in the mirror, but inside; that peculiar attitude toward beauty, her own beauty, how she both assumed it and applied it at the same time. Watching her do it as a child, from the high-skirted regions of my parents' bed, I had thought my mother the most worldly, the most perfectly glamorous woman on earth.

I don't know when I stopped thinking that, but I remember Christmases growing up, my mother always put lipsticks in my stocking—shades of rose ("for a young lady"). I'd try each one, but no matter how pale the shade, my lips always seemed garish to me, grotesque. Blot it, Ellie, she'd say, and then, It looks nice—but I always blotted and blotted till the color was gone. Catching me on my way out the door once she said, In my day you wouldn't *dream* of leaving the house without lipstick on—

Mother, I had said, fifteen and nasty, your day is over.

I'd meant it to be a joke, but she didn't laugh, or tell me not to use "that tone." Instead she pretended to become absorbed in something . . . what was it? The plants maybe, she always fussed at the plants when she wanted to ignore you . . . and I had stood there, watching her, overcome with remorse, too sullen to apologize, hoping she'd snap at me, tell me I couldn't go anywhere till I'd cleaned my room, but she didn't. And I left.

That night I went into her bedroom while she was reading, asked if she wanted a cup of tea. My father was working late shift.

A cup of tea. She put the book down on her lap. What an old lady I am, in bed at ten o'clock and drinking tea.

You're not old, Mom—

Yes I am.

No, you're not. You're the youngest-looking mother of all my friends'—you're the prettiest one.

She let her breath out in disbelief, and wouldn't look at me.

It's true—George's mother thinks you've had a face-lift . . .

She made that sound again but it wasn't real anymore, the feeling behind it—I had lifted it out with those words as cleanly as a surgeon with a scalpel.

A face-lift. Hah. She got out of bed and went to sit in front of her vanity. She turned on the magnifying mirror and blinked before its harsh white glare. We both stared at her reflection, and she pulled the skin on her face back and held her fingertips behind her ears. Maybe it's time, she said.

Right, Mom—and I was myself again, the mistress of sarcasm. She let go her face and turned the mirror off. Make mine with lots of honey, she had said then. And don't use that tone of voice with me.

———

I press my lips against a napkin, a hard kiss. On the napkin the imprint of my lips comes off, intricate as a fingerprint. Picking up my bag, I walk out, moving fast so Sandra won't see me.

"Got a date?" she calls from the other side of the restaurant, and although no one else is there, I blush.

"I'm hoping," I call back, and stride on through the screen door.

The air is cool outside, the light easy on my eyes. I walk quickly, my tennis shoes springing up from the road, suddenly sure that he's found someone else in the rain, another girl. I picture a high school dropout, a seventeen-year-old who's hitchhiked out of some obscure town, someone brown and lithe with thick black hair, a girl who gets wild on JD, a girl who loves to go down.

I break into a jog.

———

No one's home when I get there, the bike is gone, the door is locked. I feel as if all the light's been sucked out of the day. I can't stand the thought of going home, can't stand being there, the house stifles me, it seems a mausoleum to me now, haunted and strange, full of dead plants and unused rooms collecting dust, and my father and I live there like two roomers in a boardinghouse.

I start to sit on the steps to wait, but the cars going by make me nervous, and after a few seconds I stand up again. I'm walking around to the back of the house when I remember the nails that lead up to the roof, and I double back to find them. The light makes it easier to see and this time I don't look down.

The roof is hot, gritty, but I stretch out on my stomach the better to see the road. I feel incognito and the sun shines down on the back of my head, the roof heats me through my clothes. I can hear birds singing from the tops of the trees. I put my head on my hands and close my eyes.

Jesse's bike wakes me. I jolt upright from a dream and for a second think I'm not awake because I have no idea where I am, or how I came to be here. Looking down I see Jesse roaring up; he doesn't see me. Behind him is a pickup truck, and it rattles to a halt in front of the house. I lie low, my heart pounding, wondering if I should call out, but I don't. Jesse cuts his motor, swings off the bike like he's getting off a horse. The man in the pickup doesn't get out. Without a word Jesse walks up onto the porch, so close I'm sure he'll sense me, look up and see me—but he doesn't. I hear the front door open and shut. The man in the pickup waits. After a few minutes the door opens again, and Jesse moves back into sight, carrying a brown paper bag. He opens the passenger door and slides it in, saying something I don't hear, but when the man answers, I recognize Eddie's voice. He hands Jesse something, and I glimpse the thick green of folded cash. I close my eyes for a second, wish I hadn't seen it. When I open them again, Jesse's stepping back and Eddie drives away.

In the silence that follows, I hold my breath, watch as Jesse lights a cigarette. He stands there for interminable minutes, smoking and watching the road. When he's finished, he tosses the butt out on the grass and goes back inside. I strain to hear his footsteps, press my ear against the tar, but they don't come up through the roof.

I lie there paralyzed, terrified that Jesse will catch me coming down, think I was spying on him. The sun is much lower on the horizon, it must be around six or six-thirty, close to suppertime. Still I lie there, stiff, waiting for something to release me . . .

But nothing happens, and after a while I can't wait any longer. Moving very slowly, inching myself across the tar, I make my way over to the side of the roof and start down. I pause on every nail and hold my breath, but I can't hear a sound. Three nails from the bottom I jump down, crouch against the side of the house, then quickly straighten and walk out, away, as if approaching from the back.

I haven't taken five steps when I hear the front door open, and Jesse's there, in sight. He stops when he sees me, his eyes narrow.

"Hi." I walk up to him, elaborately casual. "Busy?"

"Where'd you come from?" His pupils are just pinpoints in the piercing green of his eyes, eyes that glint like the sea on a sunny day, full of light and depth, and when I point behind me I turn around because I can't take his stare.

"Over there." I smile, slide my hands into my back pockets. "Wanted to surprise you."

"Yeah?" His face finally relaxes.

"Did I?"

"Yeah," he says, "you surprise me." He grins at me and for a moment I think he's going to kiss me and I stand perfectly still, but then he turns around. "You want a beer?"

"Sure," I say. "Okay."

I wait on the porch and breathe deeply, trying to slow my heart. Jesse comes out with two cans of beer, opens mine before giving it to me.

"God, this is *cold.*" It feels great on the back of my throat.

"Keep it in the freezer."

"Don't they explode?"

"Don't have time to." He drinks it with one hand on his hip, his legs slightly outstretched, as if the minute he's finished he's going somewhere.

"Rain stopped." I lean one hip against the porch railing and sip at my beer, only now beginning to feel safe inside my lie.

"Yeah. Some storm."

"Started the day I met you." I say this as if it is an event in need of context. He doesn't say anything, just nods.

"That why you didn't come back?" He asks this as if it, too, is strictly a matter of fact.

"No . . ." I hold my beer with two hands, I can feel the can bending beneath my fingers.

"No, huh." He tips his head back and finishes his beer, then looks directly at me. "Why didn't you come back then?"

I shrug, trace a circle of dirt on the knee of my jeans. "Because . . ."

"Because why?"

I look at him. "I don't know. Why didn't you come see me?"

"Don't know where you live."

"You know where I work."

He tosses the can on the floor behind him. "You want me to come see you where you work?"

I think about it for a second and smile, shake my head. "I guess not."

"Yeah, that's what I figured." Both hands on his hips he faces the road so that I see his profile, his nose straight, his hair long.

I take another swallow of beer and then I put the can down on the railing and walk over to him, put my hand on his arm, slide it up the inside to his bicep and back down to his wrist. The skin there is smooth, hairless and soft. He doesn't shift but I can feel how still he becomes under my touch; eyes half closed, he takes it like a cat. After a minute, he opens them, gazes at me, and my heart starts pounding. I am amazed at his effect on me, his presence overwhelms me each time as if it were the first, and the light pouring through his eyes seems an impossible luxury, one I can't imagine I deserve and don't remember what I ever did to acquire. I drop my hand, hold my fingers together and look away, but I can still feel his eyes on me, unwavering, and, still not touching me, he says, "Let's go inside."

I follow Jesse into his room and watch while he stretches out on the bed, fingers laced behind his head. I lean against the doorway and he grins at me.

"Come in."

"Take your shirt off."

"What for?"

"So I can see." I walk over to him and throw one leg across his lap, start pulling his T-shirt off. He lets me, inclines his head forward to make it easier, but as soon as it's off he lies down again. I let my weight rest on him and read the tattoo out loud: Ride Hard, Die Free.

"What's this?"

"That?" He cranes his head up for a moment. "Just somethin they say. Like a motto."

"They? Who?"

This time he sits up on his elbows and looks at me as if I'm stupid. "Hell's Angels, that's who."

We stare at each other, my hands immobile on his chest. His face is serious, but I can see something dancing in his eyes.

"You're an Angel?"

"Not really." He lies back down, closes his eyes.

"Not really? What does that mean?"

He shrugs. "Never really joined. Just lived with 'em awhile."

"How long?"

"Few years."

"Why were you living with them?"

He shrugs again. "I was broke, met an Angel in a bar, started crashin at the house."

"Why'd you leave?"

"Hey." He sits up on his elbows again. "What's this, some kinda interview?"

I don't say anything, just trace the tattoo with my fingers; it's broad but delicate, made up of fine and indelible points of blue and red ink. "Die free," I say it out loud. When I look at him, he's lying on his back again. I can't tell if his eyes are open or not.

"Jesse."

"Mm."

"You're cheating on somebody, aren't you."

"Cheatin?" He lifts his head, squints at me.

"You've got another woman, don't you."

He grins, puts his head back down. "What would I do with another woman with you comin round here all the time?"

"Three times. This is my third time."

"I ain't countin."

"The other night . . . when Eddie was around . . . you were waiting for someone, I could tell."

He snorts. "It weren't no woman."

I put my cheek against his tattoo for a second and listen to his heart beating, slow and deep. "Jesse."

"Mm."

"How many other girls've you had . . . bet you can't even count."

No answer.

"Jesse."

"What."

"Didn't you ever meet one you wanted to keep?"

"Can't keep all of em."

"I mean one. One over the rest."

"If I did, you wouldn't be here." He looks at me. "Ever think of that?"

I lace my fingers on his chest, prop my chin on my knuckles. "How come you never answer my questions?"

He reaches down for me. "You ask stupid questions—"

"I just want to know . . ."

"Baby, this is it. What you see is what you get." Mouth in my ear, his words tickle, I twist my head to kiss him, pull back.

"No history?"

"What history." His hands slide underneath my shirt, I can feel him hard against my hip. "Makin history right now . . ."

I lie still on top of him, I keep expecting him to roll me over, to pull my clothes off, but instead he just keeps touching me, fingertips sliding over skin, up along my sides, thumbs stealing over to my breasts to make slow circles, down along my back, inching underneath my jeans, up again to my neck, fingers reaching into my hair. I press my weight against his lap and he tenses his hips up to meet mine, in no hurry, just responding, so I do it again and he does it again, that hardness feels good, solid through the faded denim of his jeans, and we start a slow grind. I lift myself off his chest and reach down for his zipper but he takes my wrists, won't let me, and I hear myself groan, hear how shallow I'm breathing . . . he lets go my wrists and takes my tank top off, puts his hands on my hipbones and holds me up so he can look at me. He doesn't say anything but I watch his eyes consume the sight, and can't believe it's me, my body that makes him look that way—

When I stop moving his eyes move up to mine: I'm not sure, is it me or would it be anybody, any woman, is it me or does it just happen to be me because I'm here—still breathing in short takes, still sitting on his lap, I am immobile. I need to know. I can't ask but I need to know, and I look at him, stare at him, look from one eye to the other, trying to read them, trying to see into his soul—he becomes still beneath me and then neither one of us is moving at all, we're just looking. I watch a slight frown change his face, and then he sits up. I fall back slightly, off his lap, I'm sitting in between his thighs on the bed, and we're face to face.

He raises one hand and puts the palm flat against my cheek, thumb on my cheekbone, little finger hooking underneath my chin. He holds my face and looks at me, I think my eyes are turning colors, his are green, that brilliant green, steady brilliance pouring in, but mine are turning, I can feel them turning from gray to blue, turning to indigo, to violet, climbing up the spectrum till there's nowhere else for them to go.

He kisses me. It's me. He kisses me. One arm reaches around and he pulls me in until our bodies are touching, my breasts pressed flat against his chest, and I wrap my arms around his neck, devour his mouth. We fall back on the bed and he pushes my jeans down and then his hands are on me, fingers digging into me—I hear his zipper and I gasp inside his mouth, at the feel of him inside me, still wearing his pants, denim slides rough against my skin, half-dressed we merge and hold there, very still, and then he rolls over and slides me down on top of him. Impaled, I ride him like a surfboard on the ocean, holding his hands for balance, our eyes locked until, coming, mine close.

Jesse smokes a cigarette. The smoke mingles with our smell, raunchy and sweet. Time, a slow molasses, has to filter its every second through this feeling, and I lie with half-shut eyes, unwilling to relinquish my state of mind to sleep.

———

I wake up suddenly, alone in bed. My legs are twisted in the sheet; I'm sweating all over. Instantly, I think of my father . . . and then I remember. He's working late tonight. Untangling myself, I rise and dress, walk down the hall to the bathroom and wash my face before I go outside.

Jesse's kneeling next to his bike. I sit on the steps. "Hello."

"So Sleepin Beauty finally woke up." I smile at him and he grins back. There's a slight breeze in the air, it feels delicious on the back of my neck. I pull my hair up and knot it.

"Is it running?" I ask.

"Of course it's runnin."

"Are we going for a ride?"

"No."

"Why not?" I sit forward a little. "You never did give me that ride, Jesse." He pretends to be absorbed in his bike. "Remember, the night I came up here—I asked you for a ride. You never did give it to me."

"I gave it to you," he says, and stands up, grinning. He walks over to me and putting his hands under my arms, he lifts me up with one fluid motion.

"I'm not talking about *that,*" I say. "I want to go on the bike."

"Where you want to go?"

"I don't care where—I just want to go fast." I put my arms around his neck and jump up so my legs wrap around his waist. "Please, Jesse."

"Okay," he says. "Let's go."

———

It's like riding a helicopter, the sound seems to break the air itself into a thousand shards, it makes the heat vibrate around us. We go so fast the wind rushes down my throat, making it hard to breathe. My hands are clenched tight around Jesse's waist and my hair unravels beneath the helmet and streams loose. We swoop down deserted country roads flanked by forest, and life has never been so simple, so clear; it's a curved line veering off the horizon up ahead, a rush of pure ecstasy traversing my body through the seat of the bike. Pushing ninety miles an hour I throw my head back to see the first stars glittering down, and knowing the wind will whip the words away I shout, God bless me! and feel tears I can't name rise to my eyes.

We stop because he's hungry. He parks outside the only all-night diner in town. It seems to me the whole place pauses, waitresses, cook and customers, when we step inside the door. I see us through their eyes and looking at Jesse I remember what a savage he appears: long hair and narrow eyes, the open sleeveless vest with the skull on the back, the tattoo on his chest showing through—and me, I could be anybody's daughter with my clean, straight teeth, my healthy hair. I feel the shudder that runs through these good people at the thought, and I grin, exhilarated.

We order cheeseburgers and milkshakes. I haven't eaten red meat in two years, but suddenly I crave it, and the first bite is heaven, hot grease smearing my lips. I wash it down with cold, thick chocolate and across the table, wordlessly, Jesse and I stare at each other, me still grinning like a child, insanely smug: I own the secret of life, the fountain of youth—living purely within my senses like a creature of nature, I've shed my second self, each moment bursts into the next and me I burst with it, and there is no question of why. No question of what's the point, and where will this lead. Everything just is.

On the way back we go so fast I think we're going to actually lift off and fly, either that or shatter into a million bits. I imagine what it would be like to rocket off the back and smash into a tree—I squeeze my eyes closed and pull up tight against Jesse, lay my head on his back and think it would be okay to die now, like this. I would die satisfied.

W H E N I get home my father is out on the front porch, waiting for me, his face dark.

"It's late."

"What time is it?"

"You want to tell me where you been?"

Heart pounding, I look at him, widen my eyes. "Out with some of the kids from Melanie's party." The lie comes out easy, smooth; it's a matter of survival.

He doesn't say anything, just stands there, arms folded.

"Daddy, you don't have to worry about me. I'm used to taking care of myself."

"Where've you been?"

"Oh, we just went out and had a few beers . . ."

"You all drivin drunk?"

"No."

"Bars been closed over an hour."

"We went out to the lake afterwards . . . they wanted to go swimming."

Face still dark, he says, "Next time, call."

"I thought you were working late tonight."

"It's Tuesday. I don't work late Tuesdays."

"Today's Tuesday? . . . Oh my God, you're right . . . I guess it is. It felt like Wednesday to me. I don't know what I was thinking of—" I cut myself off and smile weakly at my father, but he doesn't smile back. We walk inside.

"Did you eat?"

"Had a sandwich." He follows me into the kitchen and sits at the table while I pour myself a glass of water. "D'you have a good time?"

"Yeah, it was okay."

"Was the Schaeffer girl there?"

"Melanie? No. I don't know where she was. Probably with Danny MacIntyre. They're getting married, you know." Hoping to steer him off the subject.

"Who was there?"

"Oh, Dad. You don't know them, what's the difference?" I turn my back to him, take the ice tray out of the freezer.

"Just curious." He looks at me and I know he expects an answer; for one wild moment it occurs to me that he suspects.

"Oh . . . Chuck and Evan and Kathy . . . that's all."

"Nice kids?"

"Sure. They're okay."

"Bet you're glad your old dad made you call over there after all, huh? Got yourself some new friends."

I don't say anything.

"Whyn't they drop you off?" I bend the tray, force the ice out into the sink, pretend to strain, buying time.

"I wanted to walk a ways . . . walk some of the beer off." Without looking at him I fill the tray, busily, and walk with exaggerated balance back to the freezer.

"I was just out in the car. Didn't see you on the road."

"You were out looking for me?" I have a sudden vision of my father's headlights, two cautious beams of light going twenty miles an hour, him hunched close to the wheel, scanning the road, and I lean against the refrigerator, arms locked by my sides. He doesn't answer, nods toward the sink.

"Ice's meltin."

I want to put my arms around him, kiss him, reassure him, but I can't seem to move toward him, I'm sure it would embarrass him, and I walk over to the sink instead, fill a glass with ice and pour water over the top. He lights a cigarette.

"Which way'd you come?"

"Over there." I gesture vaguely in the direction Jesse dropped me off, can't stop thinking what if he had seen us, what if my father had caught me riding on the back of that bike, speeding on the back of that bike.

"Next time, call." He says it again, as if this brief imperative is the only way he can express his worry and his fear, his need to caution me, to keep me safe.

"I will, Dad. I'm sorry."

———

That night I dream that I am in the bottom of a lighthouse and the caretaker comes to meet me with a shovel. He takes me outside and forces me to dig, which I do until I start uncovering bones . . . they're bleached white and silver, like driftwood, and I recognize a shoulder blade and then a collarbone . . . I beg the man to let me stop, but it isn't till I'm hysterical that he relents and lets me put the shovel down. He has a small, cruel smile and I know he is pleased to have broken me down. He says, I like to see that attitude change, from looking around and thinking everything's yours.

I W A K E up with my mother's presence like a cloak, a three-dimensional shadow, all around me. At work I drink cup after cup of coffee, thinking that if I can just get my eyes open wide enough, I will dispel the feeling . . . but the caffeine just makes me jittery, and serving the customers, I spill water, drop knives, break the point of my pencil against the pad, until, finally, I think I'm going to cry.

In the bathroom my eyes look hooded, charcoaled, and I wash my face with cold water over and over again, trying to keep the tears down. I lean my elbows on the cold porcelain of the sink and let my head hang, knowing I should go back out, it's only one o'clock and Sandra can't deal with the whole place by herself, but my breath keeps coming ragged, and I'm scared of breaking down, out there, in public, in front of everybody.

"Ellie!" Sandra sticks her head in. "What's goin on? You sick or somethin?"

Taking a paper towel I scrub my face dry, the harsh texture like punishment across my skin. "No, I'm okay. Sorry."

She hesitates, then steps in and the door closes with a soft, pressurized *whoosh* behind her. "Really?"

I want to tell her, for the first time I want to talk to her about it, thinking that maybe she could comfort me, that maybe Sandra's whiskey-voice, the warmth of her arms around me, *would* comfort me—but when I open my mouth to say the words, everything else comes rushing up behind them, a torrent, and I shut it again before it can flood me, I put my fingers up to cover my lips, to seal them.

"Honey," she says then, "I know about your mom."

I look at her and shake my head. Don't talk about it. Not now.

"Sandra. The tables."

"Let them wait." She takes a step toward me but I duck back, tears starting to bubble up, and smile at her.

"Later," I whisper. They spill over onto my cheeks, and I turn my back on her, reach in for some toilet paper in the stall, sit on top of the john and blow my nose, hard, hoping that this loud human noise will reassure her. "I'm okay," I croak. "Be out in five."

"You take your time, honey," she says. "Ain't nothin out there that old Sandra can't handle."

"Thanks." I hear that *whoosh* again, and then I'm alone, and as suddenly as they came over me, the tears are gone. My grief gone dry, I sit inside the vacuum it left behind, and hang my head back, stare up at the cracked plaster of the ceiling. Oh, God.

Later, when all that's left is a tableful of teenagers drinking Cokes and tossing insults back and forth, Sandra asks me if I want to talk about it.

"Who told you?" The crisis past, I don't want to ressurrect it, and I keep my voice even, perfectly modulated.

"It was in the papers . . . small story, but it mentioned her name."

"In the papers . . ." It had never even occurred to me, I don't know why, and the thought that anybody, anybody who didn't know her, who didn't know us, could have read the details of her death over their morning coffee, make me sick. "I should have known."

"Your daddy didn't tell you?"

"No."

Sandra looks at me like maybe she's made a mistake, puts her coffee cup down and folds her hands together across her lap. I sense she's getting ready to say something, some kind of little speech that maybe she's been rehearsing, her regrets, maybe, an offer to help—

"Look at those kids. They been sittin there forty-five minutes, all's they've ordered is a Coke apiece."

I look at them and smile, the first smile that's come naturally all day. "I think that tall skinny kid likes the blond girl. I notice he's been talking to everyone but her."

"Uh-uh. I wouldn't be that age again if you paid me to." At this, we both burst out laughing.

"Me either. God, me either."

Sandra sighs. "Not that it gets much better . . ."

"You don't think so?"

"Do you?" She turns and looks at me over the rim of her

lipstick-stained coffee cup, her perfectly plucked eyebrows raised.
I shrug.

"Sure."

"Pfft. What do you know, anyway. You're hardly older'n they
are!"

"Oh please."

"Maybe you just had better luck with men than me. That
wouldn't be hard to believe." Sandra laughs. "Almost anybody's
had better luck with men than me."

"How come? Are you just a hard-luck lady?" I ask this teasingly,
but Sandra considers it without smiling.

"Maybe I am. I don't know. I think I just never learned to hold
on to a good thing when I had it, you know? Always lookin over
my shoulder for Mr. Righter." Suddenly she puts her cup down
again, puts her hand on my shoulder so that I'm looking at her
right in the eye. "Ellie, you got someone in New York?" I nod.
"Someone that loves you?" I look at the floor, nod again. "My
advice to you is to hang on to that, honey. Cause when everythin
comes crashin down around you, all's you've ever got left is the
people that love you. And you know who they are." She lets go
my shoulder. "You know who they are."

I wonder then if Sandra's seen me with him, if there's something she knows that she's not letting on to. I look at her but she's
busy lighting a cigarette. She smokes it frowning, and I realize
that all she's thinking about is her life, and her past . . . and
suddenly I just want to get out, out of this uniform and into the
sun, under blue sky, away from the web of other people's feelings,
unentangled, free.

"I'm going to give those kids their check."

O N   T H E   way home I'm not thinking of Jesse, I'm still thinking I want to be alone, I'm thinking of a winding path through the forest that I know, of the way the sun filters down, falling like grace on leaves and twigs, making dappled deer shadows on the ground, and of how close I can get to it, the inner sunlit depths of the woods, walking that path, feet quiet on narrow dirt tracks, no one there but me. I can stand still long enough for the rabbits to come out, learned that when I was a kid, learned how to tense my muscles into wood when the mosquitoes bit, tensing so hard they were trapped, and then I'd slap them dead. But when I pass his house, I see a flicker of movement, or think I do, and on impulse, I veer over, run up to knock lightly on his door. I can trust Jesse not to talk.

When he comes out I'm waiting on the grass, off the porch.

"Want to take a walk?" I call this over my shoulder, already beginning to move. I don't want him to think I'm here for any other reason. The screen door shuts and he disappears behind it, and for a second I think I've lost him, and I can feel my pace slowing, disappointment, leaden, suddenly a factor. I could kick myself—was running along just fine, could've done without him, left him behind . . . now the walk is ruined, I'll just be thinking of him—but then the screen is squeaking again, and Jesse comes out, catches up.

"Where we goin?"

"There's this path I know, used to walk it when I was a kid . . ."

"Where's it go?"

"Through the woods. Nowhere."

"One right over there, too . . ." He points across the road to a place catty-corner from his house. "Seen it?"

"No." I stop a moment, cross my arms over my chest, don't want to smile but I do, small at the corners of my mouth. "Take me." Always, again, he is leading. But I like walking behind him, watch how his jeans stretch tight across the backs of his thighs, I can see the lean length stretching and flexing from his calves to his ass, and the perfectly symmetrical way he walks, one foot in front of the other, easy, smooth, silent. His hair hangs down to mid-back, caught in a ponytail, chestnut gleaming red in the sun. We duck under leaves, he holds prickly branches out with one arm until I'm clear. Now and then he points, and I see a snail, a bullfrog, and once, a flurry of quail.

We don't talk and I am dimly aware that I have become absorbed inside this putting one foot in front of the other, absorbed by the sweet and heavy sunlight coming down, and the occasional cool of shadow that an overhanging tree provides, caught by the need to always be looking, watching out for the branch that might trip you, the patch of ivy that might graze a bare leg, the little thorns reaching for your clothes, your neck, your face. We walk deeper and deeper into the woods, and it gets harder, the path overgrown in parts by bramble so high we have to duck and skirt around it. The shadows overtake the sunlight, and sweat dries on my skin, evaporates, leaves me cool.

The clearing is unexpected. No introduction, we're just suddenly, simply, there. A soft bed of pine needles gone brown makes a thick carpet, and our footsteps fall noiseless. We stop in the middle and Jesse cocks his head, listens.

"A fox," he whispers.

"Where—"

"Sssh." He crouches, turns low on his heels, watching, watching—and suddenly he points, and I catch a flash of red, a furry red tail, and then it's gone.

"How'd you know?"

"Noise too big to be a rabbit," he says, as if it were obvious. Inside that circle of trees, he seems like one of them, growing tall and still and straight from some mysterious root beneath the earth. Reaching into his back pocket, he pulls out a joint.

"Ellie," he says, bending low to light it, as if testing my name. Inhaling deeply, he sits back on his heels and squints up at me. "Ellie," he says again, and hands me the joint. "You don't seem like an Ellie."

I sit cross-legged on the ground and toke on it cautiously. "What do I seem like?"

He studies me with utter seriousness for a second and I find myself holding my breath. Then he grins. "Like a Rexie."

"Why Rexie?"

"Used to call my first bike Rex. Used to tell people my name was Rex. Jesse Rex." He grins again.

"Wrecks," I say, "with a *w*?"

He laughs. "Never thought of it that way."

"I remind you of your first bike?" Handing back the joint, I pretend to be incredulous although I'm flushed with pleasure.

"Never was sure she'd start," he says. "And I never knew where she'd take me—" He holds the smoke in and looks at me. "But I knew we'd get there faster'n anybody else."

I smile at this and then we don't say anything, just finish the joint in silence.

I like sitting beside him like this, not touching, sharing a simple ritual; surrounded by the trees, amazed by the sound that is the silence of the forest, I imagine we're an ancient and primitive people with no known past. Staring at Jesse's profile, his nose perfectly straight, hair streaming back from that high brow, I picture his mother, a feminine version: same deep-set eyes, but darker, a rich chocolate brown, hair long and thick and blue-black, body sinewy and lean.

"Cherokee," I murmur. "What're they like?"

"Don't know. All's I knew was my mother, and she ran off the reservation when she was fourteen."

"How come?"

"Indians fuckin lost their place, man. They either mix or die."

"And your mother mixed."

"Yeah, she mixed." Jesse stares hard at the tops of the trees, branches swaying in the breeze.

"When did you move out of the house?"

"Split home when I was sixteen."

"And that was the last time you saw her?"

He pulls hard on the roach, nods, passes it back to me. Pinching it carefully between the tips of my fingers I inhale and watch the end flare orange, feel its burn.

"You think you'll ever see her again?"

"This another interview?" He takes the last of the joint and puts it in a matchbook.

We fall silent then and the sound of crickets seems to rise up and fill the void with a tremendous vibration. I am so far from New York City, and I am so far from home.

I have lived here all my life and I've never known this before. The landscape of my youth has offered up a revelation and I am stunned to see that it has always been here, this way.

Jesse leans back on his hands, squints up at the sky. From the corner of my eye I watch him. I'm always watching him. I watch his eyes, his hands, the way he moves when he walks, the way he stands, or leans, or smokes, even his silences—and I am surprised, over and over again, by the eloquence with which they speak for him.

I watch him so hard I absorb him, can feel his gestures, the pitch of his voice, invading my own. I'm even acquiring his habit of speech, language stripped down to the bare essentials. Nouns, verbs. Language is just another means of camouflage, I think, remembering how Dec and I used to stay up late talking; all those adjectives. They seem pretentious to me now, overcomplicated. What was it we were saying? I don't remember any of it; it was all inconsequential.

It's in Jesse's silence that I sense the purity of his spirit; in his silence it appears and I see it the same way I can see the shape of his skull, made up of clean, elegant lines . . . it seems to me that it could only have been spirit that constructed those bones. I imagine his as a typhoon wind, a wild force, irrational.

Leaning back on my hands I try to imagine my mother's, try to imagine where she is now, but all I can sense is her absence.

"I'm hungry."

"I better go home. I'm expected for dinner."

"Your ma cook good?"

"She cooks great." The present tense echoes back to me, full and sweet. "She's always been a good cook."

"When're you goin to invite me?"

I try to envision the look on my father's face if he saw Jesse coming through his front door and a small shiver brings goose-bumps to my arms.

"Never." I smile as if I'm kidding, but I know I'm not.

R OUNDING the bend in the road, I see my father's car, and I open the door carefully. "Dad?"

"In here." The voice comes from his bedroom, which surprises me because he never goes in there except to sleep, and it's still light outside. When I push the door open I see him standing in front of the closet, my college trunk and two cardboard boxes open at his feet. Clothes drift high from the bed and I can see the glare of the half-empty closet over his shoulder.

"Oh."

He looks up at me. "I'm goin to put these in the attic."

"I guess it's about time."

Her clothes look so small in his hands, he picks up her favorite sweater, a worn black cashmere, and looks at it, folding it over and over in his hands. I notice for the first time that he has yet to put a single item into either the trunk or the cardboard boxes, although he has pulled all her clothes out of the closet.

"Daddy, I'll take that."

"This?"

Reaching out gently I take it from him, press my cheek against it. A faint trace of my mother's smell, a memory of the way she inhabited her clothes, comes back to me, overwhelms me. I look at my father and he's just standing there, empty-handed. How could you leave him like this, I think. How could you.

"There's a lot here that would fit me. Why don't you let me go through these things first . . ." Moving behind him, I push at him until he starts walking toward the door, as if he were a small child. "You go on and have a drink, and I'll come join you."

I watch him walk into the kitchen and then I turn around,

determined to be efficient, and pick up an armful of clothes from
the bed. Her white slip slides from the rest to the floor, and I pick
it up, fold it into small squares.

I remember when my mother was still a young woman and me
a small girl lying on my stomach and kicking at the bounce of the
mattress of my parents' bed while she made up, sitting in that
white slip in front of her lit two-sided mirror; she used the magni-
fied side "when I'm feeling brave." I loved to see her face change
from clean and scrubbed to the most glamorous woman's in the
world: first, base ("Always spread up from the neck, kitty—the
most important thing about makeup is to look like you don't have
any on"), then rouge (the cream kind, thick and a rosy red), and
then she'd spit a little in a box of black paste and brush it on her
eyelashes. I'd stare at my mother's eyes in the magnifying mirror,
huge blue-green irises with tiny gold flecks in them, come over and
stand next to her when she put her lipstick on—in those days it
was a fire-engine red—and she'd put some on me too, give me a
Kleenex to blot it, and I'd walk around the house after they'd left
for the evening with my mouth carefully pursed away from my
face. Nights they went out my mother always told the sitter I
could sleep in their bed, and after I'd brushed my teeth I would
pile up all their pillows behind me, my mother's perfume coming
off the sheets, and pretend that I was her.

I remember packing to go to college in New York City. She
didn't want me there; we'd had a huge fight about it and after I'd
won she would never speak to me about it, just acted like it wasn't
going to happen. All my life I'd read books about New York, about
its glass-and-steel giants, its fire escapes, its nightlife and crime,
and all my life I'd known that that's where I was meant to be: in
the thick of things, not stuck out in the middle of the woods,

where the most that happened was the hammock being slung up outside in April and taken down again in November, the changing of the guard.

The day I packed she left the house, didn't say where she was going but she was gone for hours, and I remember filling my trunk halfway and then sitting on the floor and crying because I was terrified and I didn't want to go either and because I needed her to come home and help me, tell me which sheets to bring and whether I'd need my electric blanket.

And then the day I left she stood on the porch with her arms crossed, her face colorless, no lipstick or anything, and watched while my father and I dragged the trunk out to the car. In a low voice he told me to ask her if she wanted to come to the airport with us but I shook my head no because I knew that's what she would say and I couldn't stand to hear it.

Well, go say good-bye to your mother then, he told me, and stood by the car while I walked back to the porch. I remember how badly I wanted to cry, my jaw ached with it and my lips were tense and white, I couldn't talk, I went up to her and I saw her chin shaking too, she held her arms out and I stepped into them, a grown girl taller than her mother but not stronger. Her grip around me seemed unbreakable. I don't think she would have let go of me if I hadn't pulled away but I did and she did, and her eyes were shiny and she held them wide open because if she blinked they would spill. I smiled and waved because I still couldn't talk and then I got into my father's car and we drove away, left her standing on the porch with her blond hair ruffling in the wind. I turned around and she looked so small to me . . .

I wish now that I had cried that day I left her. I have cried so
much since the day she left me, and none of it makes up for what
I didn't cry then.

When I finish, the only clothes for storage are in one cardboard
box. The rest are in my trunk, clothes I know I'll probably never
wear but I can't bear to pack them away like that, never to see
them again, as if they never existed . . . as if she never existed in
them.

My father helps me drag the trunk into my room, and we put
the box on a shelf in the dusty closet adjacent to the stairs. He
walks back down and I follow him into his bedroom. He stands
in the doorway and looks at his room. Through the open closet
door we can see his shirts and pants, his extra uniforms and his
winter coat hanging neatly, and beneath those, a row of shoes.
The bureau has been stripped of her jewelry box, the little china
dish she kept hairclips in, the makeup mirror packed away. He
looks at it all for a long time, until I say Let's go sit outside. Taking
out the Seagram's I pour him a stiff one, mix mine with Seven-Up
and take them both out to the back porch, where he is sitting in
her rocking chair, moving slowly back and forth. He takes his
drink but doesn't drink it, and for a long time we sit in the dark,
saying nothing.

"Thought it would be a relief, puttin her things out of sight.
All this time I was waitin . . . thinkin when that was done life
would go on." His voice carries quietly through the night air.
"What a fool I am."

In the dark he raises his glass and takes a small sip before slowly
lowering it back to his lap. I should go over to him, I think, I
should put my arms around him and kiss him . . . but he is sitting
so quietly over there, so self-contained; it seems to me any motion

I make will shatter that careful composure, and I couldn't bear that.

I know I should talk to him but I can't think of anything to say—I can't tell him I'm in love, partly because of who Jesse is but mostly because we have never spoken of these things before; we don't have the language for them. My mother is gone and I realize that save for the love that binds us, my father and I are strangers to each other; she was the bridge between us. Without her, we are mute.

W E ' R E sitting in the family room, watching the six o'clock news, when the doorbell rings. It hasn't rung in so long that for a second we just sit there, as if trying to place the sound.

"You expectin someone?"

"Not that I know of . . ." Both of us get up, and I follow my father down the hall. He turns the lights on in the living room and opens the door. Melanie's father, Bob Schaeffer, is standing there, still wearing his uniform. For a second, my father stands there, immobile. Behind him, I clear my throat.

"Bob, come on in." My father pulls the screen door wide.

"Evenin, Tom . . . hey there, Ellie."

"Hi, Mr. Schaeffer, how are you?"

"Fine, just fine—look, I don't want to trouble you folks, but as I was leavin the station I came across this here—" He pulls something out of his back pocket, extends it toward my father. It's his wallet. "It was in the men's room . . ."

"Jesus, I didn't even notice it was missin." My father riffles through it, and his mouth twists sideways in a grin. "Money's gone."

"Yeah, I noticed that. Hope you didn't lose much."

"Small change, nothin to lose any sleep over."

Although he's smiling, Schaeffer seems nervous, shifting his weight from foot to foot, and I watch him curiously. He's a fine-boned but strong-looking man, and his hair is thick and blond, like Melanie's. He isn't particularly handsome until he smiles, and then I can see where Melanie got her looks.

"Well, I saw the pictures in there and I thought . . . well, I thought if you were missin it . . ."

"What pictures? Let me see, Dad—"

"Can I get you a beer or somethin, now you're here?"

"Oh, no, no, don't trouble yourself—"

"No trouble, no trouble at all." Before Schaeffer can protest again, my father is gone, leaving me the wallet to hold.

There's a picture in there of my mother, she's a young girl, couldn't be more than nineteen. It's a professional picture, one of those studio "glamour" shots, and her hair is piled up on top of her head, she's wearing dark lipstick and her skin looks flawless, without a single mark or line. I've never seen it before.

"You sure do look like your mother, Ellie." I look up to say thank you, and then I see that Bob Schaeffer's eyes are bright, liquid bright, and the words drop back into my throat. His chin trembles and I start to move toward him, to touch him, to touch his arm—but he steps back out on the porch, turns his face away. Before I can think of anything to say, my father comes back with a beer.

"Here y'are—"

"Thanks, Tom."

We're all out on the porch then, and I watch Schaeffer take a long pull from his bottle. He swallows and clears his throat, turns to me again and smiles.

"Sorry I missed you the other night. Melanie tells me you came over for a little party she gave."

"Yes, I did. I'm—I left a little early, though . . . I wasn't feeling well . . ."

"Oh sure, well, that's understandable. Sure."

There's a little silence then and the three of us stand inside it. Bob Schaeffer clears his throat again, but he doesn't say anything, and when I look at my father, he's staring off at the horizon. I feel compelled to fill the void.

"It's wonderful news . . . about Melanie and Danny. She seemed very happy about it."

"Yes, yes she is. She and her mother been puttin their heads together all summer, plannin this wedding."

"I bet."

There's another little silence, and then Bob turns to my father.

"Well, I better be goin on my way . . . Beth's keepin supper for me. She, uh—" He hesitates and then there's that smile again, uncertain, but again I notice how it changes his face. "She was wonderin if you all . . . well if you'd like to join us sometime, for supper . . ."

"Awfully kind of her, but we're fine." The curtness of my father's tone surprises me. " 'Preciate your droppin my wallet by—"

"Don't mention it. Just wish you hadn't lost your money—"

"Not your fault," my father says, unsmiling, and it seems to throw Schaeffer completely off, he starts nodding over and over again, moving off the porch.

"No, sure, right—"

"Please give Melanie my best, Mr. Schaeffer!" I call out as he opens his car door.

"I sure will, Ellie! You take care of yourself now, hear?"

My father and I watch as Bob Schaeffer pulls out of the drive and down the road.

"I didn't realize Mr. Schaeffer felt so strongly about Mom—"

My father looks at me sharply. "What's that supposed to mean?"

I look back at him, surprised. "Nothing. It's just that for a second there while you were gone, I thought he was going to cry. I didn't realize he even knew Mom—I mean apart from through you."

He looks down the way Schaeffer went. "He knew her."

"I don't—"

"Thought you said you had a good time there the other night." He looks at me.

"What?"

"You told me you had a good time over at the Schaeffer girl party."

"I did. I had a good time. I just left a little earlier than the others, that's all." I start for the house, wanting to drop it. "Want something to eat? I'll make a salad—"

"Why didn't you tell me you weren't feelin good?"

"Oh, Daddy, I was feeling fine—I just said that to be polite, that's all. Come in and have something to eat—"

"I hope you weren't rude to Schaeffer's daughter. He told me she arranged that party specifically on your behalf."

"Dad, I was not *rude* to her—for God's sakes, I'm not a child, I know how to behave myself!"

"Because your mother would be very disappointed in you if she knew you were rude to someone who had gone out of their way to be nice to you."

"I'm going to make some dinner. You want some?" I hold the screen door open.

"Not real hungry right now, Ellie." He turns his back to me, reaches into his pocket.

"You'd rather smoke, right?"

Lighting up, he ignores me.

"If I make something, will you at least try it?" I let the door bounce off my toe a couple of times. "Dad?"

He doesn't turn around. "Sure."

When I come out with a tuna salad, he's sitting on the front step, looking at something. Over his shoulder, I see that it's his wallet; he's staring at the picture of my mother. I put the plate between us and sit down, but I don't say anything. He grazes the face in the photo with his thumb.

"First picture she ever gave me."

"She looks so young there . . . Mom always told me she was twenty-one when you met."

"She was. Met her at a party. Couldn't take my eyes off her."

I know the story but I prompt him, never having heard his side. "But you didn't talk to her, right?"

"All the men were askin her to dance. I wanted to but I was scared I'd step on her feet. She was wearin these shoes, they had the highest, most delicate-lookin heels I ever saw, but she was whirlin round the floor like she'd been born in them . . . dancin and talkin and laughin . . . I knew I didn't stand a chance."

"But then she came up to you."

He nods. "Yup. At the end of the evenin, just as forward as you please, comes marchin up to me and says, 'Don't you know it's not polite to stare?' "

"She always told me you were the best-looking man in the room, and no matter what she did to get your attention, you never once came near her. She said it drove her crazy."

He laughs. "She thought I was playin hard-to-get. But I was just plain scared."

"So then what happened?"

"I told her I'd've asked her to dance if I knew how . . ."

"And she said men who could dance were a dime a dozen—"

"And then she put out her hand and asked me my name and said, 'Well if you can't dance, do you know how to walk?' " He laughs.

"And you said, 'Hum a few bars and I'll try it.' Mom said she fell in love with you right then and there." He doesn't say anything, so I prompt him again. "So then you walked her home."

"Walked her home and sat on her porch and we drank Coca-Colas. She talked a blue streak, and I hardly said a word, all's I could do was look at her."

"But you *still* didn't ask her out."

"Couldn't. I was headin for the Academy the very next day."

"So you asked her for a picture you could take with you."

"She said all's she had was an old one but I didn't care." Carefully, he pulls the picture out of his wallet. "Asked her to sign it." He turns it over and shows it to me. On the other side, in a spindly cursive that I barely recognize as my mother's hand, it says, "Marie Elena Roberts" and underneath that, "Call me when you get back."

"God, she really *was* forward for those days, wasn't she." I stare at the handwriting, trying to imagine it, my mother when she was younger than I am now, flirting shamelessly with a tongue-tied cadet.

"She could afford to be." He slides the picture back into his wallet. "Notice she didn't put her phone number." He grins at me. "She knew I'd find her."

"And you called her the minute your training was over."

"Nope. Never called. Never was good on the phone. Just drove up to her house wearin my new uniform, for confidence."

"And she was sitting on the porch in an old housedress 'cause it was Saturday and Saturday was housecleaning day—she told me she was absolutely mortified to be caught in it."

He smiles. "Couldn't tell you what the dress looked like . . . all's I could see was that face—had a smile that lit her up from the inside out. She smiled like that, I couldn't even talk."

I have never heard my father say anything like that before. "I wish she'd taught *me* that trick."

He doesn't answer, just keeps grazing his thumb over her face in the picture. I clap my hands together.

"And the rest is history!"

"Never took that picture out of my wallet. Used to embarrass her. She'd try to give me new ones, sayin she wasn't nineteen anymore, it was foolish to carry that thing around . . ."

I pick up the bowl of tuna salad, balance it on my knees, clear my throat, but my father doesn't take any notice of me.

"She always looked the same to me . . . just as beautiful as the day I met her."

"Well it sure is a good thing Mr. Schaeffer found your wallet, isn't it?" I say then, loud and cheerful, standing up.

Slowly, my father flips it closed, and stares down the road, saying nothing . . . and then he stands too, pulling himself up as if his weight were almost more than he could bear.

"Come on," he says. "Let's go inside and eat that supper."

W E ' R E both still up, watching Johnny Carson, when the phone rings. My father reaches over and picks it up, says, "Just a minute please," and hands it to me, but before I've said hello I know it's Dec.

"Are you okay?"

I take the phone with me into the kitchen. "I'm okay. How are you?"

"Lonely." He says this flatly, and I have a sudden memory of last summer in New York City, walking through the humid, deserted, late-night streets, one finger hooked through Dec's belt loop; the two of us, aimless, poor, easily amused, sleeping together every other night. I think of his body, small and compact, and I hunch over the phone.

"Is everyone out of town?"

"Everyone that matters." He dismisses my question; I don't know what to say. "I want to see you."

"It won't be long." Reaching into the freezer I pull out a bottle of vodka, pour it into a tall glass, drop some ice in, add milk; insomniac's cocktail.

"How long is that?"

"Only two more months."

"Forever."

"Oh, Dec." I want to talk to him, but there is so much I can't say, it rises huge and unyielding, forbids the outright lie; I want to comfort him but I'm too ashamed.

"What have you been doing?"

"Not much. Working. I tried to get together with some people from high school . . . depressing."

"Oh yeah? Did you see old what's-his-name?"

"Who?"

"That guy—your heartthrob. What's-his-name."

"Danny MacIntyre?" I'm amazed at how much I've told Dec, embarrassed to be this well known. "Yeah. He's getting married. To his high school sweetheart."

"Christ." We're both quiet for a minute and then he says, "I had a dream about you."

"Good or bad?"

"Nightmare. You were with another man."

I stand very still in the middle of the kitchen and hold my breath. Dec waits for me to say something but I can't think of anything, and after a second he goes on. "You were on top of him, naked, and when you saw me you didn't stop. You acted like I wasn't there."

"God."

"Are you sleeping with anyone?"

For one brief second I consider telling him the truth, immediately reject the idea. "Who would I be sleeping with?"

"How do I know? Danny MacIntyre."

"It was just a dream, Dec."

"It was so real."

"I've been having bad dreams too."

"About your mother?"

"Terrible dreams . . ."

"I wish I were with you."

"I can't imagine you here," I admit then, I can feel the vodka spinning my head, I want to tell him everything but I'm too scared, I don't want to lose him; he loves me, and I can't stand the thought of one less person loving me.

"You wouldn't have to if I *were* there."

"It's just such a . . . you know, family situation . . . you know."

"You're getting your accent back."

"I am not."

"You sound like a backwoods girl." Remembering walking through the high grass with Jesse today, I can feel the blood rising to my face. I don't say anything.

"How's your father?"

"Quiet. We put my mother's clothes away today."

"Oh."

"It was harder for him." I say this as if confessing a sin, but he doesn't hear it that way.

"I guess it's good for him to have you around."

"I guess." I tip my glass up and drain the drink. Tell him the truth, I think, but I don't, I know I won't. My father walks in and fills a glass of water from the sink. "Dec, I have to go."

"Why? It's my bill."

"Because I want to say good night to my dad before he goes to bed." My father turns and looks at me, shakes his head, says it's okay at the same time that Dec says okay in my other ear, and then, "I miss your body in my bed."

"Thanks for calling."

"You didn't have to hang up on my account," my father says.

"It's okay." I sit down at the kitchen table and spread my hands out.

"That your boyfriend?"

I nod, strain my fingers until the skin is taut. The tendons stand out hard and white. My father scrapes a chair back, sits down. "What's he like?"

The base of my thumb starts to cramp and I let go. "Dec?"

"That his name?" He taps a cigarette out of his pack.

"Dad, you know that's his name. I've been going out with him for a year."

"Funny name."

"It's short for Declan. It's Irish."

"What's he look like?"

"Oh . . . he's kind of short, got brown hair. Nice smile. Normal-looking guy, I guess."

"That what you like? Normal-lookin guys?" I look up quick then and he's looking right back at me, but his face is quiet. I shrug.

"It isn't so much his looks."

"What's he do?"

"He's trying to get into film." I shrug again; from here, all those ideas just seem plastic, frenzied; from here, in this house amidst the trees, that kind of striving emerges as pure and nearly senseless vanity: the need to get one's head above the crowd and shout, Look at me!

"I don't know what he's doing." My father watches me, smokes. "I don't know what I'm doing either."

"Thought you had ambition."

"A lot of people have ambition."

"But not everyone's got as good a mind as you." He smiles.

"Your mother and I used to wonder who you got that from." I smile then too, but it hurts. He leans forward, puts his cigarette out. "I hope you're not hurtin your career, bein here, Ellie." He keeps pressing the butt into the ashtray, gently moving it from side to side.

"Career, God." I push my chair back, press my fingers against my eyes hard for a minute, so hard I see small gold sparks. "What career." When I stand up, my dad does too.

"I don't like to hear you talkin that way," he says.

"What way?"

"Cynical. You never used to be like that."

"Well I guess I'm growing up."

"No," he says, and then, quietly, "You can't afford that kind of thinkin, Ellie. You've got too far to go."

"Yeah, all the way up the stairs, to bed." My father follows me out into the hall. I don't want to hear any more. I want him to leave me alone, I want him to go join my mother in their bedroom and let me go up to my room, I want us to have her back again, filling up all this empty space, I want to go upstairs and crawl into bed and not think a single one of my own thoughts, not think about my mother or my father, Dec or Jesse or myself. I want to fall into dreamlessness and wake up somehow different, wake up to see the world through someone else's eyes. I step up on the first stair, then, hesitant, turn back to give my father a kiss, but he's already too far out of reach.

"Good night, Ellie."

"Good night, Dad."

———

In city dreams, I walk alone through New York, the streets are desolate and the trees look thin, they've lost all their leaves.

Buildings tower over me, I lean back to see; the slant is dangerous, they're too tall, they've built them all too high, a hurricane could topple all this concrete, I keep wondering why they haven't thought of this—and then I'm leaning, careening off the top of the Empire State Building in a stiff wind, I can smell salt and I remember I'm on an island, and somehow this makes everything worse and my position even more precarious—I'm drunk, I'm holding on to a bottle of wine and my mother is there, she is giddy, tipping over, I have the sense she doesn't care, that she's barely aware of me, it's New Year's Eve and she starts to sing Auld Lang Syne, and the wind keeps snatching her voice away.

A T   W O R K   the next day I can feel Sandra watching me, I know she wants to talk and I keep waiting for her to say something but when I go stand next to her after the lunch rush is over and pour myself a Coke, all she says is "Hot today."

Outside the end of June presses up against the windows, I can feel the full onslaught of midsummer coming on. "And it isn't even July yet."

"Almost," she says, twisting to look at the Shell calendar tacked to the wall. "Couple more days." She leans one hip up on a table pushed against the back. "You got any plans for the Fourth?"

"I guess not. My dad always has to work that day." I find the smallest piece of ice in the glass, squeeze it between my back teeth. "I hadn't even thought about it."

Sandra picks up my Coke and drinks it. "All that sugar'll rot your teeth," she says, but she takes another sip. "Sugar, caffeine, nicotine . . . Seems I'm always makin some resolution 'gainst all this junk but then I think, So what. People weren't meant for nothin if they weren't meant for dyin."

She holds the glass in one hand and balances the bottom on the palm of the other, the way my mother used to hold her coffee cup in the morning. The gesture brings her memory back so vividly it's as if I'm looking at a picture, and I remember the way her hands felt when she put one on my forehead to feel for fever, and how she used to rub cream into them every night, guarding against wrinkles.

My eyes fill and I stare at the ground, not wanting to cry. I know that Sandra sees but she doesn't move, and for long seconds we stand there just like that.

"We should go out drinkin sometime," she says finally, her voice soft.

"Sure." Blinking, I take a deep breath. It comes in ragged but the danger's past. "Sounds like fun."

———

She comes driving by two nights later just after supper; I hear the deep bellow of her horn around the corner and then the green Ford pulls into view. She sticks her head out the window, her hair curled and piled up on top of her head.

"You up for Stingers tonight, Ellie?"

"What's Stingers?" As I'm walking down to her car I hear the screen door open behind me.

"Honey, you say you used to live here?" Sandra tips a cigarette out of a pack and pushes in the car lighter. "It's a bar on the wrong side of town, that's what—" As she's lighting up she sees my father and for a second she freezes.

"Hiya," he says. "I'm Thomas Lowell, Ellie's dad."

Sandra opens the door and steps out. She's wearing a man's white shirt tucked into a pair of jeans and red high heels. "Sandra Beck." She walks up to the porch, hand extended, and they shake. "I work with Ellie over at Parker's."

"Sure," my dad says. "I've seen you."

He's got what my mother always used to call his public manner on: low voice, easy smile, reassuring. My mother called it the "serve" part of "serve and protect."

"You mind if I kidnap your daughter, Mr. Lowell?"

"Thomas," he objects. "S'long's you don't hold her for ransom."

"Ransom ain't my kind of crime," Sandra says. "I usually stick with disorderly conduct."

My father smiles and so does she, her hands in her back pockets, her chin high. With a shock I realize she's flirting with him, and looking up, I see my father's face the way she might: deep smile lines around his mouth, dark circles under his eyes, a square jaw, lots of gray in his hair.

"Well I got permission Ellie, you in or out?" Sandra turns to me and although they're both watching me, I am still aware of her proximity to him, sure that she's just as aware of it as I am.

"Sure," I say stiffly. "Just let me change."

As I'm walking in the house I hear my father politely offering Sandra something to drink.

Upstairs I change into jeans and a clean T-shirt so fast I'm sweating when I'm done. Grabbing my sandals I run downstairs and wash my face and the back of my neck, don't stop to put lipstick on.

". . . there long?" my father's saying as I walk out.

"Parker's? Yeah, too long. I been thinkin it's time to move on, but it's summer, you know?"

"Sure," he says, nodding. "Sure."

"I'm ready." I balance myself on the top step to strap one sandal on, holding on to the other.

"No hurry," Sandra says.

"Ellie, whyn't you sit and do that?" my father asks. I don't answer, full of a strange agitation, finish doing the other one up. When I look up both of them are watching me.

"Ready?" I start walking toward Sandra's car. She rises slowly, her bottle three-quarters full.

"Well, Thomas, nice talkin to you." My father stands too and they shake again. "Stop by the restaurant sometime. We make a great iced coffee."

"Will do. Have a good time."

Sandra starts the car and I buckle my seat belt, mostly for my dad to see.

"Hey," he calls out. "If you need a ride home, call."

"Sure thing," Sandra says, and presses on the gas. Irritated, I think, He meant *me*, but I don't say anything. She waves to him as we drive away, but I don't look back.

"I knew your daddy was the law," she says as we turn the corner, "but you never told me he was cute."

I flip the radio on. "AM all you get?"

I can feel her eyes on me but I keep turning the "tune" knob. She reaches out and slaps my hand away lightly. "You gotta stop at a station if you want to hear the music, Ellie." I let it go, stare straight ahead.

"Want to tell me what's eatin you?"

"Nothing's eating me."

"What was the big rush back there then, that we had to leave your daddy by his lonesome so quick?"

"I just wanted to go, that's all."

"You thought I was flirtin with him, didn't you."

"You *were* flirting with him!" I face her for the first time, my back pressed against the door.

"Honey, you can calm down right now. Old Sandra has no designs on your daddy."

"Then why'd you say he was *cute?*"

"He's a nice-lookin man, Ellie. Women're gonna look at him. You oughta be glad."

"Well *he's* not going to look at *them.* If you'd known my mother, you would know—"

"No one's goin to replace your mother, Ellie," she says then, gently, reaching over to put her hand on my knee. "But your father has the rest of his life ahead of him. You don't want him to be alone till he dies, do you?"

I shake my head. "I don't know what's wrong with me, Sandra. Sometimes I feel like such a monster."

"Don't worry, baby. Everythin's goin to be all right." She pats my knee again and then she turns the radio on, finds a country station. I don't know the tune, but she does, and when the chorus comes, she sings along.

"So where is this place?"

"East." Flicking her eyes at the rearview mirror she speeds up till we're going seventy. I sit back and let the wind blow my hair all over my face, dry the back of my neck. We drive like this for a good ten minutes, neither one of us speaking, the volume on high. When the disc jockey comes on with a commercial, Sandra flips the radio off.

"Hate that shit." The road forks and she takes a left, slowing down. "So you never been to Stingers really, or you just sayin that in front of your daddy?"

"I've never even heard of it."

"Girl, you ain't lived in this town till you been to Stingers, I can tell you that much."

"What's so great about it?"

"It's what's *not* so great about it that puts it on the map, honey: everythin." Sandra laughs. "It's what my mother used to call a lowlife bin—full of types, you know what I mean."

"What kind of types?"

"Every type. You got your rednecks, you got your teenagers, you got your truckers, and then you got a little of a lot else . . . like Jeanie and Eunice—they're a pair of dykes, like to come in and drink whiskey sours, sit in the back and nobody bothers them— and there's Big Sid, they call him slow, but what he is is retarded, I'll tell you that right now—" Sandra makes a sharp right and then we're on a narrow one-way road, full of potholes, and we jounce on our seats. "Can you feel them springs? Holdin up pretty good for this old baby, huh? Watch out, it gets worse—" Yanking on the wheel she turns left, and she's right, this road is half paved, half dirt, and all craters. Sandra navigates the holes expertly, and at considerable speed. Hanging on to my seat I grin at her.

"Come here often?"

She grins back. "Look, you can see it now . . ." She points with her chin and I lean forward to see a big rusting sign proclaiming STINGERS, hung over the porch of a falling-down shack. As we approach I can see cars parked haphazardly around the place, their hoods nosing into the woods. Sandra finds a spot between a pickup so covered with mud you can't tell what color it is and a beat-up motorcycle.

"It's no Harley," I say, opening my door carefully so as not to touch it.

"No," Sandra says, slamming her door shut. "But I seen 'em here before."

"Really?"

"Just once or twice." She pushes the door open and I follow her in. The place is dark and a tinny radio plays the same station Sandra had on in the car. There are two fans in the corners, a bunch of small wooden tables and chairs. The floor is gritty beneath my soles.

The place is half full, with most of the clientele leaning up against the bar. Sandra muscles her way in between two men, reaching a hand out to hold me behind her.

"Hey, Joe, get me two margaritas, sweetie, huh?"

Someone calls something back to her but I don't hear it. She turns around and grins at me again. "Hope you like tequila 'cause that's what we're drinkin."

"Sure." I look around while she's paying. A bunch of kids, no older than fifteen, I'm sure, are crowded around a table in the back, drinking beer. Close to one of the fans there's a middle-aged couple, their faces red. The woman is talking, nonstop it seems from here. Occasionally I can hear her voice rising, the accent so thick I can't understand what she's saying. The man says nothing, just drinks, impassive.

"Come on, let's find us a table." Sandra hands me a drink and I let her take the lead. She goes over near the front, where the other fan is blowing. "Stay by the door case you need a quick exit, that's my motto." She winks at me and sits down.

"Cheers, Ellie." We lift up our glasses.

"To Stingers," I say.

"Lord help us," she says, and we clink. She takes two sips in rapid succession then puts her glass down, eyes the lineup at the bar. "You see any talent?"

I let the liquid down my throat slowly, wondering if there's anything else in there besides tequila, and squint over at the bar.

"What about the guy at the end? In the red-checked shirt?"

"Nah. No good. Know him." She picks up her glass, takes another hefty swallow. "In the biblical sense, too." She smiles, wry.

"Who is he?" Bravely I take another sip too, determined to match her.

"Jimmy Ricks. Works in the tobacco factory. Got a nice body, no future. I don't like to string 'em along. End up hurtin everybody."

"I know what you mean." Thinking about Dec I feel shame, a hot flush up my neck, and I look down. She sighs.

"Playin the field when you're over thirty ain't no ladies' sport, Ellie, I'm here to tell you. I don't recommend it."

"I'm surprised you're not married, Sandra."

"Oh, that. I done that." She drinks again and so do I; it goes down easier this time. "Even had a baby. The works."

"You had a baby?" I stare at her, unable to picture it.

"Sure. Still do. Well, I mean he's grown-up now, pretty much, but he's still my kid."

"Grown-*up*?"

She sits back, obviously enjoying the surprise on my face. "Nineteen years old. Near's old as you are, I bet."

"I'm twenty-five, Sandra."

She bursts out laughing. "Honey, you don't need to look so mournful about it."

"Well, what's his name? Where *is* he?"

"His name's Elvis and I don't know where he is." She picks up the glass and this time she downs the rest. She looks away and for a moment I think the subject's closed, but then she looks back at me, square in the eye. "I was seventeen when I had him, he weren't what you call planned." I watch her but I don't say anything, and after a minute she goes on. "I could've had an abortion, too, that weren't it. I wanted the baby." She shakes her head. "Stubborn as a two-headed mule . . . I'm surprised my daddy didn't kick me right out of the house. But he didn't."

"You lived at home?"

"All the way up till Elvis was old enough to go to school I did. Then I moved us out to our own place. Me'n my ma always fought too much. Bad for the kid."

"What about . . . the father?"

"Jackson." Holding her glass by the base, Sandra pushes it around in small circles on the table. "Oh, he left town when I was three months along. Couldn't handle it. He was just a kid . . . guess he must've been twenty years old . . . he was a musician. Played the guitar. He was real good, too. He had his whole life ahead of him." Looking up she catches my eye, smiles. "Don't worry," she says, "I ain't always been this big about it. For years I swore up and down I ever found him I'd put a bullet through his balls."

"God." I finish my drink, fish a ten out of my pocket. "Another round?"

"You're fittin right in here, Ellie, just like I knew you would." Sandra lifts the bill and winks at me. "Be right back."

I watch the door while I'm waiting for her to come back. A tall man in blue jeans comes in, a rangy man with a craggy face, a face that makes me think of mountains, gray skies and mountains. I sit up, anxious to point him out to Sandra. Picking up the drinks from the bar, she starts to head back to the table and I try to catch her eye, incline my head toward the man. She doesn't see me but suddenly she stops, staring. I follow her eye to see the man at the bar buying a beer. He smiles at Joe briefly, then turns around. Sandra is walking over to the table very carefully, as if every ounce of her attention must be concentrated on not spilling the drinks. When I look at the man again, he's got his back to us.

"Who's that?" I lean on the table and whisper the question. Sandra digs into her purse, rummaging for cigarettes. I wait, but when she finally looks at me she just lifts one shoulder, her eyes hard.

"You don't even know his name?" I lift my glass with both hands, watch her face over the rim while I sip.

She starts to shrug again, then says, "Carter."

"Oh." I stay quiet, hoping she'll say more, but she doesn't, and the set of her face forbids questions. I watch while she lights up, and catching my stare, she pushes the pack over toward me.

"Want one?"

"No thanks, I don't smoke."

"You could start. No time like the present." But she pulls the pack away, drops it back into her purse. "I'm just jokin."

She slouches down in her chair, crosses one leg over the other. I notice how studiously she avoids looking toward the side of the bar Carter's leaning up against. She keeps tapping her cigarette against the ashtray, a nervous gesture I've never seen before. Suddenly she leans forward.

"Oh, Christ. Crazy lady Perry's workin herself up to a fine rage.

Get ready for some volume." She points over to the couple I saw
before and as I look I see the woman standing up, nearly knocking
the table over.

I strain to make out the words but "Yaw dawg's an shee!" is
all I hear. Her voice screeches up to the top and breaks, she
gathers in another lungful of air and screeches again. The man is
still sitting there, but his glass is empty. He looks around dumbly,
as if he doesn't know how he got here.

"Who's that she's with?" I ask Sandra.

"Old man Perry, they been together for years." Sandra shouts
to make herself heard, and we both cover our ears. She nods over
to the bar and I twist around to see Joe stepping out, his face a
mask of patience. Walking over to crazy lady Perry, he puts an
arm around her, hustles her out. She keeps screaming but allows
herself to be led. Her husband stands up and shuffles after them.
People watch but nobody seems perturbed. The kids in the corner
are falling apart laughing.

"Jesus." I can still hear her out in the parking lot. I take a big
swallow; this second one tastes smoother, I'm surprised how easy
it goes down. I can feel the tequila in my head now; behind me,
the music seems to have taken on texture, a richness of tone.

"Marriage," Sandra says. "Ain't it wonderful?"

"Some people's," I answer. She tosses her cigarette on the floor,
snuffing it out neatly with her spike heel.

"Your parents happy?"

"They were happy." I push at the ice in my drink with the tips
of two fingers. "I really think they were."

"You were lucky," Sandra says. "So were they."

"Lucky?" I think of my mother out on the road that night in
the VW and I shake my head. "I just don't think of it that way."

"I know it seems like chance," Sandra says, leaning over the table and speaking low, "but I don't believe it."

"I don't know what I believe."

"I think everythin happens for a reason," she says. When I look at her she meets my gaze directly and for the first time it occurs to me that she knows things I don't.

"What kind of reason . . ." I don't finish my question, pick up my drink instead.

"She had someplace else to go, Ellie." She leans back. I stare at her, my hands cupped around my glass. "It must have been very important," she says softly, "for her to leave you and your daddy like that . . ."

I can feel something coming loose inside and I pick up my glass and drink quick, one, two, three swallows. It burns going down, brings tears to my eyes. Sandra lifts up her glass too.

"To her spirit," she says. "Wherever it may be."

I lift mine again too and we both drink all of it down.

"Whoo!" Sandra gives a yell that turns all the heads at the bar. She stands up. "If you call attention to yourself," she says, heading over there, "you might as well give them somethin to look at."

Joe gives her two more margaritas in record time and she brings them back to the table with a waitress's balance and efficiency, setting mine down before me with a flourish. Holding hers, she waits for me to lift mine and then she says, "To what?"

Suddenly I want to talk about Jesse, but I don't know how to bring it up. I become aware of a burning in my bladder.

"I have to go to the ladies'." Sandra points to the back corner, reaching behind for her purse.

"Here, you'll need these." She hands me a small package of Kleenex, smiles. "That's Stingers."

The bathroom is primitive, a single lidless, seatless toilet, and the floor is mildewed, wet. I crouch over the seat while I go, careful not to touch it, and hold my breath.

When I open the door I see the man Carter standing next to our table. Sandra is lighting another cigarette, saying something. I walk back slowly, conscious of people's eyes on me, wonder how out of place I look; raking my hair back from my face, I feel careless, daring, ready for anything, riding a tequila high.

As I come up to the table they fall silent and turn to me, both of them smiling, but I sense something tense between them, something anguished.

"This is Ellie," Sandra says. "Ellie, meet Carter."

"How are ya." His clasp is hard and dry. When he lets go of my hand he steps back, nods. "Ladies."

"Nice meeting you . . ." I watch him walk out of the bar. Sandra doesn't turn around. I notice she's almost finished her drink, and sitting, I study her for signs of all that liquor inside, but she seems just the same as when we came in.

"Is everything okay?"

"Everythin is okay, darlin." Sandra stubs her half-finished cigarette out hard in the bottom of her glass. "Everythin is A-okay." She crosses her arms on the table and smiles at me, and suddenly I want to give her something.

"Here . . . help me with this." I push my glass toward her but she shakes her head, stands up. "Whoa. I think it's time to go. If I don't get you home, your daddy's goin to nail me."

"Sandra, I am an adult in the eyes of the law," I tell her, but I stand too.

"Maybe so, but in the eyes of your daddy you're a baby." She waves toward the bar. " 'Night, Joe!"

"Y'all come back now!" We can't see him but his voice carries over the din. Following Sandra outside, I notice she's walking carefully, putting one foot in front of the other, but it's the only sign of drink she shows. In the car I lean my head back and close my eyes and immediately everything goes into a fast spin. Sitting up, I open them wide, roll the window all the way down. She drives slow the whole way back, never once passing the speed limit, and waits till I'm in the house before taking off.

Inside, my father's bedroom door is slightly ajar, I can hear him breathing, but when I walk by he says, "Ellie, that you?"

"It's me, Daddy." I push the door open and he looks up from his pillow, squinting a little.

"Everythin okay?"

"Everything's fine, you go back to sleep."

He puts his head back down. " 'Night."

" 'Night, Dad." I start to climb the stairs, but halfway there I stop to sit and wait, straining for the sound of my father's breathing. I wait ten, fifteen, an eternity of minutes before creeping back down and sliding past his door. I open the front door with immeasurable caution, and push the screen open the way I learned when I was in high school, just so, so the hinges wouldn't creak.

In the silence that follows, I wait, but nothing moves. Slightly unsteady, I creep off the porch and down the road.

W H E N I get there the house is quiet but the bike is outside. Tequila confident, I call out, "Jesse!"

From inside, a door opens, and then he steps out; I can't make out his face, just his shape. "What're you doin here?"

"Just stopping by." I reach up and stretch, and blood rushes to my head. "Aren't you going to ask me in?"

He motions with his head and I follow him inside. In his room, a kerosene lamp is burning by his bed. I kneel in front of it, peer at the flame. The glass is smeared black, and a thin plume of smoke wavers straight up, still in the still air.

Jesse sits on his bed, back up against the wall. In the flickering light, his face is all angles and shadows, his profile sharp. He reaches down beside him and picks a roach out of the ashtray, lifts the glass off the kerosene lamp and lights it, swift and easy. He passes it to me and I suck on it.

"Been drinkin?" he asks.

"Tequila." I grin at him, absurdly proud.

He grunts. "Who'd you go drinkin with?"

"My friend from work. Sandra."

"She drop you off?" He's wondering how it could be that he didn't hear the car.

"At home she did. I walked here."

"This time of night, you walked?"

I shrug, lean back on my hands, light-headed, casual, reckless.

"So where you live?"

"Walking distance."

"Big secret, huh."

"It's my parents' house, Jesse."

"Why you still livin at your parents' house?"

"Because . . . I'm broke."

"Parker's don't pay?"

"I just moved back home. Actually."

He looks at me knowingly. "Uh-huh."

"What."

"Nothin."

"What, you think you know something—"

"Yeah, I do."

"Really? What do you know?"

He grins, leans over and reaches a hand up the inside of my thigh quick, with that catlike way he has, sneaky and smooth, so you don't know he's going to touch you until he does, and then you don't stop him because you like it. He runs his hand up, stops just before the crux, and then I realize I'm holding my breath. He laughs. I jerk my knee and his hand falls off.

"What I look like naked. That's all you know."

"Yeah, baby, that's everythin." He shakes a cigarette out, lights it. I flash my hand out to snatch it from his lips, but he ducks his head and I miss, clean. Cat eyes, too: he sees it coming.

"Give it—"

"You don't smoke."

"That's for me to decide." I reach for it again but he holds his hand up, out of my reach.

"Yeah," he says then, smug, sly, "I know why you moved back home."

"Why?"

"Some dude gone broke your little heart." He measures these words on my face, but I keep it flat, closed. He takes a drag on his cigarette and nods. "Yeah, knew that the first day you come walkin up here, past midnight. Can't sleep, she says." He blows his breath out, a small scoff. "Yeah, right."

Sitting back into the space between his thighs, I pull my knees

up to my chest, wrap my arms around them, wedge my chin
between them, stare down at my dirty toes.

"Girl's got a broken heart—" I hear him inhale again, deep, and
then exhale, soft and slow—"and I'm just the man to fix it."

From the corner of my eye I see the cigarette hit the floor, see
the toe of his boot reach out to snuff it, grind it out . . . and then
he's sitting up, I can feel his breath on the back of my neck, his
lips—

"Ain't that right, baby—"

"Mmm . . ." I stay still, curled up tight as if I don't care, as
if I don't feel him touching me, but he knows, he can sense it,
I have never met a man with such a sense, a man who can make
my body sing this way. I let him undress me, soft in his hands,
I let him do everything. He moves inside me and I taste raw sugar,
thick and sweet and deep, he moves inside me like telepathy,
everything opens . . .

"It's your Indian blood," I whisper, hoarse, "sneaking into me."
We move, we find the same place, and then we both explode, in
perfect concert.

Sweat drips into my hair, my eyes, salty as tears. He stays in,
leftover hard, me still tight around him. I can feel my mind
drifting to places blank as snow, unrecoverable images sliding by
on some mysterious screen behind my eyes . . .

I want everything, the thought comes to me—not just his
mouth, his hands, but all of his nights, his days, I want his past
and his future too. I pull his head down on my chest, run my
fingers through his hair, blink up at the ceiling above me, full of
some strange, newly minted feeling. I'm in a place I've never been
before, with a man I could never have imagined . . . a strange sense
of liberation overcomes me, as if a halo, some secret code of

conduct, has been lifted; I am no longer my mother's daughter. I am my own.

––––

It's close to four when I get home, my father's door is closed, and I sneak past holding my shoes in my hands. In the bathroom mirror my neck is streaked with dirt, my hair is wet and tangled, and I decide to take a shower.

As I'm taking off my clothes, I hear the squeak of the doorknob turning; panicked, I bundle the clothes inside my towel, saying, "Just a sec, Dad," thinking I'll tell him I couldn't sleep—that I was too hot, that I couldn't sleep, that I was sweating, having a bad dream—

But when I open the door he just mutters, "Excuse me," and walks past me into the bathroom. Underneath those sterile lights, his face is a map of ever-deepening lines that frightens me, puts me in mind of the pictures they showed us in high school of the presidents' faces before and after they served a term, decades of age compressed into four years.

Pressing my clothes up against me I go upstairs, crouch at the top waiting to see if my father will call out, but when the toilet flushes and the door opens again, I hear him padding back to his room, and then the creak of his door closing.

Coming from work the next day, I spot the Harleys from far away, four, maybe five of them, I can see the sun glinting off the gleam of them, they look like a team of horses, of tanks, well oiled and ready to move, sleek, parked low to the ground, and as I move closer, I see the three men on the porch, one of them sitting on the steps and rolling a cigarette from a package of Drum tobacco, the other two just standing there, leaning back on their heels, arms crossed over the chest, as if wearing some official stance. I don't recognize any of them, but their presence is imposing; they seem to be standing sentinel, and I get the feeling they've been here before.

The one sitting on the porch has matted hair and a thick beard. His bare stomach hangs out over his belt, and when I walk up he eyes me, at once hostile and leery.

"Is Jesse around?" I direct my question toward all of them, but only the fat one speaks.

"Who're you?"

"I'm a friend of his."

He laughs, and tobacco flecks his lower lip. "You're a *friend* a his, huh?"

"My name's Ellie." Climbing up the first step, I address the one standing closest to me, and then I step all the way up onto the porch and hold out my hand, determined to establish diplomatic ties. At first I don't think he's going to take it but then he does. I can see the tendons in his wrist and the back of his hand is covered with a dragon tattoo whose tail extends all the way up his forearm to his shoulder. It gives me the creeps, but I smile when he tells me his name.

"Randy."

"I'm looking for Jesse."

"Aren't they all." Behind me, the fat one spits. I keep my eyes on Randy.

"Is he here?"

Randy shrugs, mutters something I don't catch and turns away. I stand there for a few seconds, arms and ankles crossed, biting my thumbnail, hoping for help. Nobody says anything. With effort, I drop my arms down to my sides and take a deep breath.

"Excuse me." I start to walk in, sure that someone's going to stop me, that the one sitting is going to stand in my way, but he doesn't say anything, just turns around and spits again. The spit is flecked with wet tobacco and it splatters all over the ground.

Walking down the hall I hear low voices coming from his room. Hesitating, I trail one hand along the wall. "Jess? Jesse?" The voices fall silent, and I clear my throat. "It's me. Ellie."

I hear something scraping, and then a bump, and then Jesse steps out into the hall.

"Yeah." Standing face to face he doesn't touch me; both thumbs hooked in his pockets, he drums against his legs with his fingers, kicks one heel back against the wall.

"Just came by to say hello."

"Yeah, it's not such a good time." He doesn't look at me and I realize I'm inconveniencing him, that I'm the last thing he wants to deal with right now. Crushed, I stand there, know I should leave, but I don't. Jesse's bedroom door opens then and Eddie walks out. Seeing me he nods, just a half-inch dip of the chin.

"Hi Eddie." I smile at him, hoping to make an ally. He nods again but he doesn't say anything, just glances at Jesse, who moves away from the wall, and suddenly I realize that Eddie's an Angel, too, that they're all Angels . . . maybe even Jesse.

"You take care of it?" he asks Eddie.

"Yeah, I got it."

"Okay." Without a word to me, he heads out to the porch. Eddie waits for me to follow before moving, but then I hear his boots, heavy behind me. Outside, Jesse lights a cigarette. The fat one stands up and smiles; his teeth are brown with nicotine.

"Was just keepin your lady friend some company." Jesse grunts, but he doesn't say anything; although his face is expressionless, I imagine I can see dislike rising in his eyes. "You gonna introduce us?"

"Ellie—this's Chip."

Chip puts his hand out, and I am left with no choice but to put mine in it. To my horror, he raises it to his mouth and kisses the knuckles with wet lips. I pull it back and quickly turn to Jesse.

"Goldilocks comin to the party?" Chip asks, looking at him. Jesse shrugs.

"What party?" Nobody says anything, and after a second I ask again, staring at Jesse.

"Fourth of Ju-ly *Hell's Angels* party," Chip says then, and laughs. Jesse's smoking in fast little tokes, as if he has to finish his cigarette in the next five minutes, as if his life depended on it. He doesn't look at me, it's as if I'm not even there, and I realize he had never even intended to tell me about the party, he was just going to disappear for a day, two, three, and reappear without a word of explanation; he doesn't think he owes me any explanations. About anything.

Moving heavily, Chip stands up. He looks at Eddie, licks his lips.

"Everythin taken care of?" He glances at Jesse but Jesse's staring off down the road. Eddie nods, and as if by signal, all of them move to their bikes. Jesse takes two steps off the porch and flicks his cigarette butt down. He stands very close to the bikes while the men start them, one by one setting up a deafening roar, a noise like volcano buried under blacktop and beginning to erupt . . . and it seems to me they idle there longer than necessary, enjoying the disruption their machines make inside the early evening air . . . until, one by one, Chip leading and Eddie going last, they take off, a pack of cheetahs, bearing down on the curve of road that leads away from Jesse's house so fast I think they're going to skid, skid and crash and burn, but all they do is disappear; only their sound trails behind them.

I turn around to face Jesse. He's bent down near his own bike, poking his fingers into it, ignoring me completely.

Crossing my arms, calling out to him, I say, "I thought you said you *weren't* an Angel."

He doesn't indicate an answer, doesn't acknowledge the question, but I watch him, make it clear that I am waiting. He glances up at the sky and I follow his eyes. A bird flies low, you can see its throat tremble as it sings, cries something out, and suddenly Jesse answers, and when he whistles the bird pulls up to a tree, stops, cocks its head.

"How come they're always around?"

"Who's always around?"

"Those Angels. Eddie."

"Eddie's my brother."

"Real brother?"

At this Jesse scoffs and shifts his weight, impatient.

"How come you're going to their Fourth of July party?"

"Business." He pulls his cigarettes out, opens the pack and extracts one with his teeth, spits the bits of wrapping on the ground. I can see the brief gleam of cellophane from a blade of grass.

"You're an Angel, aren't you."

"No, man, I am a native! I am a fuckin Cherokee—" Leaning his head back he pulls his breath in and then lets out a sound, wild and high, it makes the birds fly, and it raises the hair on the back of my neck, but I don't let it show.

"You don't know anything about me, either."

"You got somethin to hide?"

"You never ask me anything—"

"Don't seem you're holdin out on me."

"Well, it seems you're holding out on *me*—" I stick my chin out, face him. "What kind of business is it, exactly, that you do with them?"

"What I do is *my* business." He starts to walk toward me and his eyes look dangerous, but then he stops, points two fingers at me. "And I don't answer to nobody about my business . . . not you, not them, not nobody!"

"You don't trust me, do you."

"Look." He takes another step forward, and then a step back, as if there's some kind of force around him, as if he's sidestepping inside an invisible cage. "What are you, my wife?"

"I'm your girl, that's what I am." I stare at him, hands on hips, I pretend I'm not shaking, I stand there sure he's going to laugh, tell me to go to hell, walk away, but he just stands there too, measuring me with those eyes, and then he shifts his weight again, he wants to leave, I can feel it, and the thought panics me—

"Jesse."

"What."

"Let's go in the house." I try, but I can't keep the pleading out of my voice. He shakes his head, mutters something. "Jesse . . ." In three steps I'm next to him, I want to touch him, want to grab on to his belt and hold him, reach up and kiss him, but every instinct tells me not to, everything tells me that if I do that he will run, he will turn around and leave me here, standing solo in the smoke. We stay there like that, neither one of us moving, and my breathing sounds loud in my own ears, I wonder if he hears it that way too. I search for the thing to say, the thing that will make it all right, the words that will set him free and make him mine again, but nothing comes, nothing comes to me at all.

"I got to go," he says then, and moves away, aside, so swift I'm left looking at the space he just inhabited, it seems to shimmer with his presence, the length and breadth and depth of his body, for just a second before it dissolves. I hear his footsteps on the porch and then I turn and run after him, grab the door before it closes and catch him in the hall, bumping into him, stepping on his heels, and he jerks around, annoyed. He starts to say something but I've got my mouth on his before he can get it out, I swallow his words, throw myself at him, and he staggers a little against the force of it, grabs my hips for balance. I've got his face in my hands, standing on tiptoe, standing on his boots to kiss him, kiss him like I'm eating him whole, eating him alive, and I reach one hand down for his belt buckle, I can't let him go, I have to have him, I have to have him now, want him inside, and when the belt comes undone I find him hard against the palm of my hand, he pulls my shorts open, pulls me up and straddles his legs, yanks my underwear to one side and then I'm on him, pegged, him in so high feels like it's going to pierce my heart, and I gasp, think, this is it, this is him, sucking on his tongue I think, I've got him, he's mine—and I love the way his breath comes out, sharp, ragged, he presses me up against the wall and then I'm not thinking anymore, my mind is submerged inside me, conscious only of the peak I'm climbing, velvet black mountain, hands clawing his shoulders I push off and come down, once, twice—and then black bursts, throat so tight my breath's a scream, small scream, hot white sparks and stars, stars burst in my face . . . he reels back a little, his knees bend and I slide off him, and in that narrow hallway we look at each other, panting, and say nothing.

Jesse goes into his room and I put my shorts back on. The button's torn off and I can't find it on the floor. When he comes back out his belt is buckled, he's tucking something in his pocket, he says, "I got to go," again and I nod, I still can't speak, but walking behind him, I reach out and take one of his hands, and when his fingers close around mine it's as if the world, once torn, has suddenly become whole again.

H O M E again. I let the screen door slam behind me, walk through the living room and into the kitchen, open the refrigerator and stare into it although I'm not hungry; and if I were, I would hardly find anything to eat here. The back wall glares whitely at me, looks strange, probably because I've never seen it before; when my mother lived here, the fridge was always full of food, marmalades, different kinds of cheese, bottles of mineral water, vegetables. Now all we have is a little milk, a little butter, a jar of mustard, half a carton of orange juice and a few solitary eggs perched in their places on the door. None of it adds up to anything.

My father's car pulls up the drive, and I sit at the kitchen table and listen to him coming inside the house, his footsteps slow and heavy.

"Hi, Dad."

"Hi, Ellie. Gonna have some dinner?"

"There's nothing to eat."

"Nothin?" He opens the fridge. "Hm. Guess we oughta make a grocery run, huh?"

"It's okay, I'm not hungry anyway."

"There's some bologna in the meat drawer—"

"That's okay, I ate at the restaurant already."

"Oh." He shuts the door.

"Aren't you going to have anything?"

"Had a coupla sandwiches at the station."

"You're getting thin, Dad."

"Yeah, how 'bout that." He pats his belly, smiles, but it's forced; he's pretending to be okay, pretending to be happy for me. Sitting at the table I want to cry, want to take his hands and promise him that everything is going to get better, but I can't imagine how that could be true, how my father will ever be happy again without her, and instead I wind my fingers together and sit quietly, determined not to cry in front of him, to be strong in front of him; determined not to let my pity show.

"How's everything at the station?"

"Little short-staffed these days, but everythin's pretty slow."

"So are you filling in for missing people?"

"Well, we're gonna hire someone pretty soon but I figure I can do some extra hours till it happens."

"Uh huh."

"Oh, that fella from New York called you the other night . . . when you went out with Sandy." He takes the bottle of Seagram's out, pours an inch and a half into a glass, no ice, no water.

"San*dra.*"

"Sandra, right. Forgot to tell you." He looks at his watch. "Hup, news's on."

"Was it late?" I follow him into the family room, lean against the doorway while he settles in his chair, picks up the remote.

"Don't know, I was asleep when he called."

"I told him not to call late." I keep thinking, What if he calls and Dad comes up to get me and I've sneaked out to meet Jesse. "I'll tell him again."

"Didn't matter to me, I just went back to sleep anyway."

"I know, but still." We both fall silent for a minute, listening to the headlines. When they cut to a commercial, he turns to me again.

"He pretty stuck on you?"

"We've been friends a long time."

"He goin to visit?"

"He's pretty busy."

"Well, you oughta call him back. Sounded like he wanted to hear from you."

"I will. I'll go up and call him now."

"Goin to bed?"

"Yeah, I think I'll skip the news tonight." I look at him, sunk deep into his chair, the glass of whiskey propped against his thigh. Every line in his body spells fatigue. "You ought to go to bed too, Dad. You're not getting enough sleep."

He nods. "Soon's this's over I will."

Crossing over, I bend to kiss my father's cheek.

" 'Night, Ellie."

I can still hear television-bright voices promising whiter teeth and fresher breath when I'm halfway up the stairs.

Still dressed, I lie across my bed and let my head dangle toward the floor. Tears fall upside down, but I sit up and quit before I can really start. I can't stand crying anymore, I don't want to think about my mother and I don't want to think about him downstairs either, because both things make me cry and they're so useless, what good are all those tears, they don't change anything anyway. I blow my nose once, twice, and reach down for the phone to call Dec, but then I think that he'll want to know how I am, he'll ask me how I feel, and I don't want to talk about it because it's the same thing, it's always the same thing, she's still dead, and sometimes it seems to me there's never been a time when this hadn't happened, when this wasn't true; when my mother wasn't dead.

When I'm with Jesse I never think about it. When I'm with Jesse I am a different person, living in a different world, and it seems to me that I can choose different things; he exists in my life as something alien, something apart from everything else, something secret; I can't imagine integrating him into my normal existence, telling my father about him, and I certainly can't imagine telling Dec. I've stopped struggling with my conscience; Jesse is simply something I need, and that's as far as I get with it. If Dec could feel the way I feel, I'm sure he'd understand; lying in bed with my clothes on, television chatter drifting faintly up the stairs, this is what I tell myself.

I WAKE up from a swamp of dreams, tangled dreams full of people and things people have said to me that I don't want to remember. I sit up with an effort, glad to be awake. The slanted

ceiling of my room oppresses me, I can feel the day's heat beginning to beat down, and as I shower, I'm already anticipating the
end of my shift, and the rush of adrenaline that always accompa-
nies the first sight of Jesse.

At work, time crawls. My impatience builds, and the only thing
that alleviates it is motion. I stay busy, filling up everybody's coffee
cup, everybody's water glass, and then I refill the water pitchers,
make new pots of coffee. Even when Sandra stops to talk to me
I keep moving, wiping the counters, separating the silverware,
stacking the napkins.

"What time is it?"

"Jesus Christ Ellie you ask me that one more time I'm gonna
brain you—"

"Sorry."

She tucks a bit of hair behind her ear, takes a fresh pack of
cigarettes out. I watch her go through the ritual of unwrapping
the cellophane, tapping the bottom of the pack against her wrist,
taking one out and lighting it, and for a minute I envy her the
habit.

"Does smoking calm you down?"

"It does if you're havin a nic fit." Sandra exhales out of the
corner of her mouth, watches me. "What're you so nervous
about?"

"Nothing. I just want to get out of here, that's all."

"You got somethin special waitin?"

I shrug.

"Boy, you sure are close-mouthed, Ellie, I'll say that for you."
I don't know what to say to this and she goes on, "No locker-room
talk from you, no sir. Uh-uh."

"It's not that . . ." I can't explain it to Sandra because I'd have

to explain it to myself first, and I'm afraid to face the contradic-
tions, afraid that if I think things through something will change,
that somehow I'll lose him. Picking up a pitcher of ice water I look
at her helplessly. "Excuse me." I don't turn around to see her
expression but I can imagine it, how she stands there, smoking and
shaking her head. I keep moving around the restaurant, circling
like a fish, until finally Sandra grabs my sleeve.

"Okay, you're free."

"What time is it?"

"Time for you to get out of here—for *my* sake." She gives me
a little shove toward the back room. "And don't come back till
you've gotten it out of your system, you hearin me?"

"Thanks, Sandra." Grateful, untying my apron, I'm on my way.

———

Wearing a pair of shorts and a sleeveless shirt, sneakers and no
socks, I head for Jesse's, free at last, but still uneasy. I remember
yesterday, how he nearly dismissed me, the sense that he could,
that he wanted to, leave me—I'm beginning to lose control over
my feelings for him, and even as I think it I realize I've never had
control, but it's beginning to matter now, matter more than
anything else. Starting to sweat, I try to slow down, but I can't
quell the feeling that I have to hurry, that I'll miss him if I don't
speed up, and finally, I break into a run.

When I get there, his bike is gone. Come on, Jesse, I think,
disappointment sharp as a stitch in my side, you have to be here
. . . but as I walk up to the porch I'm already slowing down,
because I know he's not, and I don't want to confront his absence.

"Jesse?" I walk up to the house, knock on the door, then try
the knob; it's locked tight. At the window, I cup my face against
the glass, but there's nothing to see, just shadows in an empty
room.

"Jesse!" I pound on the window, once, and then turn around. "Goddamn you." Leaning against the house, lacing my fingers behind my back, I decide to wait. Maybe he'll come home, like he did the last time, the thought occurs, but something's already whispering that this time it's different. I consider climbing up onto the roof but it's too hot still, and I know I won't sleep, I'll just lie there underneath the sun, sweating on the tar, waiting and waiting, squinting at the road . . .

I slide down into a sitting position instead, and my T-shirt rides up the wall so that my bare back is pressed against brick, rough and cool on my skin, abrasive; moving, I lean into it, the abrasion feels good.

In my shorts pocket I find the joint I rolled earlier this morning, thinking maybe Jesse and I could take a ride somewhere and smoke it, could go swimming maybe, maybe take a boat out on the lake . . . With a pack of Parker's matches, I light it.

Cars drive by, a station wagon, a big blue Cadillac, a shiny new Toyota. Smoking, I watch them, count them, try to see who's driving them, but from the depths of Jesse's porch I'm too far away to see any features, and this comforts me: if I can't see them, then certainly they can't see me. As I finish the joint, this becomes more and more important, and I scoot over toward the far side of the house, draw my knees up to my chest, and sit there. It's not even five o'clock yet, the sun is still high in the sky, and I wish it were later, wish it were almost dark and Jesse were home by now, happy to see me, glad I saved him the roach. A mosquito whines in my ear and I spend a few minutes watching for it; when it comes again I reach out and clap it dead between my palms. I think about Sandra, how she pushed me out the door, and wish I had stayed, finished out my shift, because it was better to be waiting there, while I still had something to look forward to, than waiting here, full of foreboding . . .

I start to count every other car, start making bets with myself; if I only count every other one for fifty, he'll be here when I'm finished. It takes surprisingly long for fifty cars to go by, and still, no Jesse. I decide the trick is not only not to count every other car, but not to even *see* every other car, and I start closing my eyes and waiting for the sound of an engine coming down the road. I become expert at gauging them, expert at keeping my eyes shut until they've just passed me, so that when I open them they have just passed the stretch of road in front of me, but I've successfully managed not to see them: not the driver, not the make, and not the license plate.

The sun moves across the sky and Jesse doesn't come home. The high wears off and I'm left still sitting there, still counting, mechanically, burned out. I should go home. The thought surfaces for the first time, and when it does I know it's been there all along, from the beginning, a seed of hopelessness planted much earlier, earlier than this morning even . . . planted sometime last night. It was in my dreams, and when I rose, I thought I'd escaped them. I should have known better. Resigned at last, I stand up and start the long, familiar walk home.

When I get there the driveway's empty. I walk into the house; the screen door slams hollow behind me. I don't want to be here, the feeling closes around me as I walk down the hall—I don't want to be alone.

I'll call Dec. The thought pops up and I am instantly soothed, relieved to still have the option. Taking the phone from the family room, I untangle the extension cord so that it reaches into the bathroom, and then I run a tub, fill it with cool water. I lean over and dial his number, and then I sit down. The water rises up to my chest, and ripples softly off my chin.

He answers on the second ring.

"Well, if it isn't Ellie the elusive."

"It's good to hear your voice, Dec."

"I'd almost forgotten what yours sounded like."

"Sorry I didn't call you last night." With one wet hand I push the hair away from my face. "I didn't feel like talking."

His tone softens. "That's okay. How are you?"

"I'm okay. I'm in the tub."

"You're naked?"

"Last I checked." I like talking to him with my whole body submerged; I feel clean, truthful, full of gratitude.

"Don't torture me, Elena."

"It's the furthest thing from my mind."

He groans. "I knew it. You don't even miss me."

"I do miss you. I miss you right now, this very moment. That's why I called you." (Because you couldn't have Jesse, the thought hisses itself at me, and I sit up a little, press the phone against my ear, hoping Dec's voice will absorb me.)

"I talked to your dad the other night."

"He said you woke him up."

"I did? I thought I had, but he said he'd just gone to bed—"

"He told me you woke him up." I tell myself I'm just sticking to the facts.

"Ellie, it was only ten o'clock."

"I told you, when he's home he goes to bed early."

Dec is silent on the other end, and I know he feels bad, thinking he's kept a grieving man from his only escape. I sink back in the tub.

"How's work?" I change the subject, wanting to get on neutral ground.

"It's great—I have a new project. This woman called me up last week, she's an independent, and she's doing a short on gang wars in the Bronx. Wild stuff. She wants me to film." The excitement in his voice is audible, and I remember how bright Dec's ambition burns, that he has a life in New York, that he's leading it without me.

"That's nice," I say, but he doesn't hear the coolness in my tone, he's off and running, he tells me everything.

"It's a real break," he says. "This woman's got a great reputation."

"Does she have a great body, too?"

This stops him for a second, and then he laughs. "I don't know. I haven't met her yet." When I don't say anything, he goes on, "What about you? Were you really out with that waitress the other night, or was your dad covering for you?" I know he's just kidding, that he doesn't really suspect me of treason, but the question makes my heart beat faster.

"Her name is Sandra. She's older than me but she's wonderful. Funny."

"So you found a friend."

"Yeah, it's nice to have someone to go out with after work." Setting up my alibis, I'm surprised, a little dismayed, at how smoothly it comes out.

"Are you and your dad spending a lot of time together?"

I think about the time we spend together, mostly in front of the television, evenings when he comes home, and I press two fingers, cold and wet, against my eyes. "Uh-huh."

"That's good."

We're both silent then and I know Dec's waiting for me to say
something about my mother, but I don't. I can feel him hesitating
at the other end, wondering if he should ask, and I clear my throat.

"Well I'm turning into a real prune here," I say, speaking
before he has a chance to. "I better get off the phone and out of
the tub."

"I can call you right back—"

"No, that's okay. My dad'll be home soon and I want to get
dinner started."

"You're cooking now?"

"Oh, you know—salads and stuff. Summer food."

"Well, I'm glad you're taking good care of him."

"Yup." I stand up, water pouring off my body, and step out.
"Can't wait for you to come home and take good care of me."

"Won't be long." I watch while water drips down, soaks the
mat.

"Okay, baby. I love you."

"I love you too, Dec." It comes out with an urgency that
surprises me. "Don't forget."

Still wrapped in the towel, I walk out to the back porch, push
the door open with one toe. Outside, it's finally dark. I stare at
the sky, at odds with the world, and decide that I'm hungry.

In the kitchen I take out the last two eggs and mix them with
a little milk, thinking I'll make an omelette, a nice light little
omelette, but it comes out runny scrambled eggs instead. I eat
them out of the pan, still standing in my towel, and drink the last
of the orange juice from the carton. I know I should have set the
table, if only because it would have taken up some time, but I
can't be bothered. I can't be bothered to dress and I can't be
bothered with ceremony; for whom?

I finish in five minutes, put the pan in the sink, and wander through the house. I don't want to go up to my room, where the walls are still covered with posters of horses and sunsets with sentimental little proverbs captioned beneath them, and a big bulletin board tacked full of high school pictures, all of us either smirking at or twisting away from the camera, me invariably dressed in an oversized man's shirt, my hair loose and hanging in front of my face. I hated having my picture taken. I remember how it pained my mother, who collected photos and pasted them all into albums, neatly dated and labeled, and kept in a row underneath the old radio in the living room, some of them dating back as far as her great-grandmother's family . . .

Without thinking about it, I head for them now. When I turn on the light, I see the dust everywhere, getting thick in the corners and along the windowsills, the curtains gray with it, and I wonder when was the last time they were cleaned, and who will think to have them cleaned again.

And then, kneeling in front of the radio, as I reach for an album, the first album, I catch sight of the urn, and suddenly I wonder if there's anything left in it—a chip, maybe, some fine ash—and I think that I'd like to take it out and put it someplace safe, in a tiny box next to my bedside table. Resolute, I pick up the urn and balance it on my knees while I open it.

It's completely empty. Tentatively, I run my fingers along the bottom, the sides, but it's clean. The wind must have blown everything away. I am seized by an overwhelming, knifelike regret. How could I have let it, how could I have let her, slip away from me like that? I should have kept something, anything, a small relic . . .

I think of all the pictures I never let her take, all the times I snapped at her, and how I used to squirm out of her embrace. Sitting with my bare knees on the dusty floor, the urn hanging open and holding nothing, looking around at the curtains and the plants, shriveled in their pots, I think, What kind of a daughter was I, anyway? I couldn't even keep her plants alive.

A car pulls up the drive. Hastily I wipe my face and, half-standing, try to put the urn back before he comes in, but as I bend over to pick it up, my towel falls. I'm tucking it back in, the urn at my feet, when my father walks in. Seeing me there, he stops, still holding the door open with one hand.

"Ellie? You all right?"

"I'm fine, Dad." I clear my throat and turn away to put the urn back where it was. "I was just going to look at the albums . . . and then . . ." I stand where I am, half-bent over the urn, and hold my face very still; it takes all my strength. He lets the door shut behind him and starts to walk toward me, but I can't let him, if he tries to comfort me I'll break down and then he'll see that he can't comfort me and he'll feel worse, he'll feel useless—

I move across the room and into the hall without looking at him.

"Ellie?"

"I'm just going to get dressed—"

I run up the stairs and shut the door behind me, and in the airlessness of my room, I scrabble around, wiping my face with the towel, putting on a clean T-shirt and shorts, concentrate on buttons and zippers, on getting the comb through my hair. When I'm finished, I look composed. Still breathing too fast, but composed.

Downstairs, my father's in the kitchen, smoking a cigarette and looking out the window.

"You okay?"

"I'm fine. How was your day?" I walk around the kitchen, opening drawers and cupboards, making the silverware, making the dishes, rattle, just for the sound of it, the plain, mundane sound of it. It makes me feel as if everything here, in this house, is normal. As if this is just another summer's evening in another little house where things need to be put in their proper place.

"My day? My day was the same as it always is. Work." He blows smoke out. "Work is work."

Separating knives from spoons, spoons from forks, I stand still for a moment, unnerved. My father had always been proud of his work, sure that it was a civic service, sure that it added to the sum total of good in the world, and I had been raised to believe that what one does is inseparable from what one is.

"Did you get somethin to eat?"

"I had the last of the eggs . . ."

"Eggs aren't dinner."

"I'm okay. Did you have something?"

"Had a sandwich earlier." Holding his cigarette between thumb and forefinger, he watches the smoke curling upwards for a moment, and I watch him. "A sandwich isn't dinner, either. Whatsay we go out, nab ourselves some real food, Ellie?"

"Go out?"

"I was thinkin we could go on over to the Grill, get some steak. How's that sound?"

"It's a little late . . . think they'll still be serving?"

"Sure, they serve till ten."

"Okay. I'm not really hungry, but I can get some salad."

"You get yourself a steak, young lady, you'll be hungry when they set it down in front of you." He puts the cigarette out and

smiles at me, full of a false joviality. I want to remind him that
I've been a vegetarian for two years now, but I keep my mouth
shut and smile back.

"I'll just get out of this monkey suit and we can go." I nod, but
as he walks out of the room, he stops and looks at me. "Aren't
you goin to change?"

I look down at myself. "I wasn't planning on it. The Grill's
casual."

"I was thinkin you could put on a skirt, somethin real ladylike,
and we could go out . . ." *As a family,* I can hear the end of his
sentence as clearly as if he'd said it, and I remember all the times
in high school I was exhorted to put on a skirt, to dress like a
"lady" so that we could go out "as a family." I think of what I've
got upstairs, and I know the two miniskirts won't please him, but
I don't have anything else besides the dress I wore when we
scattered her ashes.

"Dad, I didn't really bring formal clothes . . ."

"What about that skirt of your mother's you used to wear—you
know, that pretty flowered thing . . . bet that still fits you."

From the time I was fourteen, I had refused to buy dresses. I
had gone through a shrill feminist stage, quoting Germaine Greer
and stuffing my bras in the bottom drawer of my bureau, but every
time we went out "as a family," my parents insisted on my "dressing like a lady," and that odious skirt would be dragged out, and
I would be forced, sullen and unforgiving, to wear it. I think of
that skirt with its pattern of pink posies, its double frill at the
bottom, the only one of my mother's skirts that fit me around the
waist; I was always bigger than she was, even after I graduated
from high school and lost my baby fat.

"Oh, God, Daddy, please . . . not that skirt again."

"Go on now, Ellie, you always looked so nice in it—go on
upstairs and put it on, please your old Dad." He doesn't wait for
me to say yes or no, he just walks out and down to his room, sure
of my obedience, and the old rebellion rises. I stand where I am,
one hand on the kitchen table, and I can't believe how little things
have changed . . . can't believe that here I am, twenty-five years
old and a woman of independent means, still being blackmailed
into wearing a hideous peasant skirt—

But things *have* changed, I tell myself, walking slowly up the
stairs, and if that's what's going to make him happy, if all he wants
is for me to wear this damn skirt, then I'll do it. And I won't
complain.

Tearing my mother's trunk apart, I find the skirt in all its
flowered splendor and wish that I had thrown it away while I still
had the chance. Studiously avoiding my reflection in the mirror
once it's on, and hoping no one I know will see me tonight, I walk
downstairs to meet my father.

He's waiting for me out on the front porch, smoking another
cigarette. When he sees me he smiles broadly. "Well now, don't
you look nice."

I grimace at him, bite down on my lip to keep my mouth shut,
and we get in the car. He smiles at me again while I'm buckling
my seat belt, and I smile back, but we're both as awkward as two
people on a blind date, each trying to act the way we think the
other one wants us to.

"Ready?"

"Yup." After that neither of us speaks, the darkness inside the
car a relief, a camouflage. I slump down in my seat and stare out
my window at the trees that flank the road, at the deeper darkness
beyond those trees, and I think of ancient cultures I studied in

college, ancient mystic rites that took place in the heart of the forest. I remember walking behind my father, my hands gray with her ash, unable to comprehend that this was all that was left; what fire had made of her flesh.

When we open the restaurant door, I don't see any customers, just one waitress leaning against the reservations podium, talking on the phone. When she sees us, her face freezes. She cups one hand over the receiver and says, "Sir, the kitchen's closed."

"Thought y'all were open till ten."

"Yes, ten o'clock," she says, still holding the phone, holding out hope.

"Well, 'cording to my watch here it's ten till." His eyes stray up to the far wall, where a round clock face indicates that his watch is right.

For a second I almost think she's going to say the kitchen's closed early and turn us away, but then she mutters, "I'll talk to you later," and hangs up. Her lips a thin line, she asks, "Smokin or nonsmokin?" and leads the way with two oversized menus to a booth in the back. We slide in on either side and she hands us the menus, but then she pulls her pad out of her pocket and just stands there, waiting. My father looks at her.

"We'll just take a minute to look these over—"

"If you want to order dinner you'll have to place your orders now before the kitchen closes," she says, her voice a monotone, staring at some point in space over our heads. My father keeps looking at her, and I nudge him under the table.

"I'll have the salad bar, please. Don't you just want a steak, Dad?"

"Yeah, steak sounds good. I'll have a sirloin steak—"

"Six eight or ten ounce."

"... Eight. I'll have your eight-ounce, medium-rare ... and a baked potato—"

"Sour cream, butter, bacon bits or chives."

"... a baked potato with sour cream and butter, and—"

"You have a choice of house salad, spinach or corn."

"And a double whiskey on the rocks. Seagram's."

"You have a choice of house salad, spinach—"

"No vegetables. Just bring me the drink."

She makes a sharp little notation on her pad and wheels around.

"Thanks," I mutter after her rapidly receding back.

"Jesus Christ," he says, loud enough for her to hear. "They got one of those suggestion boxes here? Think I'll suggest they let her go."

"She probably thought she was getting off till she saw us."

"I don't care what she thought, she has a job to do and she should do it."

"Yeah, some job, big deal."

"She doesn't like it, she can find somethin else."

"Sure, just like I did . . ." I say this under my breath, looking at my feet, but my father catches it.

"You could've found somethin else, Ellie."

"Not anything else that pays, unless it's typing, which is just as bad."

"Well, I hope you don't treat your customers the way she does. I'll tell you somethin, that young lady there ain't gettin much of a tip from me."

"That's great, Dad. First you make her hang around an extra half hour and then you stiff her. Just great." I hiss this at him because the waitress is coming back toward us, taking short, stiff, little steps, my father's drink on her tray. She sets it down in front of him without a word and turns to walk away.

"Excuse me. I believe my daughter here would like somethin
to drink too." I shake my head furiously at him, but the waitress
turns around and looks at me. "Ellie? What'll you have?"

"I'll just have a beer, please—"

"Miller, Coors, Bud, Pabst—"

"A light beer. A light beer'll be fine."

"Miller, Coors, Bud, Amstel—" She stares at me without expression, but I can feel the hostility radiating toward us.

"Miller. Please." Without a word, she heads back to the
kitchen. My father shakes his head grimly, watches her walking
away. He picks up his drink, downs half of it. "That young lady's
got a bad attitude. She has a very bad attitude, and if she doesn't
change it, I'm goin to speak to the manager."

My fingers are knotted together under the table. "Dad, please.
Just relax, okay? Let's just have dinner and forget about it."

"How can I forget about it when every time she comes back
she's got that ugly face on?"

"Daddy, please."

"There is just no call for that kind of rudeness. No call at all."

"I'm going to get some salad. I'll be back in a minute."

Standing at the salad bar, I wait until the waitress has taken my
beer to our table before I walk back with my plate.

"That all you ordered?"

"I already ate tonight. I'm really not that hungry." And if I
were, I feel like adding, I would have lost my appetite.

"Eggs aren't dinner, Ellie," he says again. "That's not dinner
either." He points at the pile of lettuce and the three cherry
tomatoes riding on the rim of the plate. "You better have somethin else—"

For one awful moment I think he's going to raise his arm and
call the waitress back, and I half-stand, saying, "Dad, I am not

hungry! If you order something else I won't eat it, because I'm just not hungry."

"Yeah, well, I'm eatin." And then suddenly he puts two fingers in his mouth and lets go a whistle. I see the waitress whip her head around, and as my father raises his empty glass and nods at her, I sink down in my seat.

By the time his steak arrives, he's had two drinks, both doubles, and is working on a third. She sets his food down in front of him with a bang and I stare at my plate, picking up small bits of lettuce and chewing them with the utmost concentration. He thanks her, too loud but sincere now, and I know he's drunk. Instead of picking up his knife and fork, he fishes for the cigarettes inside his shirt pocket.

"Daddy, eat your steak."

"I will, I will. Just goin to finish this drink here first." He fumbles with the pack, a fresh one, his fingers too clumsy to extract one from the rest.

"Don't smoke, Dad. Your food'll get cold."

"Just goin to 'company my drink here. Nothin like a little smoke to 'company your drink."

"You're smoking a lot more these days, aren't you."

"No, no, no. Just like a little smoke when I drink, that's all." I can't bear to watch him fumbling, still trying to get one out, while the butter congeals on his baked potato.

"Here—" I take it out of his hands and do it for him.

"Thanks, honey."

"Doesn't mean I condone it. I just want you to get it over with so you can eat some of that food." Sitting up I lean over the table and poke the meat with my fork. It bleeds a little. "Mmm, looks good." His eyes screwed up against the flare of the match, he's not even listening. "You need *protein*, Dad, not nicotine."

"Jesus, you sound like your mother, Ellie. Always naggin about the cigarettes. Each one takes time off your life, she'd say—days, weeks, maybe even years—her with her silly menthols—"

"She was right."

"Always told her I didn't want to live that long anyway—who wants to be seventy? What for?" He looks at me through a thin haze of smoke. "You know what she'd say then? She'd say, Tom, you're selfish. Only thinkin of yourself, she'd say, and what about me? How am I supposed to get along if you go and die of some cancer?" He reaches for his glass and picks it up carefully, tilts it back and swallows what's left. "That's what she'd say." I stare at the food on his plate. It's stopped steaming. The sour cream has slid into a puddle on the plate and mixed with the juice from the steak to form a runny mess.

"Daddy, you should eat."

"Selfish." His elbows propped on the table, he stares out the window, past his own reflection, at the taillights of cars going by. "How do you like that."

I look around. The waitress is back on the phone, hunched over it, and I'm sure she's telling her boyfriend or her sister or her mother about the awful customers who came in half an hour ago and won't leave.

"Think I'll have another drink."

"No Daddy I think we should go home now."

"One more drink—" He raises his arm to flag the waitress, but when she turns around I motion for the check.

"Let's just go home, okay, Dad?"

"What the hell, why not smoke, right? Maybe it'll take years off my life, huh?"

"Here's the check, Dad—"

"Yes, waitress, another drink please—"

"No, we're just getting the check. The restaurant's closed, Dad."

"Closed? What d'you mean, closed?"

"See? No one here but us."

"Oh. Look at that. We closed the place, Ellie. Wouldn't you like another beer, honey?"

"Do you want this food to go?" The waitress picks up his plate and directs her question at me. I shake my head no.

"Yes, wrap it up. For the dog. We'll have it in a doggie bag, okay? No sense wastin it. Somebody'll eat it." He takes his wallet out, squints at the bill. I read it to him and he puts three bills down, ten dollars over the amount.

"That tip okay with you, Ellie?"

"You're going to leave her all that?"

"Sure. She was a good sport, wasn't she?" He winks at me and I nod. "Sure, why not. We'll surprise her." He slides out of the booth slowly, as if his weight were more than he can manage. The waitress hands him an aluminum bag, says, "I'll get your change."

"No need," he tells her. "No need."

The soft, humid night air feels good after the air-conditioned refrigeration inside, and I take my father's arm. "I'll drive home, Dad."

"No, no. Squad car, nobody can drive it but me."

"No one's going to know—"

"No, Ellie. It's against the law." He reaches into his pants pocket for the keys, starts walking to the driver's side.

"So's driving drunk—"

"I'm not drunk, Ellie, all's I had was three—"

"Three *doubles*, Dad."

"Didn't realize you were countin." He opens the door and

reaches across to unlock mine. "Buckle up now." But I just stand there, arms crossed, unmoving. "Ellie, get in the car."

"Daddy, let me drive."

"I told you, it's against the law—"

I walk around to his side and push at him. "Come on, give me the keys. No one'll see us."

"Ellie—" But I can feel him weakening, and finally he slides over.

Driving home, he leans his head against the window and I reach over to make sure the door is locked. I think he's fallen asleep when he says, "D'you think I was selfish?"

"What, Dad?"

"Sometimes I think if I'd listened to her, if we'd done more what she wanted to do, maybe things would've turned out different . . ."

"There was nothing you could have done to change what happened, Dad. It wasn't your fault."

"I think, sometimes, if we'd had a different sort of life, maybe she wouldn't have been . . ."

"Wouldn't have been what? Driving that night?"

"If I worked regular days, like other men, if she hadn't been alone so much at night—"

"Daddy, stop. You're just torturing yourself. There's nothing you could've done to change things."

"I never even saw it . . . never even saw it comin . . ."

"Nobody did. It was an accident." I glance over at him but he's staring out the window; he hasn't heard a word I've said.

"The empty nest, that's what she called it . . . you were gone and there she was, rattlin round the house by herself, me workin nights, college bills . . . she said she felt old, saw the rest of her life stretchin out and nothin new in it . . ." Lurching slightly, he pushes the car lighter in, pats his pockets looking for his cigarettes. "That's why she did it, she said. To kill that feeling."

"Did what?" Sitting up high and stiff behind the steering wheel, I can feel my whole body tensing, as if against a blow.

"She cried and cried . . . cried and cried . . ."

"That smoke's making me dizzy." With my thumb, I press the automatic lever and my window whirrs all the way down.

"Swore she loved me. I swear it, she kept sayin, I swear it," he mutters, but even with the air blowing through the car, I can hear it, what he's saying.

"Dad, what are you talking about? She *did* love you."

"She could'a been somethin else, you know, her style, her brains . . . used to think sometimes she wasted herself on me."

"There was no one else for her but you." I say this forcefully, and my father looks at me for the first time. "That's what she always told me." He smiles then but it's remote, the smile you give a babbling child.

"She told me one day she woke up and she realized she didn't want to live a single day without you. She said, Ellie, when you find a man you feel like that about, that's the man you marry."

He says nothing, just smokes.

"If you find a man like your daddy, she said to me, you catch him and you keep him. Don't you ever let him go." I look over at him and he's still smiling that way, putting his cigarette out in the car ashtray, smiling but suddenly silent. He doesn't say another word all the way home; it's as if he'd never spoken at all.

———

You were gone for three days. I walked down that road looking for you every night, and every night, the house was barren. Wanted you so bad. Couldn't remember the last time I wanted anything so bad. Made me want to claw my throat, tear my hair. Wanted to rip the feeling right out, the way it filled me up, the way it drained me. I had no energy for anything but wanting you. And every time, though I walked home, slow, backwards, straining for the sound of your bike, I would rather have lain down at your doorstep. Stretched myself out flat, pressed my cheek against the floorboards, hoping to hear the buzz of your bike. Walking back I kept thinking, what if you were gone. I stamped the thought down. No. But near dawn, I was still awake.

What if you were really gone.

O N   T H E   morning of the Fourth of July, I tell my father I'm going to a party that night. I tell him one of the kids, he has a cousin, there's a farm.

"I'm workin the night shift," he says. "I can't come get you."

"That's all right, he says it's a big place, we can all stay. Sleep on air mattresses outside."

"Where's this party at?"

"Somewhere past the river." I wave a hand. "Out there."

"You goin with Melanie's crowd?"

"Some kids. But I don't think she'll be there."

"Why not?"

"I don't know. Wedding stuff."

Walking to work toward Jesse's, my hands are fists, tense with hope—but when I get there, the bike's still gone. I stop and stare at the house, as if the intensity of my desire might materialize him. I remember the last time I saw him, standing there with those other Angels—talking about the party.

I don't know how I'm going to get there, but I know I'm going to go.

———

I'm serving one table their third round of coffee when I hear him, his bike, and jerking my head up, I almost pour coffee on a woman's lap, but I don't see him. Swiveling, I check the clock; my shift's not over for at least another hour, maybe two—

"Sandra!" I catch her placing an order in the kitchen. "Sandra, listen—I have to go."

"What?"

"I can't explain right now, but I really, I have to go—"

"Ellie, you still have three tables left!"

"I know, I know, but one of them's about to leave—" Scrabbling in my uniform pocket, I pull out a wad of singles. Change tinkles on the ground, but I'm in too much of a hurry to pick it up. I press the money into Sandra's hands.

"I'll make it up to you, I swear—" She stares after me as I run into the Employees Only. I'm out again in less than five minutes, running through the restaurant, holding my shoes. I can feel everybody staring but I just keep running and I don't look back.

When I get to Jesse's, he's just coming out of his house.

"Jesse!" I sprint the last fifty yards and throw myself against him. He catches me and I hear the breath leave his body. "Take me with you." He tries to disentangle himself, but I lock my fingers around his wrists. "Jesse, please."

"Ain't no place for you."

"Why not?" Finally catching my breath, I notice for the first time how bright his eyes are, how dilated the pupils. His pulse races beneath my fingertips.

"It just ain't."

"Yes it is—"

"Can't be lookin out for you—"

"I can look out for myself—"

"Uh-uh." He shakes me off. "It ain't a good idea."

"Jesse, I promise, I promise I'll take care of myself. I can take care of myself. You don't have to babysit me. I'll be fine."

He shakes his head and throws one leg over his bike.

"Jesse, please!" He stands poised, ready to kickstart the engine. "I just want to be with you—"

It catches and he revs it, once, twice, three times. Tears spill on my face while he picks up his helmet. I step back, fold my arms across my stomach, but suddenly he shouts "Catch!" and then the helmet's flying at me. Holding it with both arms, I look at him, disbelieving.

He smiles at me, crooked white and dazzling. "Get on."

———

When we pull up to the Angels' headquarters, a good half hour out of town on the highway, there's already at least two dozen bikes there. Jesse parks his alongside one that has Virginia plates and a real saddle nailed on low instead of a leather seat. I stare at the row of bikes, each one different from the rest, all of them polished to a shine.

"Most of those been rebuilt," Jesse says, nodding at them. "The Angels can take 'em apart and put 'em together again in two hours."

"Can you?"

"If I had to."

Walking up to their house, I feel as if I'm entering a fortress. They have looped barbed wire in a wide circle a good hundred yards out, and a bunch of men are hammering together what seems to be a small platform, some kind of stage. Music blares from two speakers on either side. By this time, we have to shout.

"What's that for?"

"Band."

He heads straight for a keg of beer that's already been tapped. When they see him, the Angels nod, but nobody says anything much. One of them, a short, paunchy man with a dagger tattooed on his left cheek, spits on the ground and leaves. I hang back, trying to act nonchalant, trying to make it apparent that I am with Jesse, although he seems to have forgotten me already. Suddenly from the house I hear a whoop, a high, female voice, and when

I look a woman is charging straight at me, moving so fast her features are a blur.

Ducking, I jump back, and Jesse turns around just as she leaps on him, legs wrapping around his waist. He almost falls but then he catches his balance and starts to laugh. She kisses him all over his face.

"Fuckin redskin, where you been!"

"Hey Rose, you're lookin good—"

"*Feelin* good, you mean to say!" Letting go, she steps back, and it's only then I see, quite clearly, that she's part, if not whole, Indian, too. He grins at her.

"Knocked my beer down, too." He stoops to pick up his cup, but she grabs it from him.

"I'll do that—"

Furtively, I study her while she holds the nozzle into the cup. Her hair is red-brown and cut short, close to her head, and her eyelids are painted white. She has the same high, hard cheekbones that Jesse has, and I wonder if they're from the same tribe; wonder if they're related. Her body is lean as a young girl's. But when Jesse takes the cup she's filled and hands it over to me, she turns and looks at me, and her face, her eyes especially, are obviously older, certainly older than Jesse; I gauge her to be at least thirty-five. She studies me as if I were a statue, incapable of perception, and then her mouth twists up sideways in a smile.

"That yours?"

Jesse doesn't say anything, just grins at her again, and takes the second cup.

Behind us, a mike screams. Rose turns around.

"Band's here."

Four guys wearing skintight jeans and heavy-metal T-shirts, all of them sporting huge manes of frizzed-out dyed black hair, are picking up their instruments and climbing up on stage. There are two electric guitars, one of them purple, the other black; both of them are designed to look as if they were cut from lightning bolts.

"I'm goin in." Walking past me, Jesse motions toward the house. "Got some business to take care of first."

I nod, both hands wrapped tight around the plastic cup of beer. I can feel Rose looking at me, but I stare fixedly at the band while they set up the stage. Five minutes later, when I glance back to see her, she's gone. Keeping to myself, I walk down to the edge of the stage. When they start to play, I'm deafened. Around me, people congregate, Angels and their girlfriends, or, for all I know, their wives: narrow women on whom thinness looks scrawny, thirty-year-old women with straight waist-length hair parted down the middle and falling flat on either side of their faces, wearing jeans so tight they have to swivel their hips to take a step forward, wearing spaghetti-strap T-shirts and open-toed high heels, their nails painted brilliant shades of crimson. They drink beer and stand as tough as the men; occasionally, I catch their looks, but I deflect them, look right through them, and keep turning around, trying to make it clear that I am waiting for someone. I stay where I am through two sets, although the music has begun to give me a headache.

It isn't until it's beginning to get dark that I head for the house. A clot of Angels are blocking the doorway, drinking beer. They look at me when I walk up, and two of them exchange glances, but nobody says anything.

"I'm looking for Jesse . . . any of you seen him?"

"Saw him in there awhile back," one of them volunteers, inclining his head toward the doorway.

"Can I go in?"

At this, they all laugh; I have no idea why.

"Just don't steal anythin," the same guy answers, and they all laugh again. Smiling uncertainly, I move past them.

In the hallway, somebody's smoking a joint. He eyes me with bloodshot eyes. "What you want?"

"I'm looking for Jesse. They said he was in here . . ."

"Indian?" He takes a long toke, holds it in. I nod.

"That room." He points with the joint down the hall a ways, where a door stands ajar. Grateful, I smile at him, and he holds out the roach.

"Want some?"

"No, thank you." Walking quickly I go over to that room, knock on the door; when there's no answer, I peek in. There's no one there. I step in and shut the door behind me, glad for a moment's solitude, and then I see Jesse's jacket in the corner. When I walk over to investigate, I see that he's left his T-shirt there too—I drop the clothes where I found them and head back out.

I walk through the house and out the back, tense, wary, my head swiveling, peripheral vision straining, looking for Jesse. It's dark now, Angels who've been drinking all day in the same place are moving; there's a sense of a plan being put into action. I want to find Jesse before anything happens, but I don't see him any-where, and I feel as if I've been doing this all afternoon, all day, all my life—looking for Jesse, and not finding him.

Out back somebody's built a fire and I approach, peering over the lick and rise of the flames for his face, that profile—and then I think I see it, my body jumps forward—

"Girl, you got to quit it." It's eerie how she looks like him, she could be his sister, and when I stop I know she's been watching me, that she saw me before I saw her. She looks up at me, eyes dark, focus blurred, and then I see she's gripping a half-empty bottle of tequila by the neck, her fingers claws.

"Quit what?" I stand near her, kicking one toe into charred dirt.

She smiles, wise, says nothing: she knows. When she tips the bottle up I stare at her, furtively—that faded beauty like dried roses, pressed and crumbling, dusty scent still sweet. I can imagine her younger days, before tequila burned her eyes low and deep in her head, made her mouth twist sideways, helpless and bitter. Her hair is cropped short but still thick, I picture it hanging to her waist, and that waist flat and narrow, navel a shallow ripple he put his thumbs in—did he do her like he does me—she reads my mind, knows I'm burning, says, "He gets 'em like a bitch in heat, but I knew him first.

"Had him when he was fifteen," she says, eyes slide to the corners, and then she laughs.

"Did you know his mother?" One hand clutching the other, rolled into a fist, I hunker by the fire, want everything, want to know everything she knows, suck it out of her like juice from a lime, thin and sour.

She tips the bottle up again and I watch how her throat opens for the amber, how she lets it flow; she doesn't offer me any. Her skirt's hitched up to mid-thigh, her knees are bony but the bones still good, underneath forsaken skin. She doesn't answer, knows what I'm after, knows the value of her secrets, dug deep.

"Got the firewater syndrome," she says, "like me." She looks at me and I get the feeling she could move faster than I could see, even drunk, and I take a step backwards, just a tiny step, but she's watching with those narrowed eyes and suddenly she laughs, high like a rooster, like a crow, pleased to have scared me.

"His mother?" I move forward again, clear my throat.

"Mother. Huh!" Rose puffs her lips out in disdain, takes another slug. "Never was the mother type anyway, always lookin to escape what was in her. Let the men fall over her, feed her brew—he'd come home, find her spread on the couch, half-naked, out cold . . . and then he'd hit on me—" She stops, drinks again.

"He hit you?"

She laughs her raspy laugh again. "Wouldn't you like to know." Her eyes slide sideways, this way, that way, she hunches low into herself, I get the feeling she's forgotten me. "Always had that fuckin grease on his hands . . . comin over an' slammin into me, curl up sleepin . . ."

Picking up a stick, scratching in the dirt, I have to ask, jealous even of his past, "Did he live with you?"

"Live with me—" Rose grunts, throws her head back and then the bottle, her eyes rolling white. "Yeah, he lived with me. Like an animal't's crawled into your hole to save his strength."

She falls into an abrupt silence, staring at the fire, moody and bitter. I sit where I am, scratching circles, one inside the next, over and over into the dirt. The bottle dangles from her fingers, and we stay as we are for long minutes, me waiting for her to drink again. I know she'll tell me everything if I just hold out for it.

Someone comes out of the house, we both look up; he's too short to be Jesse, and as he comes closer I see he's got a mustache, he's holding a beer. He looks over at us, eyes hidden inside his squint, and when he sees me they widen a minute, he looks me over, I know he wonders who I'm with, if I'm game.

"Rose." He barks her name out but she doesn't even look up,

and he comes walking around, passing close to me, smells like sweat. He grabs her by the hair, pulls her head up, and her lips curl back in a snarl. I half-stand, don't know whether I should leave or try to protect her, knowing even as I think it what a stupid idea that is.

"Leave me alone." She jerks her head and he loses his hold.

"Stop drinkin." He reaches down for the bottle but she's too fast for him, she moves it out of his reach and then pulls it in, holds it to her chest, folds herself around it.

"It's Fourth of July," she says, defensive, and I realize he's her old man, trying to look out for her. "Leave me alone."

"Who's that?" He jerks his head at me, feet planted wide.

Rose looks up at me as if she's seeing me for the first time. "Look at her. He's fishin big water these days, ain't he?"

Turning his face, the Angel spits suddenly and it's like an insult, aimed and sharp. "Fuckin worthless Indian."

Making a guttural sound Rose turns around, teeth bared, and the Angel laughs, but he takes a step back. She hisses at him and he makes another swipe for the bottle, but she's still faster than he is, and he misses again.

"Ah, fuck it," he says then, disgusted. "Drink till you die." Without looking at me, he turns around and walks away.

"That fuckin worthless Indian's better'n you any day," she mutters. "I'd take him over you any day."

"Why did Jesse leave you?" I keep my eyes averted.

"Never did leave me!" She sits on the log again, takes another drink. "Left his mother. Found some white asshole with her one day and he lit into that man, was goin to kill him sure—" Rose shakes her head and lifts the bottle up again. Her eyes have a hazy look. I'm not sure she remembers why she's saying this, or to whom. I stay quiet, for fear my voice will jolt her from her trance.

"The guy was screamin, someone called the police . . . they got there, she had a gun pointed at him, pointed at her only son, the guy moanin half-dead on the livin-room floor and Jesse backed up against the wall . . . cops slapped the bracelets on him and locked him up for seven days and seven nights. He got out, lived with me. Till he turned sixteen and took off for good, he lived with *me.*" The bottle dangles from her hand, liquid sliding up the neck but never spilling over.

"I taught him the slow love." She looks at me, eyes narrow. "Taught him good, didn't I?"

Ashamed, ashamed, I look away, never wanted to share him like this. Her words fall and his life rises from them, full and far beyond me, I can't hold it in my hands, I want to find him, corner him, shove myself up against him and hear his groan, low and forced, inside my ear.

Standing, my heart fluttering, I wipe my fingers on my jeans and look around. Rose stares dull-eyed into the fire, knows I'm leaving her. I stand there for a second, wanting to say something, wanting to give her something, but there's nothing, I know there's nothing. I say, "Well . . ." but she doesn't look up, she knows there's nothing too, and then I walk away, turn my back to the fire and walk back inside the house.

J E S S E ' S jacket lies crumpled by the bed where I left it. I pick it up and dig into the pockets, don't know what I'm looking for until I pull out a small cellophane bag of shiny black capsules. It rips and they spill into my hand, five of them. I stare at them, roll them against each other in my palm, watch how they shine, thinking, They're in Jesse right now, racing through his veins, pumping inside his head. I stare at them and want to think his thoughts, want to be where he is, want to know where to look. I am aware as I shake two of the pills from my palm into my mouth, as I pocket the other three, that I don't know what I'm taking. The thought slides serenely across my mind without registering. Saving up spit, I swallow them, and then I sit on the bed with my hands braced against my thighs and my back to the wall, waiting.

An explosion shatters the air outside my window and I'm up off the bed and crouched against the wall so fast I don't even realize I've moved until I look down, surprised to see the floor so close. I wait, a hunched-up hunted war victim in a bomb shelter, for my pulse to stop racing until it dawns on me that it isn't going to, and when I stand my knees jerk me upright so hard my neck snaps.

A high blast of music leaps out suddenly from inside the house, hard-sliding trippy guitar and a tense backbeat, Led Zeppelin making me think of every murky sex dream I've ever had and I'm speeding, speeding, moving around Jesse's room, my body one step ahead of my mind, his knife shines at me suddenly from underneath the bed and I snatch it as a bottle rocket whines and blasts itself right over the roof. I try to stop grinding my teeth while I sort through a mound of clothes until I find what I'm looking for, the T-shirt he wore here, a black one with a white skull with eagle's wings blazing on the front of it. The floor feels cool against the backs of my thighs while I slash the T-shirt, cutting off the collar and the sleeves before taking off the bottom half with one long jittery yank of the knife. I pull my shirt off and put the T-shirt on and then I'm out the door and the music deafens me—there's no one in the house, and the last of the daylight is filtering through the windows. I stand by the door too scared to go out, I can feel the air contracting and then the deep bass boom, it's Beirut out there and Jesse's loose, it's this that gets me out and into the smoke, the smell of sulfur acrid up my nose.

I move around to the side of the house, men I've never seen before are standing inside the smoke, their thumbs hooked in their belt loops, eyes hidden behind dark shades, unmoving as if invulnerable to fire. I watch them unnoticed, squinting for a glimpse of Jesse, but everybody looks alike, overlarge and leathered, hair in ponytails and bearded faces—a series of sharp reports go off right near me and I leap into the air with a small scream but no one hears and when I turn I see him, I recognize his walk, hips low-slung and fast, and the need to possess him grips me like thirst. I watch him moving across the grass to the raised-up wooden stage, watch sparks shower down around him—he doesn't look up, not once, as he jumps up on the platform and seizes the drumsticks. He's wearing nothing but his jeans, and his face is streaked with sweat and smoke, he looks like a wild man, like an Indian warrior, crazed, displaced—

A bonfire burns in a garbage can in the middle of the road in front of the house. Over on the stage Jesse's still beating at the drums, arms flying, I try to hear his rhythm in my mind and wonder how many black beauties *he* took. Crouched behind an overturned crate I'm thinking so fast it all comes together in one blinding hum, electrical currents colliding, I count to ten and then, hands up over my head, I go for the stage but I haven't even made two feet when something flies at me, a flash of green light; caught by the impulse to move both right and left, forward and back, I'm transfixed and then I feel white heat searing into the leg of my jeans, and screaming, I twist away before it burns my skin and run for the side of the house and cover.

Everything's happening at once, I see Chip moving up to the garbage can with an armload of something at the same time that the flashing blue lights appear and then everybody's taking cover, flames are whistling through the air and the noise explodes against me in waves. I cover my head with my arms, something hits me and I twist sideways, all I can think about are my eyes, visions of sizzling sparks burning through my pupils, and the whole world feels brittle and jagged, ready to break into pieces beneath my feet.

Someone reaches down and shakes me. I look up into Eddie's face and he says, "Cops're here," and then he turns around. Using his body as cover I stand, don't see Jesse anywhere. I shout his name in Eddie's ear but Eddie shrugs and moves forward, I see another cop car pulling up, men in helmets and blue uniforms—

Moving faster than I ever have before I sprint for the door. Inside a woman is swearing, on the edge of hysteria, I can tell she's drunk and when I pass her she reaches out as if to grab my hair but I zigzag away and race down the hall.

The room where Jesse changed is empty but through the window things are still exploding, the glass is cracked in two places. My breathing sounds high and ragged in my ears and every time I blink it's as if the world is crashing to black, I see jagged blinding white edges everywhere when I open my eyes again, and when I put my hands up over them my fingers come back smeared with black. In the hallway a fight erupts, I can hear the dull thud of bodies against the wall and men's voices, animal grunts.

I dive under the bed dragging the sheet with me and curl up into the smallest ball I can, praying I won't be found.

T I M E goes by, minutes and minutes, stretching like wire into each other. The noise has stopped, I can hear voices through the house but I don't move, I feel like I've been there all night, cramped and terrified, breathing dust, waiting for something, an inner signal that everything's okay, but the signal never comes. I hold my breath and let it out, I don't move. Jesse, please come, please come, the words run over and over through my head, a rhythm, a litany, a spell—

The door opens. Heavy boots walk my way, and then someone's hand grabs my foot. Kicking, I scream, it comes out small and bounces off the bottom of the mattress.

"That you?" Someone's face appears. I recognize Eddie upside down, I can see the light of his eyes, and then the grip on my foot tightens, he starts to drag me out. I let him, not helping, just limp weight along the floor, I don't want to come out, I'm sure my father is going to be out there, waiting for me . . . but I don't want to stay under that bed anymore either, I wish I were home and in my bed, alone, safe, asleep.

I squint under the overhead light, a single bare bulb, I stay crouched, I have a cramp in my leg, I throw one arm over my eyes.

"Are the cops gone?"

"Yeah."

"Where's Jesse?"

"Took off."

I take my arm away. "He left?"

"Cops came and he took off." Eddie seems immensely tall from here, his hands on his hips, his face inscrutable as rock. I want to cry, I think I'm going to cry but I don't want him to see it, and I sit there biting my lip and rubbing at the cramp in my calf, digging my thumbs into it hard.

"You okay?"

I nod, keep my face averted.

"Let's go."

"Go where?"

Eddie reaches down and pulls me up by the elbows. When I'm on my feet he lets me go but when I try to walk, a sharp pain shoots through my leg and I start to crumple. He catches me and lifts me as if I were a bag of garbage, and with a grunt, throws me over his shoulder. We walk out of the house, I see it all upside down, it's destroyed, bottles smashed into hundreds of shards of glass, puddles of beer everywhere, broken chairs, heaps of unrecognizable debris. He carries me outside and then I see figures moving, and firelight. I close my eyes and hold on to the cloth of his jeans until he gets to his bike.

He doesn't have an extra helmet, he says, We'll have to risk the cops, and I grab his shirt, say no, please—he kickstarts the bike, he says we'll take back roads, get on. Get *on.* And then he shrugs, says, stay here, I don't care, and I jump on, pull up close behind him, clutch his belt loops. We take off and the wind raises goosebumps on my flesh, the shirt I tore flies up and my stomach is bare, I hold on to Eddie and my teeth chatter.

We go down roads I've never ridden on before, winding roads,
dirt roads, roads with no lights. Scared, I close my eyes. He shouts
into the wind, "Where do you live?"—and leaning into him,
trying to get close to his ear, I shout, "Take me to Jesse's, I'll walk
from there."

———

When we get to Jesse's, the house is dark. His bike isn't there.
Eddie cuts the motor and the sudden silence sounds a roar inside
my ears. He looks at me.

"You walk from here?"

Pulling my shirt down over my stomach I nod, keep looking up
the road.

"You sure?"

"Maybe I'll wait here a little." Stepping toward the house.
"Maybe I'll just catch my breath." I walk up to the porch but the
door's locked. I try the front windows, but they're shut tight.
When I turn around, Eddie's watching me. I don't say anything,
just lean against the house, and after a second, slide my back down
the wall till I'm sitting on the floor. My heart's still pounding,
pounding, I wish it would quit, I wish I could make it stop, it
makes my hands tremble—

Suddenly Eddie swings off the bike and walks up to the house.
He doesn't say anything to me, just wedges his shoulder beneath
a window and shoves his weight up into it with a grunt; the
window gives, he steps back.

"I'm leavin."

I watch him kickstart the bike again, readjust the helmet, and
then, with that inhuman roar, take off. The minute he's gone I'm
up and through the window, into the dark house. It feels menac-
ing, as if evil spirits lurking don't want to let me stay, and I hurry

down the hall and into Jesse's room. I go for the bed but when I get in I feel exposed, the room stretches out on all sides around me and I sit rigid, watching every shadow, until finally, taking the sheet, I drag it into a corner and hunch up, shoulders squared against the walls. For the first time I notice how warped the house is . . . warped windows, warped walls. I'll count to fifty and then I'll go, I tell myself. I'll just calm down and then I'll go. I start to count, one mississippi, two mississippi, but I keep losing my concentration, hearing things, and then I have to start over, it seems I never get past twelve. I keep thinking, When I get to fifty, then I'll go—

And then I hear his bike, it's Jesse's bike, I recognize the sound, the way he brakes, the way the engine coughs when it stops, but I don't move—I hear his footsteps on the porch and then they stop.

"Who's there!"

"It's me—" My voice comes out rusty and I clear my throat, call out again. "It's me . . . Ellie . . ."

I hear the front door open and Jesse coming down the hall.

He's wearing his jeans but no shirt, I remember now that I hacked it to pieces, that it's still on me. His body is bare, his hair is long, tied back in a ponytail, streaked with purple dye. He pulls me up, staggers, I lean against his chest and he balances on his knees. I touch his hair, it feels coarse, slick beneath my fingers. I touch the purple dye, touch the strands of silver. He looks at me, glitter eyes watching. I touch it again, just two fingers, lightly, so lightly maybe he won't feel it.

"You left me." My voice comes out cracked, hoarse.

"Cops came. Had to split."

"You left me there."

"Come on," he says; his voice is hoarse too. "I'll take you home."

"No." I clutch his arms, nails digging into his skin.

"You shouldn't'a come. You don't belong in places like that. I knew I shouldn't'a let you come."

"I wanted to go. I want to go anywhere you go."

Long silence thick between us, I refuse to meet his eyes, press my face against his skin. He smells like smoke. "You're crazy," he mutters finally.

"Me." I laugh, a choked sound that grows. When I don't stop he holds me away.

"What's funny." But I can't stop laughing, gasping, the silence now torn with it, ragged. He takes my wrists, pulls me up, still I'm limp and laughing, feeble, laughing—

He pins my wrists up hard against the wall but I won't look at him.

"Stop it." He hisses at me, face pushed up close. I can't, I'm falling, he staggers, holding me up, presses his body against me hard, I'm flat between him and the wall, I think the wall will give first, they're squeezing the breath out of me, squeezing and squeezing . . . if I don't stop laughing I'll die, I'll suffocate—

"You take somethin tonight? You take those pills in my jeans?" He shakes me, I want to answer but I can't get the words out, my lungs hurt, my heart feels weak from pounding so hard, and Jesse shakes me again, harder. "How many'd you take?"

"Two . . . just two . . ." He eases off and I start sliding, I'm not laughing anymore, just sliding down against the wall and I think how nice it would be to give up, to close my eyes and fade away, float up somewhere and never come back. "I wanted to know what it felt like . . ." I whisper, and Jesse catches me, holds me underneath the arms and clasps his hands, a hard knot against my lower back, holds me up against him. "I wanted to know what that kind of speed felt like . . ."

Later he holds me in the shower, doesn't ask me why I'm crying. Turns me around gently underneath the stream. Don't know which is water and which is tears. In bed we drink half a bottle of Wild Turkey, hitting on it methodically until it's gone, taking turns. The jaggedness starts to recede, muffled by alcohol.

I love you, I whisper. He's asleep. I love you. I say it over and over and over again, and then, just before dawn, I slip out. I walk down the road to my house. My body feels leaden, as if it belonged to somebody else, and me, I feel invisible.

I T ' s four o'clock and I'm inside the Employees Only, changing, when Sandra comes in and shuts the door, holding her palms flat against it behind her, as if she is afraid of being followed. Her eyes burn in the semidarkness, and I stop dressing, aware of some rent in the usual scheme of things.

"You got a visitor."

The blood rushes to my head, I can feel my mouth wavering up into a smile at the same time that my stomach knots hard in apprehension. "Oh, God." Pulling my T-shirt down over my head, barefoot, I walk outside.

Jesse's standing at the counter, drinking a cup of coffee. He's wearing his sleeveless leather vest, its edges cracked and hardened by the weather, a red-white-and-blue skull patch blazing over his left pocket. His sunglasses are gray-green squares that cover only his eyes; they make him sinister.

I am aware of Sandra watching from the back corner of the restaurant, and the last table of customers are staring openly.

"Hi." I look up at him, unable to contain my pleasure.

"I'm goin to the river. It's fuckin hot out." He finishes his coffee and digs into his pocket. "You comin?"

"I'll get it, Jesse." Still wearing my apron I fish in the pocket for tips and pull out fifty cents. "Just let me change."

He nods and turns to walk out. I run back into Employees Only without looking at Sandra, start tearing at my skirt, suddenly sure he's going to leave without me. As I'm yanking my shorts on, Sandra walks back in.

"That's him?"

"Uh-huh." I stuff clothes into my bag, start looking for my hairbrush.

"Honey, I don't think you know what you're doin."

The brush tears through my hair, I can see the streaks of sun in it now, streaks of gold. "Maybe not."

"Ellie, you know anythin about that guy?"

I stop to look at her. "I know enough to know I like him. And you're the first person to find out, so don't tell, okay?"

She shakes her head. "Darlin, you're in way over your head."

"Okay?" I snatch up my bag and go for the door but my eyes never leave hers, and finally she shrugs.

"It's your business, not mine."

"Thanks, Sandra." And then I'm out and through the restaurant, out the door and free at last. Jesse starts his bike when he sees me and I run over there without looking back. Securing the helmet under my chin, I climb on behind him, grip the leather seat with bare thighs.

We take off down the road and the thick humidity changes to a warm breeze that makes my eyes tear and tears every thought from my head the minute it's been formed. I hang on to Jesse, slipping my hands up under his vest to feel the hard ridges of his stomach beneath my palms, and we become the dip and rise and curve of the road, the deep sways and the way the trees rush by, a thick green blur.

We turn off the road suddenly, Jesse slows down and then we're on a dirt trail. He brakes the bike and we get off. He pulls it around and parks it behind a tree.

"Will it be safe there?"

He doesn't deign to answer the question, as if safety were last on his list of concerns, and we head off through the woods, the vibration of the bike still buzzing through my body.

I don't know how he knows where he's going because there's no path marked out that I can see, but I don't ask any questions, just follow along through waist-high grass, thinking we could be anywhere, thinking these are the savannahs of Africa. We veer from the grass into the forest and I pick my way carefully, watching rabbits darting out from the thick green underbrush and looking out for poison ivy. Rays of sunlight beam down through the tops of the trees; occasionally I catch the scent of pine.

Drops of sweat are trickling down my back when we finally catch sight of the water.

"This looks good enough to drink." I lick the sweat off my upper lip.

"Go ahead. If it runs over rocks, it's clean." He bends down and dips his face in the water, sucks it up with a loud noise. I kneel and scoop some up with my hands, sip it. It tastes like mountains, granite rock and sweet grass mountains, and then I do what Jesse did, put my whole face in, open my eyes underwater. I can see thin strands of green moss clinging to riverbed rock, and pebbles washed smooth by the current. When I sit up again, cold water trickles down my neck beneath my shirt, runs in icy little rivulets that make me shiver and scream. Jesse laughs.

As we walk alongside it, the river starts to broaden, and when we get to a hump of rocks, Jesse inclines his head. "Swimmin hole's over there." We climb over the rocks, which are wide and flat and hot. The river empties out into a big lagoon surrounded by forest. I have a sense of total enclosure and I look up at the sky, that deep Carolina blue, the clouds so clean and white-bright they're hard to look at. Jesse strips, his body is wet beneath the leather vest. His flanks gleam whitely at me when he dives in. I undress slowly, suddenly beset by an absurd sense of modesty.

"How is it?"

"Fuckin cold!" He shakes the hair out of his eyes and, pulling strong, swims across to the other side.

I get in the water slowly, surprised to find he's right. The top layer is warm but just inches beneath it's as though the water were rising up from some hidden half-frozen depth. Holding my breath I dive in, feel that clear coolness smooth against my sides. When I come up, Jesse's swimming back.

"See the turtles?"

Treading water I look around warily. "Where?"

"Everywhere." He comes up next to me and sights one with his finger. "There. He's stickin his nose out into the sun."

At first I only see bubbles but when I stare I can make out two little eyes, and then the shell floating just below the surface. Turning slowly around I count three, four, five. "Are they the snapping kind?"

"Guess you'll find out." Inches away, Jesse grins at me, his eyes sparkling clean. Smiling back I put my arms around his neck, press my submerged, chilly body against his. He paddles backwards to find a place where he can stand and I throw my head back to see the sky.

"Is this what heaven looks like?"

Standing he holds me around the waist. "You like it out here, huh?"

I reach up and kiss him and his tongue is like a water moccasin, wiry and alive. I taste river water, sweet and slightly muddy, and his hands move down to press me close against him while he moves backwards until we're out of the water and lying on a small dirt beach, the forest three feet away. Lying on top of him I can feel the sun drying my back while my hair drips cold drips down my side. I lick the drops of water as they fall on his stomach with the tip of my tongue. His breath quickens and I move down the length of his body, and take him in my mouth. His thigh muscles tense beneath my chest and his breathing loses consistency, comes in hitches. I feel all-powerful and I tease him for an immeasurable length of time until he's straining everything he has up into my mouth, and then I speed up and don't stop until he comes, with an agonized sound, as if letting go something precious and rare.

We stay there like that, me quiet with my wet hair in his lap, for minutes and minutes and minutes, and Jesse falls asleep. I slip back into the lagoon and float on my back for a while before coming back to sit next to him, stare down into his peaceful face for long minutes. I think about the way he strode into the restaurant and claimed me, the grip of his fingers on my arms when I kiss him.

I love him because he leaves me no choice.

I T ' S nearly six and the last table in my section is eating dessert; unless someone else comes in, I'm free in fifteen minutes. I'm tugging at the waistband of my skirt, anticipating freedom, when a blue Toyota pulls into the parking lot. Sandra catches my anguished look.

"Maybe it's just someone needin to use the parlor," she says, ever hopeful.

We're both watching the door when Dec walks in. He is so out of context here that for a minute I don't recognize his face. His eyes rove the restaurant and then find me. He smiles broadly, and I can feel my own smile, huge and surprised, as I start to move toward him.

He grabs me in a hug and I am shocked by the joy that comes over me, the joy of feeling his solid, skinny self up against mine, of smelling the faintly soapy smell of him, of his voice, clear and low in my ear.

"Jesus, Ellie," he says, stepping back. "What on earth are you wearing?"

"What on earth are you doing here?"

"I'm driving somebody's car to Florida. I answered an ad." There are dark circles under his eyes.

"You been driving long?"

"Only twelve hours or so." He grins at me. "It's beautiful here. You never told me."

"Sure I did." From the corner of my eye I see Sandra picking up my table's check. "Wait a sec, will you? I'll change and we can leave."

"Who *is* he?" Sandra asks, coming into Employees Only to give me my tip.

"That's Dec. From New York, Dec."

"He drive all the way to see you?" She's visibly impressed. "He's cute. Least we can do is keep him entertained." She winks at me and walks back out.

Wearing a tank top and jeans cut off at the knee, I come out to find Dec drinking a cup of coffee and talking to Sandra. She's laughing and playing with the ends of her hair.

"Hey Sandra, stop flirting."

"Honey, I have to flirt like sharks have to swim." She turns back to Dec. "Quit and it's instant death." He laughs, pushes his coffee cup away and stands.

"I am so sick of caffeine and driving."

"I'll drive you home." I take his arm. "You can meet my father."

"The cop?"

"Don't worry," Sandra says. "He's no hard-ass."

"That's what you think," I tell her over my shoulder. "You're not my boyfriend." We walk outside, into the wilting August heat, Dec's arm around me.

"How's New York?"

"Hellish." He throws me the keys over the roof of the car. "Hot and dirty. People are shooting each other."

"I don't miss it." Trying to open the door, I finally realize it's locked. "You don't have to do that here," I tell him.

"It's not my car."

Reaching over, I let him in. "I forgot about your overdeveloped sense of responsibility."

"It almost makes up for your total lack of it," he says, buckling his seat belt. "You never call me."

Driving away I see Sandra standing by the window, watching. I give her a little wave and she waves back. "I know," I answer, but I don't explain.

"I finally decided if the mountain won't come to Mohammed . . ." He looks at me from his pale face, eyes dark, and his presence overwhelms me, I had forgotten this, the familiarity of him, the intensity of its pull on me. He leans over and, lifting the hair from my neck, kisses me there, soft and sweet, but then he moves away, slides down in his seat . . . and I shift into third.

"I can see why you don't miss the city," he says, gazing out the window.

"It doesn't seem real." I take a detour so we don't have to drive by Jesse's house, keep checking my rearview mirror.

"*This* doesn't seem real." He gestures at the forest on either side of the road. "Nature as far as the eye can see." I feel his eyes on me. "Don't you get bored?"

"It's slow," I say, keeping my eyes on the road, "but you settle into a rhythm."

"I never knew you to settle into anything," he says, and turns so that he's facing me. "You look good, though. Healthy." I can hear the happiness in his voice and I realize that he has driven for hours, hours and hours, just to come see me, and suddenly I feel sick, nauseated almost, and I want to pull over and look him in the eye and tell him everything, tell him, Dec, I'm sleeping with another man, I can't imagine stopping, I still love you—

"Home's at the end of this road." I step on the pedal and we speed toward it. He lets his head fall back on the seat and sighs deeply.

"I can't wait to get out of this car and *stay* out."

"How long are you here for?"

"I don't have to have the car there till the eighteenth," he says, his tone carefully neutral. "And I can get there in a day."

The eighteenth, I think, my mind moving slow as a child's, is four days from now. I put the emergency brake on. "Well, this is it."

"Nice hammock." He puts his hands in his pockets and walks up to the house. Standing on the porch he looks around nervously. "Your father home?"

"Not yet. You'd see the cop car right out here."

Inside, the living room is dark and stuffy. Dec blinks when I turn the lights on. "What happened to the plants?" He walks over to the far corner, where the leaves have crumbled and fallen to the floor. He touches a spindly brown stem and it cracks between his fingers. He steps back and looks at me. I haven't stopped in this room since the day I opened the urn; it sits where I last put it, slightly askew, square and solid and silent.

"They're just dead," I say finally. "That's all."

When Dec starts moving toward me, I reach over and flick the switch so the room is dark again. "Want a beer?"

He follows me into the kitchen. "Aren't you going to give me the grand tour?"

"There's nothing grand about it—it's just a house." I take two beers out of the fridge. "We can drink these on the back porch."

"What about your room?"

"Oh, it's so hot up there right now. It's right under the roof." My stomach is fluttery, I feel nervous as a virgin, and when I twist off the beer top, my fingers are shaking.

"What time does your father get home?"

"It depends," I say, although I know that he won't be home till nine o'clock. "Sometimes early, sometimes late."

Outside, we both sit on the edge of the porch, stretch our legs out.

"So now that you're back, are you here to stay?" He leans back on one arm, the one closest to me; although I don't believe he thinks for a second that I would stay here, he asks the question straight; Dec never presumed me.

"Of course not. I'm leaving in the fall," I say, wondering if it's true. I think of my place in New York with its one square room, the tiny kitchen like an open closet to one side, the futon that folds into a couch during the day. Dec and I used to spend weekends there without ever going out, ordering Chinese and listening to the radio. Although I know my life is there, waiting for me to come back and start living it again, I can't imagine how it's going to happen. I want to say this but I can't, because I can't explain it—it seems I can't tell him anything, that anything I say will lead to something I don't want to say . . . it's so strange, this withholding; in New York, I always told him everything. He's going to know, the thought sinks inside me, heavy and fatal, but when I look at him his face is clear. He has no idea. He's sitting inches away from me and he has no idea.

"How've you been?" His voice is very quiet, his eyes on me, a steady gaze. I look away.

"Okay." He doesn't say anything, waits for me to go on. "It's . . . you get used to it." I clear my throat. "At least, you get used to not getting used to it." I meet his eyes. "I can't explain."

"You don't have to." He lifts a hand, touches my face, and I smile at him. Feeling like an impostor, an actress, a traitor, I ask him what he's been doing.

"Filming in the Bronx." He grins at me. "Not everyone's ideal summer vacation."

"Was it scary?"

"Not once the kids got to know us. They loved the camera—everybody wants to be a star. Should've seen them, thirteen-year-old black kids break-dancing so fast their faces were just a blur. When we interviewed them about the rival gang, they'd get all tough, nothing but four-letter words—the whole time crowding up close to the camera, checking themselves out on the monitor, and you'd hear them asking their friends later, 'Was I cool?' "

"So it turned out well?"

"Oh, it turned out great. We got some terrific footage. And this woman, Mary Essex, the director—what a talent."

"You liked her?"

"She's amazing. The most serious person I've ever met in my life—she walked around smoking Camels, never wore any makeup, she really didn't seem to care what she looked like . . . but what an energy. So intense!"

"Did she like you?"

He grins again, leans back on his elbows. "Are you kidding? I made myself indispensable."

"I bet you did."

I keep asking questions and he tells me about the people we know, the movies he's seen, the kitten he befriended downstairs. He talks easily, fluidly, his words washing over me while the sun slowly sinks into the horizon, and I rediscover what pleasure there is in hearing his voice, the dip in it when he says something funny, his delicate sense of irony, the range of his subjects. I don't say much, I feel rusty, as if I've been in the woods too long and have forgotten how it was I used to speak. By the time the sun's gone down we've finished a six-pack, all the beer in the fridge.

"What do you do at night?" He blows into an empty bottle and the breath sounds like a foghorn coming back out.

Wait for my father to go to sleep, I think. "Drink beer."

"We better go get some, don't you think? Your dad's going to be pissed if he comes home and there's none left."

"He won't be pissed." I stand up. "But it's a good idea."

"Where is he?"

"Working. He'll be home soon."

We drive to a 7-Eleven and buy two six-packs, and when we get home my father's car is parked in the drive. As we walk up to the door, Dec takes my hand.

In the kitchen my father's making a bologna and mayonnaise sandwich, and he looks up, surprised to hear two people in the hall.

"Dad, this is Dec, my friend from New York." They shake, Dec's face flushed. "He's on his way to Florida and he stopped to see me."

"Well now, isn't that nice."

"I think we drank all your beer." Dec pulls a six-pack out of the brown paper bag.

"Not at all, not at all—" My father looks down at the bread spread out on the table, no plate. "Can I make you a sandwich, Dean?"

"*Dec*, Dad—"

"Oh no thanks, I've been eating all day."

"How 'bout you, Ellie?"

"Think I'll just have another beer."

"You oughta eat some dinner if you're goin to drink."

"I will."

"You'll just make yourself sick drinkin on an empty stomach."

"I'm not hungry, Dad."

"Still, you oughta eat."

I contain my irritation and twist off the beer top. "I'll eat later,

okay, Dad?" My father doesn't say anything, just looks at me. Dec
stands near the door, frozen with politeness. "Want to come out
to the back porch with us?" I take out a beer for Dec without
asking.

"Soon's I finish these." He picks up his knife again.

"You could eat out there," I say, leaving. "It's nice outside."

We sit in the dark and sip at our beers, neither one of us
speaking. My father comes out five minutes later with two plates.
He puts one next to me, with two sandwiches on it, and sits in
the rocking chair.

"Thanks, Dad," I say, although I hate bologna. I don't touch
the sandwiches, but Dec reaches over and takes one. I'm sure he
hates bologna too, but he eats the whole thing.

"How long you here for, Dec?"

"Just a few days, sir . . . I'm actually driving somebody's car to
Florida for them, so I thought I'd pass through, see how Ellie was
doing." Dec sits very straight, his spine perfectly erect, as if at
attention; it's the uniform, I think, it always commands this effect,
and for a second I despise it, it seems such a costume, and my
father's part in it a charade—but then I think, No, Dec would
behave this way with any man who was my father, cop or not.

"Your family in Florida?"

"Oh no, they're in Pennsylvania . . . I'm just doing this to earn
some money, sir."

"Call me Tom, please," my father says, but I can tell he's
impressed, that he thinks Dec a young man with fine manners.
"What is it you do in New York, then?"

"I'm working in film, actually, I'm interested in documen-
taries . . ." Dec speaks earnestly, talks about his "work" with great
seriousness, as if he's making some kind of bid. Everything in

Dec's tone solicits approval, permission, and I watch in the dark, how my father keeps nodding, yes, yes, yes. It's as if they're drawing up some ancient, unspoken contract, and the contract has to do with me.

The conversation fills me with an uncontrollable restlessness. I keep getting up, emptying my father's ashtray, sitting down again, leaning back on my hands, then hunching over my knees, saying nothing, until finally I get up and take the plate with its solitary sandwich into the kitchen. Although I know no one will eat it now, I wrap it carefully with plastic wrap and put it in the fridge, as if by preserving it I am somehow complying with my father's request that I eat.

Light-headed from the beer, I fill the sink with soap and hot water, even though there's only one plate, one knife. I wash them over and over again, arms submerged up to the elbow, steam rising to make me sweat.

"What are you doing?" Dec stands in the doorway, holding two empties.

"Just cleaning up." I'm as busy at the sink as a suburban housewife with a compulsion for order; mindless, efficient.

"Why don't you come out and sit with us?" His voice is low, even, but I can tell he knows something's wrong.

"I will." My voice has a high, false ring to it, the kind of heartiness you hear in a woman's tone when she's speaking to somebody else's spoiled child.

Dec waits there, says nothing. Moving briskly I get another two beers out. "Here. I'll join you in a minute."

He takes the bottles but he doesn't move. Back at the sink, I'm still scrubbing the same plate when Dec comes up behind me.

"Give me a kiss." His voice just a whisper now, but raw, pleading, it hurts to hear it, and I turn around, he holds me, the bottles a cold pressure against my lower back, he tastes like beer, tastes like Dec, this mouth so familiar, how many times have I kissed him before, I couldn't count. A sound comes from his throat, cracked, involuntary, the sound of a parched man swallowing his first sip.

"Dec." I break it off, push him gently away. "My dad."

"You coming out?"

"In a minute." He's about to kiss me again, I can feel it, and I push at him once more, harder. "In a minute."

When he's gone I pull the plug, hold it, my hands red and waterlogged, and watch the water going down the drain. My heart feels trapped inside my chest, I need to get out of this house, I have to get *out*—

"Hey, Dec." Opening the screen door I interrupt him; he finishes his sentence, looks at me, his face lit by the light streaming through the doorway. "Want to go out?"

"Thought you said there was nowhere—"

"There's one place, a disco, we can drive there—I forgot, I haven't had a car—I'll just run and change—" I know he's tired, slightly drunk, but I don't leave him any choice; letting the door bang, I slam up the stairs, pretend I don't hear him when he calls out behind me.

In the airlessness of my room, the door shut tight and the shutters closed, I dress, pulling out clothes I haven't worn since I left New York—a beaded top, a short black skirt, shoes with heels. I clip on gaudy rhinestone earrings, put on eyeliner, purple mascara, plum lipstick.

When I come down I find Dec has changed into a fresh shirt, combed his hair. My father's in the kitchen, opening another beer, and Dec leans against the door while I move around, looking for keys, for money, for ID, blotting my lipstick and reapplying it again, moving around them like a bee.

I sense how we fill up the foreground with our youth, our vitality; anticipation seems to be a luxury, an excess of energy my father can no longer afford. He sits smoking, quiet, he smiles at us but his eyes are full of a dark wisdom, a being beyond these things. I can't think about leaving him here, like this, alone, but I can't stand the thought of staying either; I feel panicked, presented with a vision of age and aging that I can't deny. I know if I live I too will fade, I will become an "older woman," established, out of bounds, someone young men no longer stare at, whistle at—someone whose life, however wonderful it may be, has closed around her.

"You look great, honey."

"Good night, Daddy." I kiss my father and he pats my back.

"If you need a ride home, call me."

———

As I walk up to the car my heels make a smart clackety-clack, sound of a woman in charge. When I look at Dec, I am aware of my eyelashes.

"I haven't worn makeup all summer."

"You don't need any makeup," he says, still disgruntled. He liked sitting out on the porch, making good with my father, drinking beer in the dark.

"Did you bring any weed?" I drive too fast, want to impress him with my ease here, how well I know these back road curves, this town.

"I smoked it all driving—" He braces himself against the dash. "Ellie. Slow down."

"You smoked all of it?" I feel like screaming, slamming on the
brakes, making his head snap back. "You couldn't've saved some
for me?"

"I didn't know you wanted it! Goddamn it, Ellie—slow down
or *I'm* driving."

"I'd love to see where we'd end up." I mutter this but he
catches it, turns in his seat to face me, still stiff-arming the dash.

"What is *wrong* with you?"

Stopped at a red light, I glance at him, hair blown to one side,
face pale in the dark, dark-ringed eyes wounded, and I am
ashamed, ashamed, and I want to tell him I'm sorry, want to reach
over and press his sweet mouth against my neck, whisper into his
hair, I'm sorry, baby . . .

The light changes. "I don't know. Just my period coming, I
suppose."

Dec leans back against the seat, puts his head back and sighs.

"Where are we going, anyway?"

"The only place in town that stays open past midnight. It's a
gay disco, Festivities." He doesn't say anything and for a moment
I try to imagine this situation with Jesse, me in the driver's seat,
taking Jesse to a gay disco; it's unimaginable. He would be incapable of such tolerance. I feel another rush of warmth toward Dec,
but it stays, as if caught, inside me. We pass redbrick factories,
railroad tracks. Under other circumstances, I would have showed
Dec—would have told him to breathe in deep, asked if he could
smell the tobacco. His eyes closed now, he doesn't notice anything.

"We're here." The red neon sign reflects off the windshield,
and Dec's eyes open abruptly.

"Where?" He doesn't move, just looks at me, but I know the

look, know its purpose well—pitiful puppy eyes, sleepy doe eyes,
let's-just-stay-at-home eyes—and I step out briskly and slam the
door.

"Here!"

———

Inside, the deep bass disco beat makes the whole room thump,
envelops us in a womb of sound. Stunned by the strobe, the red
and purple lights, the people dancing, the heat, we stand motionless for a moment. I feel as if I have forgotten how to behave
beneath this onslaught of artifice but Dec, more newly emerged
from this kind of scene, walks up to the bar.

The place is packed with men, the young ones already drunk,
prancing around shirtless, their hairless chests gleaming, heady
with this rare opportunity for exhibitionism, graceful as cats, sure
as peacocks. They dance in pairs, heels stomping on the shiny
dance floor, or alone, sidestepping on the catwalks above, wearing
sequins, satin, leather vests, thick eyeliner. Older men stand at the
bar and I sneak glances at them, surprised to see such sturdy,
stoic-looking types, plain Joes wearing flannel shirts and blue
jeans, drinking Bud, clean-shaven, unsmiling. They almost look as
if they were here against their will, as if they are enduring the
scene for some unknown, perhaps even sacred, reason—but their
eyes give them away. Constantly roving, they scan the room like
radar, so alert they seem unblinking.

I suck my drink up through the pair of tiny straws, finish it
before Dec's halfway through his beer. On the dance floor, someone lifts a cupped hand to his partner, who inhales deeply. His
friend does the same, and I watch how their eyes close, how they
lean back into that senseless sex beat, swaying to their knees,

mouths curving in thoughtless ecstasy. Hoisting myself onto the
bar with my elbows, I catch the bartender's eye.

"Do you have any amyl nitrate?"

"What?"

"Poppers! You got any poppers left?"

"Four-fifty." He produces a vial from underneath the counter,
hardly acknowledges the dollar tip I leave him, and suddenly I feel
free, liberated by the insignificance of my sexuality here.

"Come on, Dec, let's dance!" He follows me onto the floor,
dances stiffly, an obvious straight. I crack the vial open and hold
it under his nose.

"What's that?"

"Sniff it," I shout, and when he does, I do the same.

Lights melt in my eyes, limbs melt into music, I am caught in
the center of it all, the vortex of time, everything slows and I am
trying to grasp it, I *am* it, the knowledge bursts in my head and
I want another moment to . . . the edges harden and the tempo
comes back, a hard beat knocking at my temples.

Opening my eyes, I grab Dec's hand for balance. He looks
dazed. His beer is spilling, and taking the bottle, I finish it before
letting it drop to the floor, where it rolls gently into a corner. We
sniff again, and again, everything unfolds into slow motion, and
us with it, and there we are beautiful—ease, grace, fluidity itself.

We stay on, dancing, and although I know the songs are changing, I can't discern the difference—the same, insistent beat keeps
pounding, mechanical, relentless, carving an identically rhythmic
pain in my skull. Dec takes the vial of popper from me, screws the
lid shut. I follow him off the dance floor, aware of being a curios-
ity, one of a handful of women in the pulsing mob; yet I sense
no hostility, and I feel safe, a criminal in disguise.

We grope our way to the back and up a few stairs, to a small lounge where a blue light and soft music play amidst peculiar, rounded velour armchairs. We both sink into one. Our bodies fit together without consulting us, my legs draped over his, his arm behind my head. The ceiling, I notice, is studded with tiny blue stars. My headache recedes.

"Millions of unsuspecting brain cells, dead." Dec shifts his arm so that my face is turned toward him. He grins at me. "And all for the sake of sensationalism. And here I thought you were living the clean life."

"I am!" I hold his wrist with both hands, look up at the ceiling again. "At least, I was."

"Oh, come on. Tell me you've never done that stuff before."

"Sure I did, in high school. Not since I've been back, though. Not till you came, anyway."

"Right. It's *my* influence over you. Certainly."

"Guess it's that New York City air. Makes you want some."

"New York City air is just what I drove hundreds of miles to escape. And what I want doesn't come in a bottle—" He rubs his nose against my cheek. "Ellie . . . what's the matter . . ."

"Nothing." I stay still, perfectly still, and Dec kisses an eyebrow, my cheekbone, an earlobe, my jaw. "Everything." I jump up. "Want a drink?"

"Jesus." He lets his head fall back, refuses to look at me, and I head off toward the bar at the far end of the room, come back with a beer for him, another screwdriver for myself. I sit on the arm of the chair and he takes the bottle without looking at me. Tentatively, I put one hand on his hair, let my fingers play with his curls. He doesn't look at me, becomes immobile under my touch, and I can sense his need, a nearly palpable thing. My stomach churns.

"Dec . . ."

"What?"

"Nothing." Holding the glass between both palms, I can feel it sweating, see the ice melting into the syrup of liquor. "Let's get drunk."

———

It's very late and my head is splitting when we leave. Dec drives home, slowly, and I direct him with as few words as possible, squinting at the road. I make a big deal of being quiet when we get there, taking my shoes off inside the car, tiptoeing through the front room. In the family room, I point exaggeratedly at the sheet and pillow my father has laid out on the couch, and Dec groans. When I start to leave the room he grabs my wrist.

"Dec, I've got such a headache—"

He pulls me backwards until we both fall on the couch, wraps his arms around me and holds me there, against his beating heart.

"I've missed you so much . . ."

"My father—"

"We're not *doing* anything, Ellie—"

"I know, but . . ." I disengage myself. "I feel sick."

He falls back on the couch, covers his head with his arms. "You don't want me here, do you. You don't want me at all."

"That isn't it."

"Well, what is it, then?"

"This house." My head is splitting, ax coming down, splitting. "Put yourself in my place, will you?"

He doesn't say anything, and after a few seconds, after the impasse has settled, a fixed thing, the hurdle neither one of us will jump, I slip out the door, saying I'm going to get some aspirin.

Upstairs, I lie in bed without breathing, listening to the small sounds Dec makes, and imagine what they correspond to; him, undressing. I close my eyes, remember the feel of his narrow ribcage under my cheek, his hands, fine and capable, rubbing my back, how he liked to throw one leg over me in his sleep, and how I liked to be held like that. I try to remember what it was like, sex with him, and it comes back to me as if I had been someone else, as if the memory were someone else's; every time I try to summon it as something real, something that once enveloped me, something I moved with, tasted and heard and smelled, all I can think of is Jesse. Jesse's body, Jesse's hands. Jesse's sounds. I wonder if Jesse missed me tonight. If he was home to miss me. And then I think of Dec on the couch downstairs, sleeping alone underneath my mother's sheets, musty from the linen closet . . . and my father, how unbalanced that bed must feel, with just the one side weighted down . . . and me, huddled in my attic room, unable to set anybody free.

T H R E E days with Dec. All I can think about the next morning is how can I keep hiding. Because I know I'm going to keep hiding. Dressing, I'm thankful for work, for the hours it takes from each day.

He's awake and sipping coffee when I come downstairs. I kiss his cheek.

"How'd you sleep?"

"Okay. I'm surprised you don't have air-conditioning here. It's so hot."

"I know. My mother always claimed it made her sick. Summer colds."

"Oh." Dec sits up a little, and I watch an expression of respect straighten his features; as if we were talking about a saint. It annoys me, the stiffness that death commands, makes me blurt, "Personally, I always thought she was full of shit."

He doesn't say anything, just looks at me. I pour milk in my coffee, two teaspoons of sugar. "You see my dad this morning?"

"Yeah, I got up when he did."

"Really?"

"Uh-huh. We sat and had a cup of coffee before he left for work."

"That's nice."

"He's a nice man."

"Mm-hm." I know he wants me to tell him that my father likes him, I know he would like to hear it, but I can't; encouraging him at this point, in any way, would only be elaborating on a fraud.

"Are you really going to work today?"

"I have to."

"Can't you call in sick?"

"There's only Sandra and me in the whole place. I can't just leave her in the lurch."

"Don't you have a substitute waitress?" His hair still uncombed, his shirt wrinkled, Dec as ever has a wonderful alertness about him in the morning, as if his sleep, no matter how brief, refreshed him completely. He looks at me now, woeful over the rim of his cup, and I have to smile.

"Sorry, baby."

"How sorry?" He pushes his chair back, pats his lap. "C'mere."

"No time."

"Not even one second to sit on your boyfriend's lap? For Chris-sakes, girl, you done been gettin cold out here in these damned backwoods!"

"Okay, for one second. Then you have to give me a ride."

"I'll give you a ride," he mutters, putting on an exaggerated Brooklyn accent, and when I perch on his knees, he pulls me back to sit solid on his lap. He leans his chin on my shoulder, making exaggerated sounds of bliss.

"Mm, you feel so good—"

"Dec, stop—"

"Come on, Ellie, let's just have a quickie—"

"I have to go—"

"I *swear* it'll be a quickie." He laughs. "I've been holding back so long, think I'm gonna burst—"

"Dec, I'll be late—" I try to twist off but he grabs my wrists. I can feel him now hard underneath my skirt, and it panics me. "Cut it out!" I jump up and away, and we face each other, both of us slightly breathless. He doesn't say a word, just stares at me.

"I've got to go." I pick up my coffee cup, put it down again. He pushes his chair back and walks out of the room.

I wait for him outside, on the front porch. I'm already sweating in my uniform when he comes out, dressed, his face closed.

In the car, pretending nothing's happened, I start talking, telling him where he can go while I'm at work, giving him directions, but he cuts me off.

"I think I'll just go."

"Go where?"

"To Florida."

"Today?"

"After I drop you off." He's bluffing, I know he's bluffing, but for a minute I think, yes, go—I think what a relief, and he won't find out, he won't know—but I'm surprised at how awful the thought is, the idea, that Dec would leave, that Dec would leave me. Like this.

"No, Dec. Please. Stay."

"Why?" He looks at me for the first time since we got in the car.

"Because. I want you to."

"I don't think you do."

"Yes, I do."

We pull into Parker's lot and he stops the car. Both of us sit there.

"No, I'm leaving."

"Dec—" I bite my nails and he stares out the window. "It's being here . . . and at my house . . . I'm not comfortable. With my father around."

"Your father wasn't around yesterday when I got there. He wasn't around this morning when you came downstairs."

"But the thought—that he could come in . . . that he would know . . ."

"Well then, it's still better for me to leave, isn't it."

"Oh, please. Dec." He won't meet my eyes and I grab his arm, pull at him, kneel on the seat to face him. Confronted by this abrupt withdrawal, suddenly it's easy to touch him, easy to kiss him, and the minute we make contact his resistance is gone, and then I'm wedged between him and the steering wheel, and the horn goes off. We both jump, and it goes off again.

When I walk into the restaurant, Sandra's grinning.

"Quite the farewell scene out there. *From Here to Eternity* in the front seat of a Toyota."

L ATER Dec picks me up and we drive to the lake, rent a boat for nine dollars with a motor that looks like an eggbeater, it makes him laugh, and we whirr out away from the dock, away from the other boats, passing a black woman and her two children, all three of them swinging homemade fishing poles, passing a young couple rowing, passing the No Swimming sign, until we round a bend and find ourselves alone, surrounded only by deep green lake water, and the forest crowding up along the beachless shore, and the sky a hard blue dome above. Dec produces a skinny joint, "the dregs," and we cut the motor and dangle our feet over the edge, smoke it underneath the bleaching August sun. He doesn't touch me, makes no moves, and out here, dazed, floating, I feel cut adrift from my own life, and for the first time, the sick apprehension that's been dogging me ever since Dec walked into the restaurant evaporates.

Furtively, we strip and jump overboard, swim in circles around the boat, dive down and touch each other underwater. When we laugh, it bubbles upwards. The water is cold beneath the surface, it numbs me, feels like it's penetrating through every layer of skin, and I keep submerging myself to forget the texture of polyester, of sweat and grease and smoke, and the feel of Jesse's skin. His beard when he hasn't shaved, the calluses of his palms, the scars across his knuckles, the silky undersides of his arms, the flat ridges of his belly. The feel of Jesse's skin.

In the boat, we have fast and rocky sex, quick, like he said it would be. I keep my eyes closed, dig my nails into his wrists. When he pulls out, I turn my head while he dips his T-shirt in the lake and wipes me off. I lost my virginity in a boat, I tell him, and he smiles at me. I know, he says. I know all about that.

On the way home he announces that he's going to take my father and me out to dinner. I don't say anything. Okay, Ellie? he asks, driving, glancing at the road then looking at me. Okay, Dec.

Back at the house, when he asks us where we want to go, neither my father nor I mention the Grill. Instead, he asks Dec if he's ever had "real" Southern food, and at seven-thirty, all three of us showered, we drive to Aunt May's Bar-B-Q and have barbecued pig, grits with butter, hush puppies, sweet iced tea. Dec raves, about the food, about the lake, about the lushness of the land, and I watch my father drinking bourbon on ice.

———

When we get home, my father pulls out a bottle of brandy, three glasses.

"Thought we'd have us a little nightcap." I can tell from the way he's speaking that he's already tight.

"Dad—"

"You drink brandy, young man?"

Dec grins. "Whenever it's offered."

"There you go." My father hands him the bottle. "Take this on out back, I'll join you kids in a second."

"It's a little late, isn't it?"

Heading for the porch, Dec turns around to give me a look. "*Late?* Ellie, it's only—"

"Ssh—" I push him through the screen door. "He's getting drunk, Dec."

"Oh, come on. He is not drunk."

"Look, he's *my* father! I think I can tell if he's getting drunk better than you can—"

"So what if he's getting drunk? Why the hell shouldn't he?"

"Because . . ."

"What—is he nasty when he's drunk?"

"No . . ."

"So let him drink."

"That's easy for you to say. He's not your father."

"No, Ellie, he's yours, I think it's safe to say that you've firmly established that."

"Dec, you don't know—"

"Have some brandy." He hands me a glass just as my father emerges from the bathroom. "Have some brandy, sir!" Dec pours him a glass and they both sit down. I stay where I am, blinking in the dark, holding on to the small glass globe with both hands and not drinking.

"Well, I'm wonderin if I should ask you what your intentions are regardin my daughter, Dec."

"Oh, please!"

"Honorable, sir. Completely and totally honorable," Dec answers.

"Would you stop acting like I'm not here?"

"Well, good. Good." He lifts his glass toward Dec. "Cheers."

"Cheers." They both drink, neither of them looking to see if I do.

"I just wish I could have met Ellie's mother," Dec says then, his voice quiet, but the words hit me hard. This is what I was scared of; this is exactly what I wanted to avoid.

"She would have liked you, I can tell you that," my father says, nodding. "Would've enjoyed your sense of humor."

Still standing, shrouded in the dark, I lift my glass and drink it all down at once. It brings tears to my eyes.

"I'm going to bed."

"Why?" Dec looks directly at me.

"Because—I don't want to sit here getting drunk and maudlin."

"Nobody's maudlin, Ellie."

Because I don't want to cry in front of either one of you, I think, and I don't know why. Putting my glass down carefully on the floor, I turn around and go up the stairs. I can hear their silence stretching behind me, and I close my bedroom door against it. Lying in bed, I close my eyes against it, but the tears slide out anyway. If he weren't here, I could sneak out and go to Jesse's. For one brief moment I consider doing it anyway—climbing out my window and onto the roof, sliding down the oak tree—I picture the run, the breathless run to Jesse's house, the knocking on his window, and him there, inside, the kerosene lamp etching plumes of black smoke on the ceiling. I keep my eyes closed and I imagine lying next to him, stretched out sideways to fit on the mattress, and how his eyes have an almost almond cast to them. I imagine the shadows the lamp makes on the planes of his cheekbones, and how even the air feels different there, sweeter, softer. I keep my eyes closed and I imagine everything.

I WAKE up late for work the next morning, still groggy, eyes glued shut. I can't remember my dreams; I feel as if I've come up from a blackness so deep it had substance, a thick, tarry ooze. Even though I know I should hurry, I stay in bed ten more minutes, reeling my life back to myself, each thought coming in slow, as if through a fog . . . I remember leaving Dec with my father downstairs. And then I remember: today is Dec's last day here.

Downstairs, I find him still sleeping on the sofa. He's flung the sheet off in the heat, and one foot dangles on the floor. His face looks smooth and young, unlined. I move very quietly so as not to wake him, and leave a note on the bathroom mirror. Although I'm sure he's working the night shift tonight, my father is already gone. I walk to work with dark glasses on, my limbs still feel gelatinous. Approaching Jesse's, my heart beats faster. I speed up and then slow down, hoping to see him and hoping he's gone.

The Harley is parked by the porch, but the house is shuttered, motionless, Jesse probably sleeping inside. Reflexively, I veer toward the house . . . I could just slip in for ten, twenty minutes . . . I'm already late anyway . . . but twenty yards from his house I stop. He would sense it . . . the feel, the scent of another man on me.

Tomorrow, I think. I'll see him tomorrow. I have to wait one more day.

Dec shows up just after the lunch rush, hair still wet from the shower. He sits at a table near the kitchen and Sandra insists on serving him breakfast: two hotcakes and two eggs, sunnyside up, bacon, a side of grits, four slices of buttered toast, orange juice, coffee. Dec protests but he eats it all, to Sandra's delight. She makes sure the syrup is hot and she pours his water sideways so the glass fills up with ice.

"What a cutie he is," she says to me while I total up a check. "You found yourself a good one there, Ellie." I smile and nod, pretending to be too busy adding to answer. I can hear the undertones in her praise, something that sounds akin to warning: don't blow it.

When the last three people in my section leave, I sit with Dec and have a cup of coffee.

"Slept pretty late, didn't you?"

"Yeah, went to bed pretty late, too."

"Hmm." I lift the cup to my lips with both hands and blow lightly across the liquid's surface; I don't want to ask any questions about last night.

"We killed that bottle of brandy."

"God. You must be hung over."

"No, I think I slept it off. I bet your dad feels like shit, though."

"He can handle it."

"No kidding. At the end I was slurring my words and bumping into the walls but he sounded like he'd just been drinking seltzer all night. He's hard-core."

"He drinks too much."

"Is it a problem?"

"Just lately. He's started drinking a lot more lately. I don't know why. At first he hardly drank at all . . ."

"I guess the shock's wearing off."

"I guess." I can't look at Dec, I just keep blowing on my coffee although it's hardly even steaming anymore.

"Do the two of you ever talk about it?"

"No."

"Why not?"

"I don't know. We just don't. He's not much of a talker, my father."

"He was doing all right last night. You're the one who went to bed."

"I told you—I didn't want to sit around getting drunk."

"Ellie . . ."

"What."

"Nothing."

We sit in silence for a minute and then someone comes in, sits in my section. I stand up, grateful for the interruption.

"Listen, Dec, you don't have to stick around waiting for me to be finished here. Why don't you go have a swim at the lake or something? Come back and pick me up later."

"Okay. Will you get me the check?"

"Oh, Sandra won't let you pay."

"I know, that's why I asked you."

"Forget it. Breakfast is on the house."

When he's gone, Sandra waves a five spot at me.

"Big tipper, too. Doesn't get much better."

Watching Dec's car pulling out of the parking lot, I feel a vague dread, something cold around my heart. All day I am extra attentive to the customers and I keep asking Sandra questions, hoping that other people's voices will dispel the feeling, replace it with the mundanity of everyday life, but by the time Dec's back the feeling's worse.

We go to the movies and watch a double feature, Katharine Hepburn and Spencer Tracy, back to back. The theater is old and beautiful, a dark and cool dome, and Dec and I sit with our feet up on the seats in front of us, eating popcorn. I'm almost comfortable then, sitting and watching a movie with him as I have so often in the past; I'm almost absorbed by the plot, the grainy black-and-white flickering, but I can't quite shake it: the sense of something bad coming.

When we get out it's dark.

"Let's go home," Dec says.

"Home? Already?"

"Your father's working all night, isn't he?"

"I guess . . ."

"Good." He takes my hand, holds it firmly. "It's our last night together for the rest of the summer, and we have the house all to ourselves."

"I don't want to go home yet."

"Why not?"

"I just don't."

Standing by the car, we face each other. Dec starts to say something then stops. He digs in his pocket for the keys and then drops them in my hand.

"Fine." He walks around to the other side and waits to be let in. His face has turned to stone. I stand there, flipping the keys from one palm to the other, and try to keep my chin from trembling.

"Come on, Ellie, let's go!"

Without a word, I unlock the doors and start the car, but I don't shift to drive because I don't know where to go, and when Dec turns to look at me, I break.

"Jesus, Ellie . . ." He reaches over and pulls me to him. "Talk to me, will you?"

"That house—I've never been there without her, you know, it's just not the same—it's not home anymore . . . I can't stand it . . ."

"I know . . ."

I lean against him and cry and he smooths my hair, over and over, his hand gentle and steady and soothing, until I stop. Sitting up abruptly I find a Kleenex and blow my nose. "I'm about to get it any day now . . ."

"Get what?"

"My period." Wadding up the tissue I stuff it in the ashtray. "Let's go have a drink."

I take him to a bar on the other side of town, a bar that's clean and brightly lit, full of young people with short haircuts and button-down shirts, a bar Jesse would never set foot in. We sit at a small table in the corner and drink gin and tonic, but neither one of us says much, and after the second drink it's depressing to stay there watching everybody else having a good time, or at least faking it, so we pay and leave. He gives me the keys again but this time I drive home with no debate.

"Can I see your room now?" Dec asks as I open the front door.

"You mean you didn't go up there and check it out this morning?"

"You just think you know everything, don't you, Miss Smarty-pants."

"It's true, isn't it?"

"You're missing the point, Ellie." In the hallway he takes my wrist and when I turn around he kisses me. "Will you show me now?"

I feel slightly sick to my stomach. "Okay."

Dec starts up the stairs and I duck into the kitchen and grab the last three beers in the fridge before following him. He's sitting on the bed taking his shoes off when I get there.

"I bumped my head on the ceiling."

"You have to be careful." I twist the top off one beer and put the other two on my night table. They look oddly out of place next to the little lamp with its fringed ivory shade and the white digital clock. His shoes off, Dec leans back on the bed, arms behind his head, and watches me. The posture echoes of Jesse for a second, and I lean out the window and take three deep breaths.

"The air is so clean here you can taste it," Dec says. Behind me, I can hear him twisting the top off another one.

"I always took it for granted." I lean with my back on the sill and sip my beer.

"New York must have been such a shock for you . . . after this."

"Believe me, I was craving shock after this."

In the darkness of my room, I find it easier to talk. The sound of crickets drifts up from the ground below, and aside from the rare car passing by, there is no other noise. After a while, I start to relax, and when Dec opens the third beer and says, "Come here and share this with me," it's almost easy to take the four steps over there and ease my body down next to his.

We haven't drunk half of it before Dec leans over and puts it on the floor. I close my eyes when he starts to make love to me, feel aged beneath his fresh excitement, his breath hot on my neck. Jesse's eyes, the tattoo on his chest, how his sheets feel when I sleep on them, damp and gritty—it all keeps coming up like a question that doesn't know how to phrase itself. I put my arms around his neck to keep him from going down. He twists out of his clothes, I keep my eyes closed. But just before he enters me I suddenly think I'm going to suffocate, suffocate if I have to fake my way through this, and the nausea of his not knowing, of his not sensing it—"Wait a minute," I whisper, and slip out from under him. He groans, falls back on the bed, while I rummage through my purse. I find what I want, position myself over him. When he sees what I'm holding he starts to protest, but when I slide myself onto him he loses his words. Arching back, I hold the vial to my nose and inhale and the feeling is tremendous, I go spinning galaxies away, whirling black, and Dec holds my hips,

pushes me down on him. When he comes I am just beginning to
return.

"Why'd you do that?"

I screw the vial shut. "I read it in a short story once. I wanted
to try it."

"How was it?"

"It was pretty far out," I tell him, thinking, that's just where
I wanted to be. Calmer now that it's finished, I lie with my cheek
against his chest. His fingers graze my arm and I fall into the first
tranquility I've felt all day.

"Did your parents have sex?" The question jolts me out of my
trance and I laugh a little.

"At least once."

"You know what I mean."

"Sure, they had a sex life. I walked in on them once—came in
late one night and couldn't find the aspirin, barged right into their
room . . . I didn't see much, thank God, but I heard the springs
squeaking, there was all that flesh . . ." I shudder, remembering.

Dec laughs. "What'd you do?"

"I fled, of course."

"Did anybody bring it up the next day?"

"My mother made some crack. Something about Why do you
think I married him—"

Dec laughs again, reaches down for the beer. He takes a sip and
passes it to me. "You're lucky, you know. Sounds like your parents
were in love with each other."

"I remember one year . . . my freshman year at college. I came
back at Christmas and something was wrong. They were both so
tense with each other . . . my father was always snapping at her,
and I found her crying twice, for no reason. They wouldn't talk

about it, either—I asked her once, what, but she wouldn't say. I
remember coming downstairs the day after Christmas and he was
sleeping on the couch. That was the first time I had ever seen
them sleeping apart. I felt sick the whole time I was home. I think
that's when I realized that my parents were happy together—I
mean, that they had been happy together—when they weren't
anymore."

"What happened?"

"I don't know. It just cleared up, whatever it was. The next
Christmas everything was fine."

"Were they faithful to each other?" Dec's question hangs in
the air, and I twist away from him, irritated.

"Of course they were."

"How do you know?"

"Because I know them, that's how! My mother always talked
about how important it was. She always told me . . ." I trail off.

"Well, your parents are human, you know."

"One of them, anyway." I kick the sheet off, stare at the ceiling.
"My mother . . . I don't know what she is now."

Dec doesn't say anything to that, and a silence wells up between
us.

"She's just not around anymore," I say finally, to break it, and
it comes over me as if I've never felt it before, the knowledge that
I'll never see her again . . . I tense against it, and suddenly the
inarguable finality of her absence seems a terrible betrayal, and
every love a lie. Turning my back to Dec, I curl up against the
wall.

I wake up much later, sweating, from a dream that I was
running after my mother. She was in my father's squad car, driving it, and I was screaming at her to stop, that she had no right,

screaming at her to get out, that she was breaking the law—but she just stepped on the gas and drove out of sight.

Blinking in the dark, I realize that Dec has gone, and I'm alone.

T H E seventeenth of August dawns a heavy, white-sky day; although I can't see it, the sun presses down from behind a haze of humid cloud, and somehow the heat seems worse for this film between earth and fire; it's as if the air itself is sweating.

"It'll storm today," Sandra says, more than once, glancing up through the restaurant windows. "It's gonna be loud."

"I wish it would happen now," I answer. Even in the air conditioning, my back, my palms are sweating. "Get it over with."

Walking to the kitchen with a trayful of dishes, I stumble on myself and everything goes crashing to the floor. The sound of breaking glass sucks up every other noise in the place, and for one long moment, I am the object of everybody's breath-held attention. Bending down to pick up the pieces, I can feel my pulse racing. Sandra comes over with a broom and grins at me.

"Makin waves, Ellie."

"I'm so sorry, Sandra—"

"Shit happens."

"I wish it would rain."

Bent over the dustpan, she looks at me. "You seem a little nervy today. Bad night?"

"No . . . it's just a case of hormones, I think."

She straightens up, smiles sympathetically. "Got the curse?"

"Any minute now," I tell her, and though it's true, it isn't what I feel. She hands me the broom and we walk to the back. "Dec's leaving today."

"Ah-hah," she says then, "no wonder."

That's not it, I want to say, sorry to have misrepresented myself—but I don't know *what* it is; I don't understand the absence of relief at the thought of his going.

He comes in just after three. Sandra pours him a glass of iced tea and shoos both of us to the back. "Sit down, lovers. Smooch if you want to."

Under the table, he twines his legs around mine. "All packed. Even vacuumed the car."

"How long will it take you to get there?"

"Thirteen, maybe fourteen hours. I'm giving myself extra to pull off and sleep."

"That's good." My tongue feels glued to the roof of my mouth. I sip some of his tea. He just watches me, silent, and miserably, I am aware that he thinks I'm beautiful; that he loves me. I don't deserve you, I think—and then, all in a rush, I'm leaning across the table to hold his face in my hands, to kiss him.

A noise like thunder reverberates outside.

I'm up like a shot, I recognize it instantly, and the thought sinks into me, knowledge heavy as stone, that this is it, this is what I've been waiting for.

Jesse parks his bike and walks into the restaurant, and it seems to me that the very air around him thickens. He's wearing his sleeveless leather vest, and even from here I can see the tattoo. People stare. Dec stares. Nobody moves, and the thought flashes, They think he is a criminal. They think he's going to rob us. I

want to run to the ladies' room but I am paralyzed; he's coming
straight for me. Peripherally, I am aware of Sandra, watching.

When he's a foot away he stops, hooks his thumbs in his front
pockets. He jerks his chin at me.

"Where you been?"

"Nowhere . . ." I stand stiff as a board.

"How come you haven't come around?"

I open my mouth and don't say anything. I can feel Dec's
shock, spreading sickly. He stands up and the chair scrapes against
the floor, stammers on its hind legs for a second before settling
behind him. Without looking at him, Jesse says, "Who's he?"

Eyes like guns, drilling into me. There's only one thing he can
hear if I'm ever going to see him again, and when I open my
mouth, I say it. "No one."

"You don't know him?"

Dec's staring at me but I can't, I can't meet his eyes. "He's just
a friend."

At this, Dec moves, as if suddenly unfrozen. He walks out of
the restaurant without looking back, taking hard, stiff steps. The
bell on the door jingles softly behind him. Jesse hasn't taken his
eyes off me once.

I can hear the car starting outside.

"Just a friend, huh?"

I nod, mute. Dec drives away so hard the wheels squeal, and
Jesse's head jerks around to see. When he looks at me again, his
mouth is one tight line.

"Yeah, right." He turns to go and I grab his arm.

"I knew him in college . . . I didn't invite him, he just showed
up . . ."

Without breaking stride, he yanks his arm from my grasp.

"Jesse, please—" I follow him to the door. "I'm off in an hour."

He's out the door and the distance between us stretches, one, two, ten, twenty feet.

"I'll come by—"

Mounting his bike, he doesn't acknowledge having heard. When he starts the engine, I have to shut the door to keep the noise at bay. When I turn around, every eye is on me. Carefully, I walk to the back and mindlessly empty a full coffee pot. Sandra walks around with a pitcher of water, refilling glasses, and gradually, the tension leaves the room, but I start shaking so hard my teeth are rattling. I go into the ladies' and sit on top of a toilet seat, lock the stall door in front of me. I draw my knees up and hug them, holding myself hard in an effort to contain the trembling.

Sandra comes in, knocks on the door. "You comin out?"

"I don't know."

"It's not the end of the world, Ellie." Her voice is soft, reasonable. I push my knees into my eye sockets. They fit perfectly, press a dense blackness into my head. I'll become a Buddhist, I think. I'll concentrate on having no thoughts, ever, again.

I hear Sandra strike a match and a moment later the sickly sweet smell of burnt sulfur drifts over the door. I hear her inhale, exhale. I hear her waiting. I don't move. She doesn't say anything, and for five minutes we stay there like that, while a thin membrane of cigarette smoke permeates the air.

"Okay. You stay there as long as you like." She opens the door. "Soon's the last table leaves, I'm puttin the Closed sign up and takin you out for a drink." I can hear the sounds of glass and silverware coming in through the open door. "Okay, darlin?"

"Okay."

The door shuts behind her.

F O R T Y - F I V E minutes later we're sitting at Stingers, at a small table tucked into the back corner. I sit low in my seat, my knees propped against the table's edge. Aside from asking if I'm ready and telling me where to sit, Sandra hasn't said anything to me, but she acts as if nothing's wrong, absolving me in the light of her refusal to judge. She goes to the bar and comes back with two drinks.

"Jack Daniel's," she says, putting mine in front of me. "Swear by it. Cures everything . . . colds, curse, bad dreams. Heartaches. Drink up, sweetie."

I take a sip. It tastes smooth, leaves a trail of heat down the back of my throat. I take two more sips and Sandra nods approvingly. I smile weakly. "Thanks."

"Don't mention it." I watch her while she looks around the place, feel a rush of warmth for that face, those jaded eyes and peroxide hair, for the way she keeps me company without asking any questions; I want to acknowledge my debt to her, but gratitude has always made me awkward, left me speechless. I reach over and take one of her hands. Her grip on mine is strong and sure.

"It's not the end of the world," she says again, and I let go her hand, and take a deep breath. I will not cry. I will not.

"I wanted to tell him . . . I thought about telling him . . . but

I couldn't. I just couldn't." My voice shaking, I stop, take another sip. "It was so awful . . . but I thought everything was going to be okay . . . I mean he was just about to go . . . if he had left just fifteen minutes earlier—" I hit the table with the flat of my palm, more to distract myself with sensation than anything else.

"Just didn't happen that way." Sandra looks directly at me, her eyes wise. My face twitches under her gaze, nervous, guilty, and I look away.

"You think I deserve this, don't you."

She waits until I meet her eyes to answer. "No, honey. But it wouldn't have happened without you."

"I didn't invite him to come stay with me! I didn't ask him to come!" Even as I say this, I realize what a futile, feeble refutation it is, and I put my head in my hands, ashamed of sounding such a spoiled, whining child.

"He came because he loves you, Ellie. That's all," she says quietly. I nod, staring down.

"I know." Although I've been looking at it for a good minute, it's only now that I see the initials *J.R.*, scarred crudely into the wooden tabletop. I blink, wondering if he would have done this . . . worse, if some girl he was with would have done this. Stupid thought. I close my eyes to shut it out.

"I'm obsessed with him." It comes out soft but it resonates through my whole body.

"You been seein him all this time? Since you got here?"

"Pretty much." With an effort, I pull my head up out of my hands.

She sits back, and I watch her nails, smooth red ovals, the glue-on kind, as she pulls a cigarette out and lights it.

"He must be good in bed." Sandra says this matter-of-factly, exhales smoke from the corner of her mouth, leaning back in her chair. I shrug, not wanting to reduce him to girl talk. "I went out with a biker once."

"You did?" Relieved at the sudden switch of focus, I sit up straighter.

Sandra smiles, her lips twisting up sideways. "Honey, ain't much I *haven't* gone out with and that's a fact."

"What happened?"

"He took off." She lifts up her glass. "Story of my life."

"I don't believe it."

"Actually, I ran him off," she admits, smiling slyly. "I always had a knack for gettin rid of men when I got sick of 'em." She bursts out laughing. "And even when I didn't . . ."

I wonder if she means Carter, or even her son, Elvis, but I'm afraid to bring it up; afraid that she's making an analogy between us. He's not just a biker, I think, and I'm not getting rid of him . . . but then I think about the way he never says please, just takes what he wants, and I remember Rose, the way she kissed him when she saw him, the bitterness in her voice, how she became another part of his unspoken past—

"Sandra . . . you don't know anything about Jesse, do you?"

"I know he's trouble, baby, but it don't take nothin but a pair of eyes to know that."

"I think I'm in love with him."

"Well," she says slowly, as if she thinks she shouldn't, "he's some piece of work, that's for sure." She puts her cigarette, only half-smoked, out, and then she folds her hands on the table and smiles sadly at me. "He's goin to break your heart, Ellie."

"How do you know?"

"Sweetie, I'd put good money on it." I look away, defiant, and drain the rest of my drink, wincing a little at the burn.

"Feel better?"

"I keep thinking about Dec driving all the way to Florida by himself." I cover my face with my hands.

"Hurts, don't it."

For the first time since Dec left, tears fill my eyes, but I don't let them go. I don't let Sandra see them and I don't let them go, I just sit perfectly still, waiting for the wave to subside.

"There is no pain in this world, darlin, 'cept body pain and the pain of losin what you love." With one hand, she strokes my head.

"That's why I didn't tell him. Because I didn't want to lose him." I take a deep breath, and it hiccups through me.

"Nothin's simple, is it."

I think about riding the back of Jesse's bike and the feel of his body when I lie against it. "Some things are." I watch Sandra finish her drink. "Some things."

She's gone to the bathroom when the door swings open and Jesse walks in, Eddie right behind him. Everything shifts, my sense of the world, my place in it—how does he find me? He's not even looking.

My heart pounds fever thoughts through my brain—I'll say, I think—but instead I just slide way down in my seat. They don't notice me, order a beer at the bar, speak in low tones. When Sandra comes out, their backs are turned. She sees them, looks at me wordlessly. I want to compose myself for her, in front of her, she has seen enough wreckage for one day; after all, we're colleagues first, fellow waitresses . . . not just friends. There are façades, I think. There are necessities. Carefully, she sits, leans in toward me.

"Want to go?" Her voice a whisper.

"You go," I tell her, lowering my feet to the ground. It feels insubstantial, as if it's made of marshmallows, and I press my heels into it, hoping for resistance.

"What about you?"

"Jesse'll give me a ride." I say this with total assurance, but she knows what speculation it is, sees how I hide.

"I didn't hear the bikes."

"Neither did I."

Sandra picks up her purse, slowly drops her cigarettes in it. "Okay," she says. "I'm leavin." She doesn't. "You sure?"

Hands on the table, one over the other like a nun, calm, chaste, I smile at her. "See you at Parker's."

She doesn't answer me, lets me know she doesn't share this assumption: that everything will be fine, that tomorrow will come and I will be at Parker's on time, cheerful, eyes dry. Holding her purse with two hands she walks straight across the room and out the door. Both men turn when they hear the heels on the floor, and then Jesse sees me. I stand up slowly. He turns back, doesn't watch me coming.

At his elbow, I don't touch him. "Hello." Eddie swivels around, surprised. "Hi, Eddie."

" 'Lo." He shoots Jesse a look, inquiry, but Jesse's tipped his beer up; he opens his throat and the liquid flows till it's gone. He nods at the bartender and gets another one. I motion to Joe.

"I'll have a beer, please." I push a crumpled dollar across the table, wondering if I should pay for Jesse, if I should buy for Eddie; scared to offend.

When he finally speaks to me, his tone is cold. "What're you doin here?"

"Just came with Sandra from work. She wanted a drink."

He doesn't answer this, doesn't look at me.

"We're talkin business."

I've been dismissed, but I have no place to go; no way to get there . . . but I don't tell him this. I will not throw myself at his mercy, I think, but it isn't pride that keeps me from it, it's the feeling that it will do me no good; that he has no mercy for me.

———

The screen door shuts with a soft hitch behind me. Eddie's pickup truck faces the bar; there were no bikes. No warning. Above me, the sky is still white, smothering. Dec would be in Georgia by now. I have an image of him driving, still stunned, unblinking, and all the landscape flowing by in a blur of heartbreak.

Ahead of me, the dirt road yields nothing. I could walk down to the main road . . . hitchhike. I get as far as the edge of the battered porch and slowly squat on my heels. Can't hitch, my father would kill me. He would find out. But more important than this fear is the hole inside, black hole of yearning. Like a junkie, my whole body craves him. Jesse, love me. Look what I have done for you. Look what I have betrayed.

Like a squaw, I squat unmoving. Immobility like a prayer. Don't leave me.

———

I'm sitting on the edge, empty bottle in my hands, when they emerge behind me. Heavy boots make the floor tremble. I don't turn to see them see me. My back absorbs their glance, silent surprise. Eddie walks past with a nod, walks to the pickup. Jesse stops, looks down at me.

"Didn't ask you to wait," he says. A fact.

"I don't have a way home." Another fact.

"What happened to your friend?" I can't tell if he means Sandra or Dec; he gives me nothing, not even anger.

"Gone."

"Too bad." I hear the warning then: don't expect anything. Eddie starts the motor and Jesse descends the two rickety steps to the ground. Prideless, I follow, stop two feet from the truck, watch him get in. I don't say anything, just stand there. In my mind, I'm already walking down the dirt road to the main one, sticking my thumb out, making my way, when Jesse calls me over.

"Get in."

Although he doesn't touch me, our thighs ride against each other, pressed together in the small cab. I savor the contact, close my eyes to feel it better. I have no thoughts, wish the ride would never end. If we spent hours like this he would thaw, I think. He would have to. The motion, the churning of the wheels beneath us, would loosen his resolve. He would let me lean my head against him. He would want me.

Eddie drives down back roads, deserted twisting roads in dire need of repavement. I have no idea where we're going and I don't ask any questions when we finally turn onto a small, rutted driveway that leads to what seems a deserted shack. Jesse gets out and goes around the back. He comes back wheeling his bike. Throwing one leg astride the seat, he tells Eddie, "Drop her off, huh?"

Eddie nods, but I scramble out. "No, that's okay, I'll walk from Jesse's." About to kickstart his engine, Jesse stops.

"Goddamn it—"

"You want me to follow, or what?" Eddie asks, leaning out the window.

"Forget it. Go ahead."

Reaching behind his seat, Eddie pulls out a helmet no bigger than a cap and tosses it to me. I watch his truck backing out of sight. Jesse doesn't say anything, just starts the bike. He's pushing off with one foot when I reach him, and I know he is ready to leave me behind without a second thought. He roars onto the road and I cling to him, pressing my face against his jacket.

We haven't gone more than a mile when sirens lacerate the air. I open my eyes to see flashing blue lights. My heart turns to ice as Jesse slows down and finally stops.

"Fuckin pigs," he mutters as he takes his helmet off. "No one on the road but me." He sits on the bike while the cops park the car, lights still flashing, on the side of the road. One of them crosses over. Terrified that I know him, that he'll recognize me, I pull the helmet down as far as it will go to hide my eyes. Absurdly I wish I was wearing a bra. I look away, stare over my shoulder into the trees, my fingers twisted together.

"All right, let's see your license." I don't recognize the voice.

Jesse pulls his license from his wallet, hands it over. The cop inspects it. "You know how fast you were goin, punk?" I don't see it but I can feel Jesse shrug.

"Ninety-eight miles an hour." Jesse shrugs again. It's the wrong thing to do. Please Jesse, I think, play along. "I said, *ninety-eight miles an hour.*"

"I heard you the first time." I feel my eyes widen and I turn and clutch at Jesse's jacket. "Please, Jesse," I whisper, but he shakes me off with one hard jerk.

"All right, Bob, run a check on this clown—" He calls Jesse's license number to the other cop, and we hear the hiss and static of the radio. I look at the man in uniform standing in front of us, at the belly that hangs over his belt and the spread of his feet on the road; no one talks to him that way and gets away with it. He's the law. I can feel Jesse's rage like a living thing. A muscle jumps in his jaw. He puts his hands on the handlebars and flexes his wrists.

"Settle down, buddy, you ain't goin nowhere quick, and you sure as hell ain't goin home tonight, not if I have anything to do with it—"

"Fuck you." It's low but the cop is ready to hear it. He jumps forward.

"What's that you say?"

"Jesse," I say before he can answer, and climbing off the bike, I stand as close to the cop as I can without touching him. "Please, officer, we can pay the fine—"

"Listen, little lady, I don't know what you're doin with this shitbird but you are makin one big mistake—"

"Nick!" As soon as I hear it I recognize the other cop's voice— it's Bob Schaeffer. My blood changes temperature.

"What."

"Come here."

"What!"

Schaeffer gets out of the car and shuts the door. I turn my back to both of them and face the forest. Behind me, I hear Schaeffer pull Nick aside. A brief conference, and then both men go back to the car and stand outside it, still talking. Nick keeps raising his voice.

"I don't give a shit whose—"

Finally, it ends. I sit on the bike and keep my face averted, but I watch. Nick gets in the car and Schaeffer writes out a ticket, hands it to Jesse.

"Don't push your luck," he says. He doesn't look at me, just gets back in the car, and they drive off. Jesse rips the ticket in two.

"Motherfuckers."

———

When we get to his place, he parks the bike and gets off without once glancing at me. I stand with Eddie's helmet in my hands.

"Jesse."

"What." He's unlocking the door.

"Can I come in?"

As if he hasn't heard, he walks into the house. The door shuts behind him. I stand there, agonized. Okay. I'll go home. My lips form the words softly; as if, by speaking them, I will become accustomed, resigned to the idea. Instead, I step up on the porch. He hasn't locked the door behind him. If he really didn't want me . . .

The house is dark. I can hear him in his room, hear him lighting a cigarette. Slowly, I walk down the hall. I don't say anything, just push open his bedroom door. I know he heard me coming.

He's kicked back on his bed, shirt off, smoking.

"Did I say come in?" For the first time, his eyes flare. He doesn't sit up but I sense movement, a readiness to leap, and my eyes half close against it. I shake my head, standing in the doorway. The ember of his cigarette glows, bright orange. He waits for me to leave. I just wait.

He smokes it down to the end and then he tosses it on the floor. Sitting up, he snuffs it with his heel, one hard twist, and then he looks at me. "Goddamn it—"

I take a step backwards and he stays where he is. Fingers trembling, I unbutton the first, the second, the third, the fourth buttons on my shirt. He makes a sound, irritation, looks away— but when he looks back I have taken it off. I face him, bare-chested, mute. Although it's close in here and I can see small beads of sweat on his forehead, my skin is goosefleshed. He rises abrupty but I don't move; the air is charged, electric: I can feel his desire as surely as I can feel the heat. Slowly, I walk the five steps to him. I can hear his breath coming hard. Kneeling, I undo his belt buckle.

Everything leaves my mind except this: I'm touching him. Each moment rises up like a bead of dew and then evaporates, and I am subjugated, all of me subjugated to Jesse's pleasure, everything pitched to his response. It is atonement and I am prepared to ignore the pain in my knees, happy to ignore it, happy it is there. I have started and I will finish, like the snake charmer, first luring the asp, then catching it, milking it of its venom, pressing behind each fang till the poison, pushed, comes. I feel his hands on my head—involuntary, a reaching out for balance, because his knees are swaying. All his blood gone rushing to the low center of him, hard to stand up straight. But then I feel his fingers on my neck and he crouches, I start to bend but he takes hold of my armpits, thumbs dug in, and lifts me up. I put my face up to be kissed, blessed, but he turns me around, one hand undoing my zipper, the other tugging my jeans down, around my hips. I balance with both hands against the wall, feel him taut between my thighs, and then his fingers down the front of me and a crushed sound comes off my lips—he comes in from behind, holding my hips with two hands and I am gored, full. He stays there like that for seconds and then starts, small hard movements so that he hardly retreats a quarter inch each time. He is staking me out, staking his claim—with one cheek, the side of my mouth open against the wall, I know I would give anything, I would give everything up to be his, possessed, like this—opiates flood my brain like rosewater.

Jesse falls across the bed face down. I stay where I am, leaning against the wall, and wait for a signal from him, some sense of inclusion, of having been readmitted into his world. Just his eyes on me would do, I think, the light of that gaze on my face . . . and then I realize he's fallen asleep.

Stones in the pit of my stomach, lurching, heavy. I pick up my shirt, brush it off, carefully put one hand through each sleeve. Outside, the glare of daylight is just beginning to dim. Under the bathroom's stark, overhead light, I stare at my face in the mirror, trying to connect the look in those eyes with the way I feel. Water dripping steady from one faucet, I stand suspended, and the more I look, the more foreign the image becomes. When I turn out the light, shadows help. I slide out while I can still recognize myself.

M Y   F A T H E R ' S   car is gone when I get home. The house sits quiet in the dusk. I make a pitcher of iced tea and spike it with Seagram's, and then I lie in the hammock and drink glass after glass, swinging back and forth like something lost and purposeless, hope a vague flame that only makes my throat dry. I wait for the rain that Sandra predicted but it never comes. With night, the sky clears, a slight breeze springs up. I'm still there when the moon rises, so round it looks squashed on the horizon, gives an orange glow that makes me gasp. Good for spellin, I think, twining my fingers together on my lap. I try to remember what I ever read about witchcraft, but all that comes to me is repetition, a selfish pagan prayer: Let him love me.

I don't know who I'm asking.

———

I am lost in a subterranean labyrinth. I can hear the sound of water running all around me, small gushes, and I pick my way through a dense darkness, terrified that I will misstep and fall into a gutter. Suddenly in front of me I see an egret, snow white, delicate. It cocks its head and looks at me with one eye, bending one fragile leg close to its body. Stopping, I stare at it, and as my eyes focus, I become aware that the tunnels are full of cats, all of them as pure white as the egret. Their bodies are long and sinewy, and they move so fast all I can see are brief glimpses of cat-green eyes and white tails, coming out of nowhere only to disappear again, and it's only then I realize with a sudden, blinding flash that the earthen walls, the thick and clotted dirt ceiling, are collapsing, and the cats, they know this, they're running for cover—

I wake abruptly in bed, my stomach churning. Even before I look at the clock I know what time it is: three A.M., that time of day when suicide seems a real option, a possibility with overtones of valor, of efficiency: a solution.

When I walk downstairs to the kitchen for a glass of water, I feel sick, weak-kneed, old. Standing only seems to make the nausea worse. Gripping the sink with one hand I force two fingers down my throat and gag, but nothing comes up; there is nothing there. The nausea settles, though, a threat in my lowest abdomen, and I bend my knees and slowly squat, moving my hands and pressing hard down there, pushing the walls in, commanding them to contract. I am two weeks late.

"Ellie?" My father's voice sounds in the hallway.

"Hi, Dad." I duck into the bathroom and come out wrapped in a towel. We meet in the kitchen. Under the glare of the overhead light, his flesh appears sagging, gray, and a small shock goes through me: sooner or later, I'm going to lose him too.

"What's the matter? Are you sick?" he asks.

I should have said yes, his eyes are fixed on mine, staring through me, but I am terrified he'll figure it out, so instead I lie, stammer that I was just about to take a bath.

"A bath? Christ, Ellie, it's three-thirty in the morning—" His voice loses the sleepy edges, turns hard so fast it paralyzes me. He narrows his eyes. "Have you been doin drugs?"

Immediately tears fill my eyes; I can't help it. Whenever he treats me like a criminal I feel like one. I pity the people my father arrests, am sure that all of them, even the innocent, become guilty under that merciless stare.

"I couldn't sleep, I thought a hot bath would relax me. Is that okay with you, officer?"

"Oh, knock it off," he says. I turn to go back into the bathroom. "Want some hot milk?"

"No thanks." I run the tub, then call over the water, "You have some, though," and when I come out again I find him sitting at the kitchen table, lighting a cigarette. "Why are *you* up?"

"Heard you," he says. I go back into the bathroom. "Hey now—don't shut that door!"

"For Christ's sakes, can't I have any privacy around here?"

"I want to talk to you, young lady."

"Dad, please." I turn the water off, step in, close my eyes, hope he'll finish his cigarette in silence, leave me alone, go back to bed.

"Elena?"

When I hear my full name my throat constricts with dread;

Schaeffer must have told him. I slide my head under the water and stay there as long as I can stand it. When I come up again, my father's rapping at the door, hard, official rat-a-tats.

"You gonna read me my rights before I talk?"

"Ellie, you answer me!"

"Dad, I am a grown woman—"

"You are a child—"

"I am twenty-five years old!"

"And as long as you're living under *my* roof you will live according to *my* rules—"

"Meaning if I don't submit to interrogation I have to leave?"

"Meanin you don't use this house like a hotel to come and go from without even lettin me know where the hell it is you're spendin all your nights!" He's right outside the door. I can hear his breath coming hard, hear him inhaling on the cigarette.

"I *don't* use this house as a hotel, Daddy . . . it's my home . . . I just . . . I can't . . ."

He waits. I don't finish.

"Ellie."

"What."

"He's scum, Ellie—my daughter's sleepin with scum and I will not stand for it!" He pounds the door once, hard, and it swings open. I crouch in the tub, pull my knees up against my chest.

"Daddy . . . please . . ."

"What the hell is it you see in him? This some kind of goddamn rebellion or what?"

I shake my head miserably. "I love him," I say, and then my father's arm swings out and hits the door with such force that my knees knock up into my chin in reflexive response, and I bite my tongue so hard it bleeds. I taste salt.

"Love! Don't disgust me—do you know what Hell's Angels stands for?"

"He's not a Hell's Angel!"

"He might as well be! You think he's ever worked an honest day in his life? Bullshit! He runs speed and guns, just like the rest of them! And let me tell you somethin: you think that one you hang around with, clutching onto the back of that goddamned death machine—'cause I know, Ellie, don't think I don't know just what the hell is goin on right in front of my nose—you think *he* loves *you*? Bullshit! He doesn't love you—freaks like him just use women, use them for sex, and the younger and prettier, the better! You know what you are to him, Ellie? You're just a prize, some young skin that he can brag to his buddies about—you're not important to him!"

"Yes, I am! Shut up!"

"You think you're important to him? Open your eyes, Ellie!"

I jam my knees into my eye sockets. "Go away," I say. "Just go away."

I hear the hiss of his cigarette as he throws it into the toilet, and then his footsteps, leaving. I reach out and swing the door so hard it slams shut and then I turn around and throw up.

B A C K upstairs, wrapped inside my towel, I sit with my back against the headboard of my bed and watch the red glow of digital numbers, each minute shifting precisely into the next until half an hour is gone. Would commit crimes for a joint right now.

Moving in the dark, I fish around for a pair of jeans, find the ones I wore on the Fourth of July, under a heap of clothes in the corner, unwashed. Putting them on, I creep back downstairs. Quietly, without turning any lights on, I find the vodka and pour the last of it into a glass, no ice. Walking outside, I stop just before my father's room, stand absolutely still and listen. When I'm sure his breathing has the evenness of sleep, I inch the screen door open and sit on the steps. I'll get drunk, I think, looking at the two inches of warm liquor hopefully. I'll watch the sun rise.

But when the drink is finished, although I'm only slightly buzzed, I hide the glass behind a bush and start the long walk down the road.

———

The bike is parked outside his house. I make my footsteps loud on the sagging porch floor. I knock on the screen door. No response. Opening the door, I call his name. Standing just inside, I call it again, louder. The house is dark, but I'm sure he's there. I can feel it. I walk down the hall, one hand trailing the wall, and knock on his door. No answer.

When I swing it open, I see no one.

"Jesse?" I can smell smoke, still fresh, and I approach the bed. "Jesse?" Suddenly, from underneath it, he careens at me, teeth bared, soundless; a scream gets caught in my throat, and for long moments I can't say anything, can't even breathe.

He falls back on the bed, laughs. He doesn't touch me. I can see his teeth in the dark, quick, and then the glint of a bottle rising, him drinking. My breath comes back to me, ragged as a sob.

"Jesse . . ." I came to tell you that I love you.

He doesn't look at me. When he raises the bottle again, I can see there's not much liquor left.

That I'm sure I'm pregnant.

I stand at the foot of his bed; a thin line of sweat glistens on his upper lip. From the way he jerks the bottle to his lips and down again, I know he's speeding.

Look at me!

Watching him, I remember what Rose said about Jesse's mother. "You got the firewater syndrome too?"

When he doesn't answer, I lean over, grab his leg, his calf, dig my fingers in, through the jeans, and he moves it sharp, almost loses me but I was ready for that, knew better, and I swing onto his other leg and pull myself onto his thighs, drag my body up his legs, bite his stomach, the skin on his stomach, it tastes like salt, he twists and I twist with him and then I'm beneath him, his weight crushes the length of me, I'm flattened, I have to breathe in small, tight gasps but I lie still, uncomplaining, I feel wedged to the world, held up against it, the blood roaring in my ears, breathing so fast I'm dizzy and then he pulls back—off, back. Air rushes in between us.

He gets up and I can't predict him; he leaves and I can't follow him. I run to the door but his bike coughs up and into a roar, and by the time I reach the porch he's gone, loud, gone, I listen to the sound, how it lingers . . .

When I walk down the hall back to his room, the house is suddenly unfamiliar, full of strange creaks, noises I never heard before. I get back in bed, pull the sheet around my shoulders. It smells of Jesse, and I curl up around his scent, yearn for him. There's nothing I wouldn't do for him, the thought seizes me, repeats. I am his the way I have never been any other's. For how long, I wonder, sweating. For how much longer.

I close my eyes and picture us, Jesse and me, riding for days on his bike, driving through long stretches of forests, past coastlines, down the main streets of a hundred small American towns . . . I would do deep knee-bends when we stopped for gas, shave under my arms over restroom sinks, wear no underwear at night. I would steal food, steal sugar, cheese, his brand of cigarettes, bottles of beer . . . I would sleep outside, wash my hair with soap, and never talk about the backache. And when we got to the other end of the continent, we'd hop a ship. My fantasy starts to waver here, I don't know where we put the bike, but I know we push on, we keep moving, we put miles and miles behind us, and the past recedes. We don't mourn it.

I lie in Jesse's bed, alone, awake, and waiting. The sun rises and he doesn't come home. Dawn comes, humid, a dense light steaming up over the far edges of the sky, everything whitens; the world is a day older and I feel like I'm running in place.

S T I L L in the same clothes, I walk to work, limp beneath late August's morning heat, the dead heat of summer leaving. In between customers, I sit at a table in the back, pretending to do a crossword puzzle, pressing the pencil point hard into the page. Exhaustion burns behind my eyes, and in the ladies' room mirror, they stare back at me, red-rimmed, ghoulish. Sandra doesn't ask me any questions; she thinks her prophecy has come true. The hours go by, slow as torture, and when people start filling the place at noon, I'm grateful for the rush. My section is still full when Melanie walks in. I duck behind the coffee pots and watch while

Sandra approaches her. I can see Melanie's mouth moving, and then Sandra turns to look for me. Back pressed to the wall, I can feel the sweat breaking on my face.

"Ellie? Girl just came in lookin for you."

"I'm so busy right now—Sandra, could you serve her?"

"I offered but she said all's she wants is an iced tea. She said she'll wait for you." She puts a cool hand on my arm. "You okay?"

"I'm just tired, that's all."

"I'll get her tea."

"Thanks."

Running food from the kitchen to my customers, I smile at Melanie, make a helpless sign with my shoulders. Stiffly, she smiles back, her mouth just barely turning up at the corners. Holding a tray of dirty dishes, I walk past her table.

"Hi, Melanie."

"Hi, Ellie."

"Listen, can I get you something to eat? We have some great pies—"

"Actually I didn't come here to eat, Ellie. I came to see you."

"Oh . . . well, the thing is I don't get off for quite a while still—"

"I'll wait."

"Are you sure? I mean we could meet someplace later . . ."

"I'd rather not."

"Oh. Okay. Well . . . I'll bring you a refill."

After I've brought her a new iced tea, I leave Melanie alone, run around the restaurant with a busy little frown, hoping she'll get sick of waiting and leave. She doesn't. Hands clasped together on the tabletop, she stares out the window and doesn't move. When I've given my last table their check, I can't avoid her any longer. Untying my apron, I approach her table.

"Well, you're certainly more patient than I am . . ."

"More patient than you wish I were, you mean," she says, her voice as icy as her cold blue eyes.

"No, I'm just flattered that you waited—"

"Look, I didn't come here to be friendly. I've already tried being friendly to you, and you paid me back by sneaking out of my house without even saying good-bye, much less thank you."

Apron bunched in my hands, I stare at her, dumbstruck.

"I'm not good enough for you to be nice to, but I'm good enough to be used—"

"Excuse me—" I start to turn around but Melanie stands up and grabs my elbow.

"There *isn't* an excuse for you! My father told me your father mentioned that he's glad we're such good friends, that he didn't realize we were so close—neither did I!"

I can't keep my voice from shaking when I speak. "Look, Melanie, I work here—I am not going to stand here and have an argument with you—" I try to pull my arm away but her hold on me is so strong her knuckles are white; I can feel her perfect nails biting into my skin.

"Why, are you afraid you'll ruin your *reputation*?" She hisses this at me. "Everybody knows about you and that sleazy biker— my father saw you, Ellie—everybody knows, and if you think you can use *me* to cover up for that—"

"Let go of me, Melanie." Twisting hard, I yank my arm out of her grip.

"And don't think I don't know how you tried to seduce Danny, either—he told me how you came on to him—" She raises her voice as I start to walk away. "You're just like your mother!"

At this I freeze. I'm aware of people in the restaurant watching us as I turn to face her.

"What are you talking about."

"You know perfectly well what I'm talkin about—your mother tried to get my father the same way you tried to get Danny!"

"You're sick, Melanie—you're really sick—"

"Well, it didn't work for her and it won't work for you, either!"

"My mother never—that is a vicious lie—" My legs are trembling when Sandra comes and puts her arm around me.

"You're a slut, Ellie Lowell, just like your mother was—" Melanie starts crying. "And they're goin to arrest your cruddy boyfriend and put him in jail—my father told me—they're goin to get him!"

Sandra steps between us. "Miss, please leave the restaurant." But before she's finished her sentence, I've fled.

I N the back room, fingers shaking so hard I can't get my buttons undone, memories, bits and pieces, come flying at me like shrapnel. That Christmas, my freshman year—Christmas Eve I found my mother crying in the bathroom, I pounded on the door and she let me in, let me hug her, hold her, she let me comfort her but she wouldn't tell me what, why . . . she cried until her makeup smeared—and my father in the car on the way home from the Grill, drunk, muttering out the window. "She cried and cried," he said, and "the empty nest," he said, "that's why she did it. To kill that feelin."

And Bob Schaeffer with his thick blond hair and the smile that
changes his face, Bob Schaeffer coming over, holding the wallet,
my mother's picture, with both hands—Bob Schaeffer's smarting
eyes.

A slut, Melanie said, she screamed, just like your mother—

You fucking bitch, I think, I'd like to say it, to scream too, you
bitch, you *whore*—

The door opens and Sandra comes in, her face full of alarm. I
tug at my uniform frantically.

"Ellie—"

"I have to go, Sandra—"

"Leave him alone." She grabs my arm. "Ellie, listen to me! He's
got no future!"

I shake her off and start pulling the uniform over my head.
Strained cloth rips. "I don't care about the future!"

"Now you don't—but later you will—"

Hands flying, I find my shirt, my jeans.

"You don't learn to think about the future, you'll get caught
by surprise—caught someplace you never wanted to be. Think,
Ellie! Be smart!"

"I don't want to be smart! I want Jesse!" I fall against the wall
in an effort to keep my balance while I put my jeans on.

"He's no good for you, honey, believe me—"

"You don't know! You don't know what it's like to be me!" I
pull my T-shirt over my head and start for the door, but she blocks
it.

"Ellie—"

"Sandra, please! I've got to *go*—"

"I'll call your dad and he'll come get you—"

"No! Leave me alone!" I grab the doorknob. "Just because my mother's dead doesn't mean I need a replacement!"

Shoeless, I streak through the restaurant. I don't stop running till I get to Jesse's house. His bike isn't there; the door is locked. Fists pound war on it but nothing gives. Desperate, I back away and then run flying at the door, slamming my whole body against it. A small flare of red heat bursts inside my shoulder, but the impact jolts me out of my hysteria, and I remember the window, how Eddie opened it on the Fourth of July. Heedless of the pain, I wedge the same shoulder underneath and shove. It gives on the second try and I scramble through, tripping when I land. Running down the hall, I yank Jesse's door open.

He's not there. I glance around—his jacket's gone, his helmet, his boots. The sheet is crumpled at the bottom of the mattress. The room exhales a terrible vacancy.

Behind me, Eddie says, "He's gone."

Breath suspended in my throat, I spin around. "No—I don't— he can't be—"

Eddie takes a step toward me. "Girl, calm down." I stare at him and suddenly I think: Eddie knows where he is. Eddie will take me to him.

"I was supposed to meet him—"

"When?"

"Here! Today!"

"He never said nothin to me—"

"I know, he said he didn't tell anyone, but I was supposed—and then something happened—I didn't want to give it away, I had to act—" I grab Eddie's arms. "I was supposed to go with him!" He stares at me, trying to decipher it, whether I'm telling the truth or not. "You've got to tell me where he is—Eddie, please!"

At this, he steps out of my grasp, shakes his head, and I know
I've said the wrong thing. "Nope. Can't do that."

"Eddie, I have to find him—we were supposed to leave together—I was sure he'd wait—"

"No way he could wait."

"I know that, I know they're out to bust him, I know about the
speed—"

Eddie's head snaps up. "He told you?" I nod. "He told you
that?" I nod again. My eyes never leave his.

"Let's go."

He's parked his truck ten minutes away, up inside a dead-end
road leading into the forest. Once in the cab, I don't need to be
told to slide down till I'm out of view. All I can see is Eddie beside
me and the sky through the windshield above me. I want to ask
him why he was at the house if they were expecting a bust, and
where we're going, how long it will take to get there and how soon
we'll catch up to Jesse—but I'm afraid, afraid that in my questions
he will read my real ignorance, and realize I've lied. So I stay the
way I am, half on the floor and half on the seat, determined to
be still. I am on my way to Jesse, and it feels like a miracle.

W I T H the rumble of the truck passing through the seat,
filling my head with nothing but motor, noise, and the knowledge
that we're moving toward him, I fall asleep. Sometime I am aware
of Eddie stopping, of gas-station lights. I stay down. When he gets
back in, he hands me a Coke. I drink half of it and then I'm asleep

again, barely aware of him taking the can from my hands. I don't
wake up until we stop again. When he pulls the emergency brake
up, I know we're there. Slowly, my shoulder throbbing, my neck
stiff, I sit up. There are no streetlights, and it's pitch dark. When
I climb out of the truck and stretch, take a deep breath, I can
smell the sea.

"Where are we?"

"Near Hatteras."

We've parked behind a dark building, some kind of store. With
me behind, Eddie starts walking down a sandy trail that follows
the curve of the road for ten, maybe fifteen minutes before we
start to hear sounds—the faint beat of music, people talking. The
trail turns left, leaving the road, and then I see lights. It's a bar,
a salt-corroded old wooden building, built low to the ground. My
throat feels tight.

"Is Jesse there?"

"Maybe there, maybe at Turk's." He points behind the bar and
I make out another building, a hundred, maybe two hundred yards
back. He veers toward it.

"See you later."

"Aren't you coming in?" I call this out to his back, not wanting
him to leave me, scared now, of seeing Jesse and of not seeing
Jesse, but he doesn't turn around.

"Got some things to take care of."

"Eddie!"

"What." He pauses, looks at me.

". . . Thanks."

He nods at me briefly and then he disappears behind the building. I stand where I am, wondering for the first time how I must
look—my hair is tangled down my back, my clothes are wrinkled,

I'm barefoot, and I can feel my eyes stinging, dry with fatigue. Walking off the trail and into the shadows, I take a few deep breaths, squeeze my eyes shut, hoping to clear them, comb my hair with outspread fingers, tuck my shirt into my jeans. Inside the bar somebody shouts, a woman screams, and then people laugh, someone comes stumbling out. He's thick-bodied, has a mustache, wears a leather jacket. I hide behind a tree and hold my breath, but he is completely unaware of any other presence near him. He looks around as if he's not sure how he got there and goes back inside.

The thought that Jesse could be as close as the other side of the wall courses through me like fire. I stay behind the tree, gripping the bark with my palms, trying to work up the courage to face him. When I close my eyes, all I can picture is the way he came at me from underneath his bed, teeth bared. Digging my hands in my pockets, my fingers graze against my mother's lighter in one and something else in the other, three smooth cylinders. In my hand, the speed capsules glitter, slightly bent but still whole, smooth, shiny black. I remember when I found them, how far away Jesse had seemed then, how badly I had wanted to catch up with him—and I remember how he'd found me later, how he'd held me in the shower, in his bed. How he'd loved me.

Tilting my head back and saving up spit, I swallow one of them now.

———

When I walk inside, it seems to me the whole place pauses for just a second—and then the noise resumes again, as if I've been assessed and judged harmless. I stand just inside the door, trying to look as if I belong.

The place is full of Angels. Everywhere I look I see the colors, leather vests, boots, beards, and dark tattoos, rippling on bare arms. I scan the room for Jesse, his rangy height, the angle of his walk, but I can't see him from here. Although it's only been five minutes since I took it, I can already feel the speed kicking in; it's because I haven't eaten anything all day. Small rushes make my head light, fill my limbs with electricity. When I start moving forward, I feel charged with purpose, sure of myself. Women stare at me when I walk by, the same peculiarly specific type of women that had dotted the Fourth of July party, and they don't attempt to disguise the hostility in their looks: they suspect me of being a young and stupid Angel groupie, possibly after their old man, and I know that any one of them would fight me to protect her territory. I walk the way I've learned to walk in New York, pulling into myself, frowning slightly, intent on my own business, careful not to graze against anybody.

He isn't there. Disbelieving, I walk to the very back and hoist myself up on the cigarette machine, staring at each and every face from the slight elevation to make certain . . .

"Well, well, well. If it ain't Goldilocks." The voice comes from behind, and I jump down to see the man who's just walked out of the bathroom.

"Hi, Chip." I speak his name with great seriousness, hoping that maybe he'll return the tone. He laughs instead.

"Lookit that. We're on first-name basis." He reaches over and slaps a thin, hard-faced guy on the back. "Check it out."

"Find what you were lookin for?" With an oily smile, he comes to stand next to me; he smells like days-old sweat, stale beer and his own sour personal chemistry. Without answering, I turn away; all I want is to get out of there, but before I can take a single step, his face is pushed up close to my own, so suddenly I recoil, bumping the back of my head against the wall.

"Listen little lady you think you're somethin special, you can just walk." His teeth are stained, red-brown. "You come here followin a fuck, you think you know shit-all, reared up on your high horse—"

"I'm not on my high horse." My legs tremble, I want to take off at a run, but I refuse to let him see he's scared me. I clear my throat. My heart feels like it's pounding in my ears.

"Yeah," he says then, leaning back against the machine and smiling again. "You want more. That's the kinda girl you are." A shiver makes the hair on my arms stand up straight. Backed against the wall, I keep my mouth shut and my eyes down. I can feel Chip's eyes heavy on me, and his breath, a noisy exhalation, but I hold my pose, wait him out. The floor is littered with butts, stained with dried-up puddles of beer. The particular pattern they make engraves itself on my mind with a chemical sharpness, as if I were looking at a photograph.

"Just so's you get it straight," he says finally. Still staring at the ground, I nod, and after a few moments he grunts and walks away.

I thread my way back through the crowd, a silver thread, so light on my feet I feel like I'm flying. I follow the path that's been beaten out of the underbrush between the bar and the house that Eddie indicated, breaking into a run, overcome by a sense of urgency so piercing it's almost panic; it's the speed, I know it's the speed, and when I'm close enough to the house to see the light that seeps out from beneath shuttered windows, I force myself to slow to a walk and catch my breath.

Someone's leaning against a wall in the far shadows, smoking a cigarette. He steps forward when he sees me. A long, jagged scar extends from the corner of his left eye down to his mouth, and the sight of his face stops me cold.

"Who're you?"

"I'm with Jesse."

He flicks the cigarette away and it spins off into the darkness. "Eddie told me he'd either be here or at the bar . . . he wasn't at the bar . . ." The man just looks at me. "He's expecting me."

"He didn't tell me nothin 'bout no chick," he says then.

"Is he inside?" I take a step forward, and then another. The man moves out of my way, shrugs.

"First door on the left."

"Thanks." Trying not to seem too eager, I walk in. The house is dark, smells damp. Upstairs someone's playing Jimi Hendrix, but I don't see a soul. Unrehearsed, taking a deep breath, I knock on the first door on the left.

A woman's voice says, "Come in." When I do, she looks as surprised to see me as I am to see her. She's perched on the end of the bed as if she's just arranged herself there, one leg crossed over the other. Her hair is as long and blond as Melanie's, and she wears a tight denim miniskirt and a white halter top exposing her stomach, narrow and tan. I can see the tendons in her arms, and her feet are narrow too, strapped inside red heels. She looks at me from under dark blue lids, her mouth tight, and doesn't say a word. Looking around, I spot Jesse's jacket slung over a chair, and the sheath of his knife peeking out from beneath the bed.

"Who are you?" I stand with my back to the door, perched high on amphetamine nerves, ready for anything.

"What's it to you?"

"Does Jesse know you're in here?"

"He'll find out."

"You got no business being here."

"I got business with Jesse."

"What business?" Moving away from the door I let my right

hip jut out; my voice comes back to me like someone else's. Dimly I wonder where I learned to talk this way.

"None of yours, sweetheart."

"He doesn't want to see you." I can tell when I say this that it's what she thinks, too. One hand drifts up to the ends of her hair.

"Yes, he does." The hand drops and her voice turns mean again. "Who the fuck are *you*? His old lady or somethin?" She thrusts a tough chest out at me and puts her hands on her naked waist, her fingernails ten gleaming red ovals. I feel sure they're real.

"Yeah," I say, putting my hands on my waist. "I am."

She bursts out laughing then, pushing her hair out of her face.

"Get out," I tell her.

"The day some little wimp girl like you is Jesse's old lady is the day I die. I ain't movin."

"Look." I take a step toward her. "Jesse's mine."

"*Yours?*" She gives one sharp laugh, forced as a bark. Her eyes are slitted. "You think he belongs to anybody, you don't know shit. He ain't even an Angel! I think I'll just wait right here and let *him* tell me whether he's yours or not."

I imagine hitting her, imagine the sharp crack my open palm would make across that hard-edged face, but underneath the impulse I'm burning to know what she is to him; I know what she wants from him.

"Don't fuck with me." The words come out fast, rattling up against each other, and I say it again, amazed and empowered by the meanness streaking through me. She looks at me, takes my measure, and doesn't answer, but neither does she move. I think of Jesse's knife underneath the bed, rehearse the steps I would take, the quickstep around her and the dive to the floor, moving into the arm raised high, the sheath falling back into the shadows.

Wheeling abruptly I leave the room, nearly tripping over a half-empty bottle of Riunite. I stoop and pick it up, moving down the hall until I see the bathroom, empty. Locking the door, I sit on the edge of the toilet breathing hard, uncork the bottle and take a long drink, my voice a low hissing constant—okay, okay, slow down, slow down, it's just speed, it's only speed. I finish the wine in five or six gulps, watch the shadows my arm makes along the wall. My back is wet with sweat. Where *is* he, God, where is he, I start to think I'll never find him, that he's already moved on—but then I remember his jacket in the room—and that woman with Melanie hair sitting there, waiting for him—blond Melanie hair, thick blond Bob Schaeffer hair, hair that seduced my mother, my mother who loved me, who loved my father—

I stand abruptly and face the mirror. I look young and pale and scared: no wonder she didn't move. The thought of her sitting on Jesse's bed, her legs crossed high at the thigh, is like a brushfire in my head. Grabbing the bottle, I smash it against the back wall. Shards of glass fly back but none of them cuts me and the sound of shattered glass momentarily appeases my rage. I spot the cork over by the toilet, get it and pull my mother's lighter from my jeans. My fingers are shaking as I burn one end black, holding my breath against the smell.

Watching in the mirror I smear the black underneath my eyes and in straight lines along my cheekbones, draw one long line from the top of my forehead to the tip of my nose. I raise the cork over my head and imagine it's a knife.

Satisfied, I edge back along the hall to Jesse's room. His door is ajar; she's standing over by the window, peering out. Moving under cover of the loud music coming from above, I sneak inside and wait until she's just about to turn around, and then I let out a piercing scream, it flies out of me like a savage kite on a long string. I land with my hands on her shoulders.

Screaming uncontrollably and twitching like a small animal, she gets out from under me and goes for the hall, moving surprisingly fast on those spindly heels, with me right behind her. I go running dead into the man with the scar on his face. He grabs my wrists, pulls me up with a jerk. I catch a flash of her hair as she makes it outside, and then he throws me back against the wall.

"What the fuck are you doin!" He lurches at me again and my arms fly up to cover my face, everything tensing for the blow—

"Leave her." His voice. Adrenaline flood tastes chemical in my mouth. "She's with me."

Jesse's standing in between us when I uncrouch, holding his arms away from his body and shifting his knees; instantly, I can tell that he's been speeding for days. Although he's right there, inches away, I don't get more than a second's glance at his face because everything's moving, his hands, his fingers, his feet, even his hair.

"I never seen her face before, she comes walkin in here, makin claims, startin fights—"

"Everythin's cool now, all right? Just cool it." Jesse reaches over and grabs my arm. "She's leavin."

Jangling nerves like electric sparks, when he touches me it transfers, exhaustion burning at white heat. Fingers tight around my forearm, he takes me outside, then lets me go.

"How the hell did you get here?" There is nothing in his tone that says he's pleased, surprised, amazed at my ingenuity. I don't want to tell, lower my eyes, but he reaches out and pushes at my shoulder with the heel of his hand, a hard snap. "Don't play games with me."

"Eddie." Behind us, the door opens and the man with the scar reappears; he stands behind us, watching, and immediately Jesse starts walking. I follow him into the dark.

"Eddie told you I was here?" Standing on the lightless trail, his face is all shadows; only his eyes are bright, the accelerated bright of someone using himself up, saving nothing for later.

"He brought me."

"What the fuck—!"

"Jesse, wait—" Reaching out I try to catch hold of him but he's moving too fast, headed toward the bar, already halfway there. "He found me in your house, I told him I was supposed to meet you—"

When he turns around to face me I'm still running up to meet him and we collide, his hands fly out to stop me and when I step back my hair is tangled in his fingers, pulling at my scalp. Yelping, I move in close while he unwinds himself, and that close I can smell him, want to jump him, grab his belt and hold him, keep him near me—the sound of pine cones crunching underfoot snaps my head up.

"Someone's coming."

Ripping into the brush, Jesse starts smashing through the wooded area, and I'm right behind him, catching branches as they fly toward me, my shirt tearing on thorns. We sound like two wounded animals, I think, but we get through it all amazingly fast and come out near the road, facing a series of dunes. For the first time, I hear the dull roar of the ocean; we're right on the beach. I head for the water but Jesse moves in front of me. He wants answers now.

"I told him that we'd made arrangements—"

"Who?"

"Me and you . . . that we'd arranged to meet . . . that you were taking me with you . . . I told him I'd gotten delayed . . ."

"Bullshit. He wouldn't believe that. Not Eddie. You're lyin."

"I'm not lying, Jesse! How else would I get here? I tricked him!"

When he steps away I know he's going to look for Eddie now, to get things straight. This time I block him.

"I was desperate, Jesse—I had to find you—" My lips are cracked, mouth so dry at the corners that it's hard to talk, and when I try to lick them, even my tongue feels parched.

"Did he give you pills too?"

"No."

"What're you on?"

"I found some in my pocket."

"You look like hell."

"So do you."

Knees moving, hands on his hips, he fixes his eyes on me; a deep shiver, speed shiver, wrenches my spine.

"Why'd you follow me?" His voice is mean again, voice he might use on a man, someone who didn't know him, someone he might fight.

"Because—I have something of yours."

"You're full of shit—"

"I am not full of shit!" My voice flies away from me, becomes a scream. Fingers locking on my elbow, he starts walking toward the dunes, his boots sinking deep with each step into the sand, and then we can see the sea, spread out in front of us, each wave leaving a small ripple of white on the land before retracting into itself.

"You stop playin these fuckin games with me right now, girl." He lets me go as if shaking off a dog and faces me. The last stand.

"I'm pregnant."

He looks at me as if doesn't know who I am.

"I'm not kidding."

Looking away, he stares at the ocean for long seconds. Suddenly, he swivels around to face me again. "This's another one of your tricks." His voice is certain, full of contempt.

"It isn't a trick!"

"Fuckin hell, it ain't—"

"Jesse I am two weeks late! I am on the pill and I am *two weeks*—"

"I don't give a shit!" He starts to move again, a wildcat caught in a cage. "Don't fuckin tell me your problems, 'cause I don't give a shit!"

Scrambling in the sand, I catch up with him, and my fingers tighten like chain around his wrists. My eyes are burning in my head, I have to fight to keep from screaming again.

"Jesse, it's your baby."

His hands fly up and I'm thrown off, nearly lose my balance.

"How do you know?" He's looking directly at me now and his eyes have no color, they're just huge dark pools, black and flat as a shark's.

"What do you mean, how do I know—I know!" My voice is shaking.

"It wasn't me." He starts shaking his head. He reaches back into his pocket for cigarettes, shakes one out with one swift motion, lights it. My hair falls on either side of my face like a curtain.

Through my hair, I watch the smoke curling up through the air. Sweat trickles down from my armpits.

"Accidents happen," I whisper, finally.

"What're you sayin—you want to keep it? That what you're sayin?"

I pull my hair away from my face and straighten up. "Yes." I want to keep you.

"Bullshit! You're a fuckin liar! Woman wants a baby she don't go eatin pills! She don't go drinkin and fightin—you tell me you ain't slept with no man but me and I'll tell you you're a liar! That baby ain't mine—no fuckin way!"

"Yes, it is, Jesse. Yes, it is." I'm fighting to keep my voice even, to keep it low. I have to convince him, he has to know, desperation rising like a tide I think I'm going to shatter into a thousand pieces right here and now—

"What about that guy at Parker's—how do you know it ain't his?"

"I told you, he's just a friend! He was only visiting!"

"Don't fuckin lie to me, I was *there*!" He flies at me and for a second I think he's going to hit me but I don't move, and he stops, rakes his fingers through his hair, pulling it back. "Was it his house you've been livin in all summer?"

"What?"

"Him away on business, right, you thinkin you'd get a little extra on the side—he comes home and then you're a good girl, stop comin around so's he can get some too—"

"What are you *talking* about?"

"That why you kept your mouth shut?"

"I told you, I live with my parents!"

"That why you never gave me your phone number? That why you always *walked?*"

"Jesse . . ." I put my hands out, palms up, pleading. "Listen to me . . ."

"Lies, man! All lies!" He jerks away, dancing backwards, out of reach. "Don't touch me."

"You didn't seem to mind—" I'm losing him. "Before—after Stingers—" He looks away. "I took my clothes off for you—" Losing him. "You didn't seem to mind then—"

"It was just a fuck!" Voice a knife that cuts me off. Even ankle-deep in sand he towers over me, never looked more angular, as if underneath his clothes his body is made of planes, every muscle, every organ, sharp lines and planes.

"You're the only one, Jesse. You're the only one I love."

He flips his cigarette into the sand, and then, turning abruptly, he starts to walk, fast. Away.

"Jesse!" I scream his name so loud it tears the back of my throat, but he doesn't stop. He doesn't look back. I stand where I am, my hands fists, and scream his name again. Because it will be the last time he will ever hear me say it. My voice saying his name. My knees fold and I fall on the sand, soft, slide down. Watch his back recede. He disappears. Doesn't turn around.

I sit staring at the space where he was, waiting for something, but nothing comes. No tears. Everything dry. I should stand up. I should go. But there is nowhere for me to go from here.

The night settles around me, a starry blackness, indifferent. I am only vaguely aware of the pain in my shoulder, how my teeth hurt from grinding. He is not coming back for me. The thought breaks against me at last, a high wave, a hard wall of water. It seems to me that I will drown inside it.

Behind me, small waves wash up gently on the beach, a steady murmur, a beckoning. Moving very slowly, I walk down to the water's edge. It's cold on my toes, sucks the sand out from beneath my feet. I try to find the line that separates the sea from the sky, but I can't. It's lost. I could swim out there, I think. I could get lost inside the vastness. Having lost him, I could lose myself, too. I would be numb, I would never wake up. My mother would meet me. I feel sure, suddenly, that my mother would meet me. She wouldn't let me die alone.

I'll do it right, I resolve then, wading forward. I'll do it strong. I'll swim until my arms are wooden, and then I'll let myself sink. I'll breathe in water as if it were air. I'll do it brave.

A wave drenches me, and my clothes hang heavy against my skin, but I feel clean. My teeth start to chatter. I'll dive into the next one that comes. I stand sure, poised. But it comes and I don't move. The next one, I think, but before I'm ready it's there, it comes over me with a sudden, unexpected force, sweeps me off my feet, and then I'm under, swirling black, water in my nose, and it flashes on me through my panic that my father, my father will have to find me, he will have to say this body, it was hers, she was my daughter—

I claw at the sand on the bottom and then the wave's receding, leaving me washed up on the shore. Using the heels of my hands, I pull myself back, and out.

I watch the water moving, back and forth, the eternal motion, until my heart has slowed. Then, my fingers dangling low against my side, my hair wet and dripping down my back, I start walking toward the dunes.

My heart feels like an old, cracked gully. It is finished. I am forsaken. I have nothing left to lose, and the sense of liberation is drastic. It carries me to the highway.

S T A N D I N G on the side of the road with my thumb stuck out, I am a small thing, hollow inside. Huge trucks roar by and the earth trembles beneath their weight. If the drivers see me, they give no indication. My clothes dry, stiff with salt, and my hair is damp straw against my neck.

I don't recognize that it's a squad car passing me, going the wrong direction, until it's too late. I'm swiveling around to see where I can hide when it makes an illegal U-turn in the middle of the highway, and then comes straight for me. Pinned by the headlights, I turn my back to it and keep walking, waiting for the siren, for the flashing lights to stop me. There are worse things, I think, than being arrested for hitchhiking.

The car pulls up beside me and I stop. The cop leans across and opens the passenger door.

"Get in." My father's voice.

Under the car light, his face is haggard. Dimly, I notice he hasn't shaved. His eyes are bloodshot; for a second, I think he's going to slap me, but then he takes a deep breath and leans back against his seat. He shifts into drive, and I buckle my seat belt and wait for the inevitable, but he doesn't say anything, he just drives.

I clear my throat. "How did you know I was here?"

"Didn't."

"Then why . . . ?"

"Special case."

"This far out of the county?"

"Feds wanted us to send a car out."

"Why you?"

"Volunteered."

In the rearview mirror, I imagine I can make out the lights of the bar. He was almost there.

He picks up the radio, calls in. Through the static a voice asks for the status. Holding the mike up to his mouth, my father stares straight ahead. "Didn't find him. Headin home."

Although speed keeps sending small volts of electricity through me, I close my eyes, let my head slump against the door, pretend I am asleep, pretend I am invisible. When he stops for gas, I get in the backseat and curl up, out of his rearview mirror's range.

I will never see Jesse again. This is the only thought in my head.

W E   D R I V E   for hours, drive through the sunrise, and though I keep pretending, I never sleep. Speed won't let me. My joints are stiff when we finally pull up to the house; I feel used, obsolete. Junked.

"Wake up, Ellie. We're home." He doesn't turn to look at me, and I walk behind him, staring at the ground. Inside, he lets me pass, and I head straight for my room.

"You oughta eat."

Halfway up the stairs to my room, I keep walking.

"I'm not hungry."

"Ellie." The tone of his voice stops me. I turn around and look at him. He's standing at the bottom; his eyes are ringed dark and his shoulders are slumped.

"What you did last night," he says then, very slowly, "was a very stupid, very dangerous thing."

I have no answer to this.

"I am makin a reservation for you to go back to New York next week."

I have no answer to this, either.

"You hearin me, young lady?"

"Yes, sir."

"In the meantime, you are not to leave this house except to go to work. In the evenin, you will stay here. Is that understood?"

"Yes, sir."

"Get some sleep. You look like hell." He turns around and walks to his bedroom, and I walk to mine. My clothes peel off me like a rind, and even though it's hot, I crawl under the sheet. I can feel the hair sticking to the back of my neck and I know I should at least take a shower but then I think, what for? Nobody cares if I'm clean or not—not even me. I stay in bed, with my knees up against my chest. The speed has finally worn off, and without it, I feel drained of everything vital, as if my blood itself has turned white within my veins.

———

I'm riding in the back of a bus, I am the only one in it, and the seats are hard, they have no springs. Staring out the window, suddenly I catch a glimpse of the most beautiful, indescribably blue body of water I have ever seen; deep, vivid, steel, a glittering azure, hard and seductive. I have to get off the bus. I bang on the door and it opens but the bus doesn't stop, I have to leap, and I crash against the ground, rolling over and over until I splash into the water. Standing, I wade out. The current is very strong, but the color of the water is stunning; I am hypnotized. Looking up, I see high, ridged dunes, and atop one of them, a very small child on a bike. I recognize her immediately. She is my child. I am overwhelmed by love for her. I have never loved anything like I love her. She is propped on a bicycle that's far too big for her, her feet don't reach the pedals, but somebody's propped her up and pushed her, and the bike is flying toward the water. Beneath me, the undertow has carved a tunnel in the water, and I can see how inexorably she will get sucked into it, how surely she will be sucked under and then out to sea—drowned. I scream Stop but no sound comes out. She is coming faster and faster, I can see her face, I know it so well—it is my mother's face. If I can only say Stop I know she will be saved, if I can only get it out—I try and I try but I can't, and I realize she will die, she will die and there is nothing I can do to save her.

When I wake up, my face is wet. The room is full of sound. It takes me a moment to realize it's rain against the roof. I kick the sheet off and swing my legs around. Going downstairs, I'm so weak I have to lean against the banister.

In the bathroom, blood comes off on the tissue. I stare at it uncomprehendingly for a moment, and then I get up to find a tampon.

Junked.

B EFORE he goes to work the next morning, my father knocks on my door—loud knocks, impossible to ignore.

"Yes?"

"Ellie—it's time to get up. You'll be late for work." He steps inside but I stay with my face to the wall.

"I'm calling in sick."

"I think you should go."

"I don't feel good."

"What's wrong with you?"

"I just don't feel good."

"Maybe you should see a doctor."

"I don't need a doctor." I clench my teeth, refuse to cry. My father hesitates.

"Think I'll call Dr. Peterson anyway—"

"I have cramps." I bite the words off.

"Oh." My father is embarrassed, as I knew he would be. I can hear him backing toward the door. "You want some aspirin?"

"It doesn't help," I say. "I just want to be left alone."

He stands there, and I know he doesn't like it, me shut up in the dark like this, refusing to get up, claiming pain but needing nothing. I will him to leave. After a few seconds he does, shutting the door behind him.

I pull my knees back up to my chest and wish I were dead.

———

I have no idea what time it is when my father comes back. I only know it's night again, that I don't want to see him, that I don't want to see anyone.

"I brought you some eggs."

I crane my neck around to look and there he is, standing at the foot of the bed, holding a tray. I nearly tell him I'm not hungry, but the smell of hot food makes my mouth water; I can't remember the last time I ate. I sit up and turn on the light, prop the tray on my knees.

It's one of Mom's old wicker trays, and I wonder where he found it—I can see the dust around its rim. On top of it is a plate heaped with eggs, two buttered biscuits, a big glass of orange juice, a napkin and a little vase with three daisies in it. Although my father has never done anything like this for me before, I refuse to be touched. I concentrate on the food instead. Still standing at the foot of the bed, he watches me devour everything he's brought; after the first bite I can't stop until it's all finished, and he doesn't say a word until I finally put my fork down.

"You know how many eggs I scrambled?"

I shake my head. I don't want to look at him, and I busy myself with the silverware.

"Seven." He sits on the end of the bed. "Seven eggs." I don't say anything. "When's the last time you ate?" I shrug. "I tried to make them the way Mom used to, but I couldn't remember what she did that made them come out so good—they're just not as good as the ones she made."

I pick at the napkin. Don't talk to me about my mother now, I think at him. Don't you dare.

"D'you remember what it was, Ellie?"

"No," I say, and then, despite myself, "Milk. She whipped them with milk and a little bit of water."

"Is that all?" I nod. "I'll have to remember that."

We sit there then, me refusing to meet his eyes still, and a long silence fills the room. He breaks it.

"Cramps gone?" I lift one shoulder, as if to say So-so. "It's not really cramps that's keepin you in here, is it."

I begin gnawing on my cuticles.

"It's that biker."

"I don't want to talk about it." I look him in the eye.

"I can understand that," he says quietly. "A broken heart's got nothin to say."

I lean my head forward so my hair will hide me, but then my father reaches a hand out and tucks the hair behind my ears. I clamp my jaws together, squeeze my eyes shut, but it's no use. From beneath my lids the tears start to fall, rolling down my face.

"Ain't nothin worse in this world than a broken heart," he says, and I hide my face in my hands, unable to stop them from coming.

"He saw me with Dec at the restaurant—I went to see him and I thought—I thought maybe it was going to be okay—and then the next day Melanie came in—she said Mom and her father— she called Mom a slut—she told me about the bust—I ran over—I left everything, I ran over to find him—and he'd already gone— he'd left me, Daddy—he left me without even saying good-bye—" I rock back and forth on the bed, and awkwardly, my father reaches out to pat my back. When I finally look at him, his face is strained. I hug my knees in an effort to control myself. His chin begins to shake and I freeze, watching him. He bends his head to stare at his hands. His knuckles are clenched white inside his lap.

"Daddy?"

"I never should've let him stop me."

"Who?"

"When they called the accident in, Schaeffer was the closest. He was the one who found her. Rode in front of the ambulance. Called me from the hospital.

"They told me she was dead on arrival, but I asked to see her. I wanted to see her and he told me, Tom, don't. I knew she was in bad shape. I knew she was smashed up. I could see it on Bob's face." His voice starts to shake. "I said I wanted to, I tried—he wouldn't let me. He blocked the door. He said, There's nothin you can do. He said, You don't want to remember her like this."

He starts to cry. "I should have insisted on seeing her. It shouldn't have mattered what she looked like. I wanted to kiss her face no matter what she looked like. I wanted to hold her hand one last time—"

Putting his face in his hands, my father sobs, terrible, racking sobs that make his shoulders heave. Sitting up, I put my arms around him, and my body shakes with his.

"I'm glad you didn't see her like that, Daddy—"

"I should have said—I should have said good-bye—"

"Well, she didn't say good-bye to us either, did she—"

"No, she didn't—"

"No, she didn't."

He hugs me then, so hard it hurts my ribs. I'm the only one he's got left. I close my eyes against his shoulder and hold him as tightly as I can.

TH E day I leave for New York, the sky is a blazing blue. Before we go, my father cooks me a huge breakfast, bacon, hash browns, toast, eggs sunnyside up, coffee, makes me eat it all.

Throwing my bags into the trunk, squinting in the sun, I ask my father if we can stop at Parker's for five so I can return my uniform. He says, "Sure, but we better get going now."

Pulling up to the restaurant, I read the sign on the window. "Help Wanted." I turn to my father. "Guess they haven't replaced me yet, huh, Dad."

"Guess not." Parking the car, he leaves the motor idling, the air conditioner on.

I swing the door open. "Coming in?"

"You go on, Ellie. I'll wait." He knows why I'm here, who I want to see.

Inside, Sandra's at a table in the far corner, taking an order, her hip cocked, her back to me. I hold the paper bag that holds my uniform, clean and dry, against my legs; I am awkward here without it on. I feel huge suddenly, a great bulk against the door, blocking the light.

As I step forward, Sandra turns around and catches sight of me. I lift one hand, a small wave. For an instant, she freezes, and something wavers across her face—something like the wince you get when you swallow something so cold the hurt shoots up sharp into your head—but then it's gone, and she walks to the back, calls the order out to the cook.

When I walk toward her, she bends her head, one hand slipping into her uniform pocket, and I know the gesture, it's so familiar— by the time she's got the cigarette out, I'm there, and I raise the small flame of my mother's gold lighter up to it. Her eyes meet mine, briefly, and then she inhales. The cigarette glows bright orange.

"Thanks." Exhaling, she looks away.

"Here." Taking her hand, I press the lighter into the palm, close her fingers around it. "I want you to have this."

"It's beautiful." She touches it, turns it around in her palm, doesn't look at me.

"It was my mother's."

Sandra presses one hand up to her lips then, and through the smoke of her cigarette, it seems to me I see her fingers tremble slightly. She lets the lighter fall gently into her pocket. Her eyes meet mine, but before she can say anything, I clear my throat.

"I brought my uniform." I lift the paper bag, and Sandra's mouth twists up at one corner, smiling as if she'd rather not.

"I gathered you quit," she says dryly.

"I'm sorry I never—"

"No big deal," she interrupts, and grins at me, the old Sandra grin, irrepressible. "More tips for me."

Pale blue light hits the back wall, once, twice, and Sandra nods at the window, blinds drawn down against the sun.

"That your daddy flashin the lights out there?"

I turn around but he's stopped. "He's taking me to the airport."

"You goin back to New York?"

I put the bag down against the wall, take a deep breath. "Yup. I'm going back to New York."

She searches my eyes, and for a second I think she's going to ask me, What happened, how did it end—but all she says is "Good."

"Can't wait to get rid of me, huh?"

"You're made for better, Ellie."

"So are you," I shoot back, but she just smiles and shrugs, drags on her cigarette, one arm wrapped around her waist, her other elbow propped against the knuckles. She squints against the smoke she makes.

I take another breath, wipe my hands on my jeans, but before I can speak, she does.

"You didn't come here to say good-bye, did you?" Her voice is quiet. Startled, I don't answer, and she continues. "I got a policy. No good-byes."

"What's your policy on hugs?" I ask her, and then her arms are around me in a fierce grip; it lasts a second before she steps back, and brushes the hair out of my face. Behind us, the door opens and I turn to see a couple with their three small children coming in. Sandra picks up menus and goes forward to meet them.

Moving softly, I walk to the door. Heavy damp air greets me and I hold my breath against it. From the car, my father's watching me. He smiles. I don't turn around, but I can picture Sandra standing upright, eyes following my progress, from the door to the car, from the car to the airport, from the ground to the sky . . . and for a second a small window opens in my heart, and relief shines down, a shaft of clear light.

———

At the airport, my father walks through security with me and we stand at the gate, watching airplanes landing through the big plate glass window.

I slide my hand into his and he looks down at me, surprised, but he holds it firmly, his palm rough and dry against mine.

"You make sure to call me when you get home so's I know you got in safe."

"I won't forget."

"Think you'll need some extra money?"

"You already gave me first month's rent. I'll be fine."

"Might need more to tide you over till you find work, though."

"I can type a hundred words a minute, Dad. I can have work today if I want it."

"Hundred words a minute? How 'bout that." We watch a small plane taking off. It soars up into the clear, blue air. "Your mother was quick with her hands, too. Knitted things for you when you were a baby. Never saw anything move so fast as those needles."

"Mom knitted?"

"Sure, till she got tired of it."

"I never knew that."

"She'd get tired of things and just put them aside. Never look at them again."

"Like Bob Schaeffer?" I ask the question low, and my father lets go my hand. Still staring out the window, he nods.

"But she never got tired of you."

He turns to me and smiles then, but I can see the pain in his eyes. "No, she never did."

At the gate, they're beginning to board.

"I guess I should go."

"Got your ticket?"

"Right here." I pick up my carry-on, sling it over my shoulder. "All set."

"Okay then." He puts his arms around me and I stand on tiptoe to hug him, a bone-crushing hug. Tears spill onto my face.

"No cryin, now, Ellie. You'll be back at Christmas."

"I know."

He lets go of me. "Be good."

"I will." I kiss his cheek. "Bye, Dad."

"Bye, honey."

I start to walk away.

"And you call Dec when you get there, you hear?"

I turn and wave, and then I'm in the elevated corridor, and on the plane.

My seat is by a window facing the airport, and I stuff my bag underneath the seat in front of me, buckle myself in and wipe my face.

Leaning back, I have a sudden memory of the summer I was nine years old, the summer I got my first real bike, pink with curved handlebars, a banana-seat bike. A month later, it was stolen. My father came home from work to find me crying, inconsolable, and he turned around and left again. He didn't come back until well past midnight, long after my mother had tucked me in bed. He didn't come back until he'd found it.

Squinting through my window, I think I can make out his form, the blue of his uniform, facing the plane. I imagine how he's standing there, his hands inside his pockets, his face quiet, and I imagine him leaving after my plane has taken off, getting in the car and driving home, going back inside that empty house, alone.

I promise I won't die before you, Daddy. I promise you that.

Very grateful acknowledgments
to Jean and Teresa, who brought me in out of the cold;
to Joni, who rescued me from drudgery with one fell
swoop; to Susan, for her practiced eye and her unfailing
warmth; to René, who bought me the time; to Argyre,
who *never* said no and *always* did it free; to T., who gave
me space and so many stories; to my mother, my main
source of inspiration; and especially, to Pico, without
whom I never could have come this far, so fast.

ABOUT THE AUTHOR

KRISTIN McCLOY was born in San Francisco and grew up in Madrid, New Delhi, Tokyo, and Ithaca, New York. She has lived in New York City since her graduation from Duke University in 1984. This is her first novel.